professional
BOUNDARIES

JENNIFER PEEL

D1528079

To Delfia,

thank you for always believing in me.

Prologue

"YOU KNOW I'M CRAZY ABOUT you, right?" Ian brushed back my hair. I loved it when he did that.

Normally, I would have replied, "Yes, but I'm crazier for you." But not tonight. Believe me, I was more than crazy for him. I was head over heels, shut the front door, stop the presses in love with him, and I had decided tonight was the night I was going to tell him. Before I did, I reached up on my tiptoes, tugged on his shirt to pull him closer, and kissed those lips of his once. Then I went in for the kill. "I love you, Ian Greyson."

He faltered back and swallowed hard with a deer-in-a-headlight look.

Okay, that wasn't the reaction I wanted, but this was Ian, so I wasn't too surprised. After all, I was the one who pursued him. Even though he thought I was too young, he eventually relented. I was eighteen at the time, and he was twenty-five going on sixty. I smiled nervously and stepped closer to him. "Ian, it's okay if you don't say it back right now. I just couldn't hold it in any longer." I wrapped my arms around him, waiting for him to reciprocate, but he was stiffer than his starched collar. "Ian?"

"Kelli, you're too young to be in love."

I leaned away from him and laughed. "Did you really just say that?" Sometimes he sounded like my Dad.

"Why do you have to complicate things?" He sounded angry.

"How is me loving you complicating things? Because, FYI," I poked his chest. "I've been in love with you for months."

It was true, and I had calculus to blame. I was a pretty smart girl—I even had a full-ride to my little private college set against the beautiful Rocky Mountains in Colorado—but for some reason, I couldn't get calculus, and I needed to in order to keep my full-ride. That's when I met Ian. He was in grad school, completing his MBA, and to make some extra money, he tutored. It was the best money my Dad ever spent.

I'll never forget the first time I saw him sitting in the campus library, looking more serious than any twenty-five-year-old should flipping through the Wall Street Journal, but there was something about him. I don't think most women noticed him, and that was a shame because once you got past his serious exterior, he was a charming and considerate fellow. And he was actually quite handsome, but that was muted by his clothing and quiet mannerisms. He had dark brown hair with a slight curl that begged for you to run your hands through it, and those Hershey Kiss eyes of his were easy to get lost in. His strong jaw line that was always cleanly shaven and smooth didn't hurt either. He was like Clark Kent. He even wore the same thick glasses as him. And even though Ian dressed like a forty-year-old in khakis and polos, to me he was adorable.

"This wasn't in my plan. I'm not ready for this kind of commitment," he stammered.

Ian had his whole life mapped out, and he wanted to map mine out, too, but I refused. Sure, I liked goals and a rough outline, but I also liked the freedom to do what seemed right in the moment, regardless of plans. Besides, I was young, and he was too, but somehow, he always forgot that. Don't get me wrong, I loved his drive and dedication, but he really needed to simmer down sometimes. I succeeded, once in a while, in getting him to take it down a notch or two, but it was a hard job—a job I dearly loved.

"Ian, I'm not asking you to commit to me for life…yet," I teased.

He didn't look amused at all, so I kept talking.

"I'm happy where we're at. I just wanted you to know how I feel. I'm not expecting anything from you."

He narrowed his eyes and pressed his lips together before he began to pace back and forth in front of my apartment. I stood in front of the door and watched him. The summer breezes I loved so much ruffled his hair. The beautiful Colorado weather was one of the reasons I had decided to stay the summer term after my freshman year instead of going back home to Tennessee. But it was mostly because of the distraught man in front of me. I started to wonder if that was a mistake now.

As he walked past me, I grabbed onto his hand. "Ian…"

He looked at me with eyes as hard as stone. I wasn't sure I had ever seen him look so cold; it gave me shivers in the warm summer air.

"Why did you have to ruin everything, Kelli?" He sounded half determined and half in despair.

My eyes pooled with tears. In the nine months we had been dating, Ian had never made me cry. "Ian, what are you saying? Forget I said anything. I'm sorry."

He let go of my hand. "I'm sorry too, Kelli," his voice cracked.

And that was it. He left me standing there, inconsolable with tears silently falling down my cheeks, feeling like January in July.

Chapter One

I TOOK A MOMENT ON THE way to my car before work to stop and gaze longingly at my apartment complex's pool. I pictured me sipping cold fruity drinks while floating on the unicorn inflatable my nieces bought me. It was only February, but I could almost taste spring. I knew I should probably enjoy the season because soon enough I'd be complaining about the heat and humidity Tennessee residents suffered through every spring and summer, but I felt like saying, "Bring it on." The winter had been harsher than we Southerners are used to. But, I had survived four winters in Colorado. It was hard to believe that it had been almost a decade ago that I'd received my undergrad degree. It kind of made me feel grown up, especially today. I had a feeling I would be receiving some good news today.

My stomach fluttered at the thought of being promoted to Marketing Director of Chandler Media. I wasn't the only candidate in the running, but I was the only in-house candidate even though that ruffled some feathers at work because of my age. Maybe I was a little young to be heading up a marketing firm, but as Regional Marketing Manager I had proven myself. Our financial institution clients were adopting my idea for digital ad software rapidly and—not to be immodest—I was well liked by my colleagues, even the old-timers who got their feathers ruffled. And it didn't hurt that Gary, the owner and current director, and his wife Holly loved me like a daughter.

I only hoped now that Gary was ready to retire and enjoy more time with his wife and grandkids, that he trusted me enough to hand over the reins. I would sorely miss him. I loved sharing adjoining executive offices with him. He was more than my boss; he was like a second father to me.

I took one more second to look at the pool before heading to the parking lot. Climbing into my little convertible made me wish for spring even more. I missed the fun and the freedom of having the wind blow through my hair while the sun beat down on me as I drove. I swore the car was begging for me to push the button and slide the top down. "Just a few more weeks," I said out loud, as if the car was actually listening to me or really cared if its top was down.

As I made my way through early morning Nashville traffic, I could barely contain my excitement. I was meeting with Gary, who I fondly called Boss, first thing. I dressed up for the occasion. Our office typically took a more casual approach, unless we had clients in the office, but with the way technology was now, that was a rarity. I had done more conference calls than I could count. Personally, I liked face-to-face visits best, but they could be inconvenient and expensive. Today I looked like I was ready for a face-to-face visit with a classy charcoal gray dress that left no doubt I was a woman, and my glammed up dark hair. To pull it all together, I brought out the red lipstick. It made my fair skin and blue-green eyes pop. I hoped it screamed, *I'm ready to take on the world!* Or at least Chandler Media.

When I pulled into our office parking lot, there were already a few cars there. I noticed Boss' midlife-crisis Camaro. I laughed when I remembered Holly telling Boss she didn't mind the car, but if he ever decided to indulge in other midlife crisis activities, he would be sleeping in that car. I knew Boss never would. He still looked at Holly like a man who had wandered in the desert and she was a tall glass of cool water. I noticed Delfia's car next. She was the most fabulous executive admin assistant ever. She usually beat me to the office. Next to her car was a stylish white Infiniti. I smiled and wondered who got the new car, but then I noticed the Colorado license plates. *Weird*, I thought.

The license plate had me reminiscing. I loved Colorado. I missed the Rocky Mountains, with the hiking and camping in the summer and the amazing powder for skiing in the winter. It was the only time I had enjoyed snow. I think I would have stayed there if I hadn't been a lovesick fool. Everything in Colorado had reminded me of Ian, so as soon as I graduated, I hightailed it out of there. Ugh. What a morning to think about him. I needed positive happy vibes. I wasn't going to be rejected today by another man. I was going to go upstairs and claim my promotion.

I took a deep breath and tried to cleanse my thoughts of the evil Ian, killer of dreams and love. I began to repeat in my head, *Director of Marketing at Chandler Media, Kelli Bryant.* It sounded perfect. I chanted it to myself silently as I walked in through the empty reception area. It was only 7:30, and we didn't open until 8:00. By the time I made it to the staircase, I was feeling cleansed of the foulness that was Ian. With my thoughts back on track, I took the stairs two at a time to the executive level. This was going to be an incredible day. I could feel it.

As I walked toward Delfia's desk, which sat outside and between the adjoining offices Boss and I shared, I noticed her humming away, organizing the files on her desk. I admired her so much. She was the epitome of someone who took lemons and made the best lemonade you would ever taste. At forty-two, with practically two grown children, her husband left her. He was the world's biggest idiot, but she picked herself up by the bootstraps and did what she had to do. She'd been working for us for the last couple of years. I didn't know what we would ever do without her.

When she noticed me approach, she flashed me a smile. "Good morning, you hot little thing."

Did I mention how much I loved this woman? I posed, movie star style. "Do you love the new dress?"

"Yes, if only I could fit into it," she sighed.

I waved away her obvious lie. She looked great in her slimming pant suit and new bobbed do that went perfect with her high cheek bones. I could only hope to look so good in my forties. I noticed Boss's door was closed. That was odd. "Is Boss here?"

"Yes, he's meeting with a gentleman that wasn't on the appointment calendar."

"Huh." I smoothed out my dress. "Did you catch a name?"

"No, but he asked about you."

"Really?"

She wagged her brows. "He was quite attractive. Is there someone you're not telling me about?"

I rolled my eyes. "Yes, Delfia, I'm trying a new tactic. I thought I would have Boss interview all my potential new suitors at seven-thirty in the morning. This way he can weed out all the morons and save me the trouble." She laughed at my sarcasm, but honestly, it wasn't a bad idea. I should consider it. "So, no name, huh?"

"No ma'am, but he seemed anxious to see you. He kept asking when you would be in."

More and more curious. "Well...okay."

I walked into my office and the door between Boss's offices and mine was closed too. Just for curiosity's sake, I checked to see if it was locked, and to my surprise, it was. He never locked that door. I was more than intrigued to know who he might be meeting with at such an early hour. Maybe he was interviewing whoever it was to take my current position. That made sense, so I relaxed a little and began to think of anyone I knew who would be a good candidate. While I thought, I started up my laptop and scrolled my phone for any new messages. There weren't any messages and I couldn't come up with any ideas of who it might be, so I walked back out to ask Delfia what he looked like; maybe I could guess then.

Before I could say anything, Delfia beat me to the punch. "Are you still taking the belly dancing class at the YMCA?"

"Yes." I turned to show her my backside. "Can't you tell by the way my butt looks?" It was then I noticed, too late, that Delfia wasn't my only audience. While she snickered and stared at my backside, a man came out of Boss's office. Not just any man. It was the man I didn't need to think about this morning. I stood there not only mortified, but very confused.

"Ian," I gasped. I felt flush from the top of my head, to the tips of my toes. Probably because my heart was beating double time. I couldn't believe he was here and that he'd just heard me tell Delfia to check out my butt. Could someone please shoot me now? Or more like shoot him. I was never supposed to see him again.

His wide eyes roved over me. "Kelli."

I stood up as straight as I could and tried to regain my composure. But I was finding that difficult under the circumstances. I was sure my jaw had dropped and no matter what I did, I couldn't seem to close it. It didn't help matters either that Ian looked, um...let's say freaking amazing. I wasn't sure what he had been doing for the last twelve-and-a-half years, but it looked like a stylist had gotten a hold of him. He was in a tailored black suit that fit him to the T. The glasses were gone, and he'd grown out his hair slightly. It looked even more deserving of fingers running through it. All he needed was a runway.

"What are you doing here?" I spluttered once some of my senses came back online.

Before he could answer Boss walked out.

"Kelli, my girl, you're already here. Good, I see you've met Ian." Boss wrung his hands together.

The nervous wringing of Boss's hands had me on edge. I raised a brow at Ian wondering why Boss thought this was our first meeting. Ian cleared his throat and ran a hand through his hair.

Fine, I'd play along. "No, I haven't had the pleasure yet." I walked toward Ian with a sinister grin on my face.

Ian swallowed hard a few times.

I held out my hand. "I'm Kelli Bryant." I wanted to throw in, "Remember me, the girl who loved you, but since that wasn't in your plans, you decided to walk away and pretend like I never existed?"

He held out his hand, but he looked wary.

I kept up the act and shook it. I didn't want to touch him, but what else could I do under the circumstances? As soon as we touched, I felt a surge of warmth. That couldn't be good. I did my best while shaking his hand to ignore my conditioned response to him. It meant nothing. We were ancient history. We are talking prehistoric before the dinosaurs kind of history.

"Ian Greyson," his voice hitched. "It's a pleasure to meet you."

I smirked at his mock sincerity. For a moment, I thought he was going to smile, but that was very un-Ian like. He squeezed my hand once before letting it go. I directed my attention toward Boss. I wanted to know what in the heck Ian Greyson was doing here.

Boss was redder than a chili pepper. His balding head had beads of perspiration on it.

"So, what are you gentlemen up to this morning?" I was never one to stand on ceremony.

A pointed look passed between them before they faced me. Why did I feel like this didn't bode well for me?

"Kelli, can I talk to you in my office, dear?" Boss waved his hand toward his door.

Oh, this wasn't good. He never called me dear; honey yes, but never dear. I looked back at Delfia, and she knew too by the way her shoulders sagged.

"Delfia, could you please get Ian some coffee?" Boss asked Delfia.

What? Ian was staying?

"Gary, is there somewhere I can set up my laptop?" Ian asked.

"Delfia, please show Ian to the conference room and give him access to the Wi-Fi," Gary directed.

I couldn't believe this. My head was spinning.

Before Ian followed Delfia, he directed his attention to me, or at least I thought it was to me. "I look forward to meeting with you later."

He must be talking to Boss. There was no reason for us to meet later, and I had no intention of doing so. I looked at Boss to respond to him.

Boss was rubbing the back of his neck now. Whoa, he was on edge. "We'll all meet together after I've talked to Kelli. There will be plenty of time for you and Kelli to meet later."

Uh, that was a negative. I was absolutely not meeting with that man. Like ever. What could we possibly have to meet about anyway? I stared at Boss blankly. When he wouldn't make eye contact with me, I marched into his office and sat down in one of the leather seats in front of his desk, my heart pounding out of my chest. I heard Boss mumble something to the moron before he walked in and shut the door. He didn't sit at his desk, instead he sat next to me. This wasn't good at all.

Chapter Two

Boss took my hands in his. Before anyone thinks this was inappropriate workplace behavior, think again. I had known Boss my entire life. He and my father were lifelong friends and ever since my sweet dad passed away several years ago, Boss not only filled in as a father figure, but he became my mentor.

Boss finally found the courage to look me in the eye, but his palms were sweaty. "Kelli, my girl, you know it's time for me to try out retirement. At least that's what Holly says."

I smiled warmly. "I think you will be great at it." Presumptuously I added, "And you know I'll take good care of things here. You won't have to worry about a thing."

He gave me a strained smile.

That's when my heart sank. Any small shred of hope I had that Ian being here was only a coincidence went right through the paper shredder. "You're not making me Director, are you?" I tried to keep the emotion out of my voice.

He squeezed my hands. "Kelli, there's no question you're the most talented and dedicated employee that has graced these walls in the last twenty-five plus years. There's no doubt in my mind that you would be an excellent Director."

"But..." I said.

"There is no but, Kelli. You would be excellent. This has been perhaps the toughest decision of my career, but I feel like it's the right one, and I think you will too once you understand what Ian has to bring to the table."

I jumped up in a knee jerk reaction. "You're making *him* the Director?" I was thinking that maybe Ian was a talent finder, or I don't know, anything but this.

Boss gripped his seat and leaned back, surprised. I forgot he didn't know that Ian and I had a history and believe me that ticked me off. Ian should have told him he knew me and *how* he knew me. Maybe then Boss would have thought twice about his asinine decision. Maybe I should tell him. Or maybe I should quit. I can't and won't work for Ian.

Boss patted the seat I had vacated hoping I would sit down again. "I know you're disappointed, and rightly so, but this isn't a reflection on your capabilities. Look at this as a new opportunity."

"How?" I asked.

"Ian has extensive contacts in the technology sector. He recently sold his own technology company for millions." Boss was desperately trying to sell the idea to me.

That sounded like Ian. Looked like his plan was right on schedule. That meant he was married now, too, with two-point-five kids.

Boss stood up and took my hands. "Your digital ad software needs him. He can take this product national, maybe even global. Not only is he a capable businessman, but he knows development."

I wanted to say, tell me something I don't know. I knew Ian had a degree in software development, in addition to his business undergrad and graduate degrees. I pulled away from Boss and began pacing back and forth, running my fingers through my perfectly curled new-Director hair. "Why didn't you tell me earlier, and when did you even meet him?"

"I met him at that Marketing Technology conference in Denver last fall. I didn't tell you because, like I said, he's a savvy businessman." Boss laughed. "He made me sign an NDA before we even began discussions to explore this idea."

I rolled my eyes. That sounded like Ian—always cautious and in control.

Boss approached me and led me back to my chair. "Kelli, please sit down."

I sighed and reluctantly complied.

Boss took my hands right back as soon as we sat down. "Kelli, look at this like a partnership. Without you on board, this isn't going to work. The office staff loves you too much."

"It's too late to butter me up."

He laughed nervously. "That sounds like my girl."

I didn't find this humorous at all. "I'm going to have to think about this. There are other factors to take into account." I stood. "I'm going home for the day."

His head hung with a loud exhale.

I walked toward the door that joined our offices together.

"I'll give you a raise," Boss yelled out.

I didn't even bother looking at him before I opened the door. "If I stay, you bet you will."

I didn't know if any increase in pay was worth working with Ian. I couldn't believe he was going to be the Director. The big question was why he wanted to be. It sounded like he had plenty of money now, and he darn well knew I worked here. Ian always did his homework. I bet he already knew every employee's name and his or her vital statistics.

I walked over to my desk and looked around my office lovingly. It was spacious and stylishly decorated with dark wood furniture; I even had a private bathroom. The view was great too. It overlooked a small lake and walking path. It was going to really suck to give it all up, especially for the man who did some major damage to my heart. It had taken me a long time to get over him, but you never forgot your first love, especially when you felt the way I felt about Ian.

As a precaution, I swiped the pictures of my nieces and cat from my desk and placed them in my satchel. The thought of never coming back made my stomach roll. How did this happen? I was expecting a promotion this morning, not a figurative slap in the face.

When I walked out of my office, Delfia looked up from her computer. "Should I transfer your calls to your mobile?" she asked with trepidation.

"That won't be necessary." I had to rush past her or the tears I'd been holding back were going to fall. Unfortunately, I had to pass the conference room on my way to the stairs.

I swear it was like Ian was waiting for me. "Kelli," he called out.

I ignored him and walked as fast as my high heels would allow. It wasn't fast enough.

He easily caught up with me on the stairs. "Please stop."

I stopped on the landing and faced him. Looking at him invoked a deep hatred and an overwhelming desire to slap him, but I decided lashing out verbally would probably be more appropriate. "Why? So you can gloat about stealing my job?"

He walked down the stairs like he really was on a runway and met me on the landing. I'm not going to lie, it kind of took my breath away and that made me even more furious.

"I would never do that." He drew closer, hitting me with his clean, intoxicating scent. "I didn't know you were being considered for the position until this morning."

"Oh, so this was a perk for you?"

His brows furrowed. "You know I'm not that kind of a person."

"No, you're wrong. I don't know what kind of a person you are. I don't think I ever did. You already lied to Gary. You should have told him you knew me and how you knew me."

"I didn't lie to him," he said flatly, offended I would think such a thing.

"Still using the Greyson white lie, I see." He was great at not telling the truth, all while telling the truth.

"He never asked, and I didn't see why it was important to bring it up. This is business. It has nothing do with the fact that you and I knew each other previously."

I shook my head at him in disbelief. I knew it shouldn't bother me, but that was a little cold. We more than knew each other, but I had to remind myself that our relationship had meant more to me than it had to him. He obviously didn't even regard it as a relationship. This wasn't going to work; maybe it was just business to him, but for me, it was personal. "You can make this your first order of business then. As of this moment, I resign." I turned and flew down the stairs.

By this time, the foyer was alive with activity. I tried to remain calm and unemotional as several people wished me good morning. I faked it the best I could, but once I hit the parking lot the tears came as well as a strong urge to throw a rock at his pristine, white Infiniti. I refrained from acting on that particular violent thought. Instead, I took off in my car like a bat out of Hades.

I headed for my sister Amanda's home. I hoped her kiddos were already off to school. I loved my nieces, Courtney and Samantha, but I needed their mommy this morning. She was only five years older than I was, but she had been mothering me since I was little, especially after our own mother walked out on our family when I was only six. Occasionally Joan, our mother, would contact us, but for the most part, we didn't have any kind of a relationship with her. It was sad, but we had dealt with it for so long, we just considered it our life. We'd never expected anything from her. Besides, our dad was the greatest, and he made sure we turned out all right.

In fact, I think we turned out better than all right, especially Amanda. She was the best mom and wife. My brother-in-law and dentist, Zane Culver, hit the jackpot. Honestly, he was great too, but no one held a candle to Manda Panda, as I endearingly called her.

As I pulled into the drive of her perfect suburban home, I realized I had several missed calls on my phone. First, it was Boss, then Delfia, and a number I didn't recognize, but I did recognize the area code as being from Colorado. I could only guess who that was. It didn't matter; the only person I wanted to talk to shared my genes. It showed too. As we got older, we had frequently been asked if we were twins. I wished we were twins, the identical kind, because Amanda was gorgeous inside and out.

I turned off my phone and threw it in my satchel. It felt weird to me. My phone was like an extra appendage and I wasn't used to being off on a weekday. If I thought about it, it was kind of freeing in a way. Too bad I liked to eat, pay my bills, and be a responsible adult. At least I had a good amount in savings. I had never touched the life insurance money I received from Dad's passing. I was saving it for a house one day. Amanda frequently bugged me about buying instead of renting, but to me, buying a house now was saying I was planning to be single forever. Like a schoolgirl, I imagined house hunting with my husband and strolling through each home talking about which rooms our children would have. And honestly, I didn't want to live in a big house all by myself; it would only remind me more of how lonely I was sometimes.

I walked up to the front porch and retrieved my key. "Manda Panda, are you home?" I yelled out as soon as I opened her door.

"Come on back, Kelli Jelly," I heard her yell from the kitchen.

I rolled my eyes. Maybe someday we would come up with new nicknames. I slipped off my heels and walked back to the kitchen to find my sister, Betty Crocker, baking away. It smelled like homemade bread. Perfect, I needed a carb coma.

My floured, apron-clad sister spun around as soon as I entered. She took one good look at me. "Who died now?" she teased.

Suddenly, the full weight of my on-the-spot decision really hit me. I burst out into tears.

"Oh my, did someone really die?" She wrapped her arms around me.

"No, only my career."

She stepped back. "What do you mean, honey? Gary would never fire you."

"He didn't," I stuttered through sobs. Then I told her the entire ridiculous story. She had never met Ian, but she knew what he had meant to me and how devastated I was when he broke up with me.

"Well, that's quite the story. And you're sure he knew you worked there?"

"Positive."

"Hmm." She tapped a finger against her lip.

"What does that mean?"

"I find it interesting, that's all. Is he married?"

"What does that have to do with anything?"

"You don't find it weird that your ex-boyfriend suddenly shows up after how many years and becomes your boss?"

"You don't know Ian; this has nothing to do with me. It's purely business for him. He's an opportunist."

"I bet he is," she responded.

"Seriously, sis, you don't know what you're talking about."

She shrugged her shoulders and led me to her kitchen table where we both sat down.

"So, are you really going to let this guy take what you've worked so hard for?"

I laid my head down on her table and moaned. "What else can I do? I can't possibly work for him. I used to make-out with him. And let's not forget I told the guy I loved him, and he said that was a complication and never talked to me again, until today."

"Was he a good kisser?"

I lifted up my head slowly. "What kind of question is that? And what does it have to do with this situation?"

"It's all in the kiss, right?" She gave me a toothy grin.

I thought back to some of those kisses. I could still feel the way he would caress my cheeks—peering into my eyes like that's all he ever wanted to do—before pressing his lips against mine. He always took his time before his tongue would tempt my lips to part. Each time I gave into the temptation, which was every time, I was rewarded with tingles down my spine. "You have no idea." I wish I didn't either.

"That good, huh?"

"Best ever. You see why I can't work for him?"

"Are you kidding me? Show this guy who the boss is and what he's missed out on all these years."

I tapped my fingers on her perfectly cleaned table. "I don't know, sis." From the looks of it, he didn't seem to be missing out on much. I hated that he was even more attractive now.

She stood and assessed my pathetic figure while taking off her apron. "I say we go shopping and get our nails done while you're contemplating."

I wiped the tears out of my eyes. That was the best idea I'd heard all day. "You really are the most terrific-est sister ever."

She pulled me up out of my seat. "Tell me something I don't know, Kelli Jelly."

Chapter Three

STILL WASN'T SURE WHAT I was going to do, but a day of shopping and being pampered at the spa with my sister was therapeutic, to say the least. She lived up to her most terrific-est title. All day she kept encouraging me to go and get my job back, even though I wasn't sure I should. In my head I had completely gotten over Ian, but there seemed to be some murky water under that bridge in my heart. Why else did I have such a strong reaction to him? I didn't think you could truly loathe someone unless you had truly cared for that person. And did I ever loathe him. It was probably because he was the only man I had ever loved. That wasn't my plan, but for some reason, try as I might, love had eluded me. Not to say I hadn't had a man or two tell me they loved me, but I'd never been able to reciprocate. I'd never been able to find a man who made me feel as cherished and safe to be myself as Ian had. Well, you know, until he walked away when I told him I loved him. So maybe it was all a lie.

Or maybe I was defective and could only fall in love with men who would never love me back. Or maybe I had trust issues because my mother abandoned us and the first person I expressed my love to also abandoned me. Amanda said I was making something out of nothing. "Look at your life—you're the most trusting and open person I know. You just haven't met the right guy yet," she would say.

Easy for her to say, she met Zane when she was eighteen and was married at twenty-one. I wouldn't say I was jealous of her; it was more like I had holy envy. Is there such a thing? I don't know, but what I did know was that I wished for what she had - a house full of people to love. I would have traded in deal-making and conference calls for PTA meetings, soccer games, and diapers in a second. Don't get me wrong, I loved my job, or at least I used to love it. I kept forgetting I didn't have one anymore. I just wanted more. No, that wasn't it. I think I wanted more personal fulfillment. Belly dancing could only give me so much, no matter how good my butt looked.

By the time I arrived back at my apartment, the sun was beginning to set. While I unloaded my haul for the day, I looked over the plethora of bags and thought maybe I shouldn't have shopped like I was still gainfully employed. Oh well, you only live once, right? Besides, it was for therapeutic purposes, and if I had to look for a new job, I needed to look my best. Or if I didn't find a new job soon, I needed to look good lying out by the pool; my new red swimsuit would do the job nicely. So, maybe I would have to eat ramen for the next week or two.

With my heavy load—I was embarrassed to say I had a dozen bags in my hand— I walked across my complex, only stopping for a second to pay homage to the pool. I needed spring now more than ever. Thankfully I lived on the first floor and not far from the parking lot. My sister reminded me again today that it would be even more convenient if I had a garage to pull into. I told her I would think about house shopping…maybe. I needed a job first. Oh, that thought hit me in the gut. I loved Chandler Media.

Before I turned toward my apartment, I noticed a man sitting on the other side of the pool in a suit and tie, staring down at his phone. My first thought was wow, someone is more desperate than me for the pool to open, but as I got closer and realized who it was, I thought some other words I shouldn't say out loud. I couldn't believe Ian was here. I started double timing it to my apartment. Too bad the loud clicking and clacking of my heels alerted the jerk to my presence.

Ian stood hastily and headed my way.

I ignored him and kept walking toward my apartment, hoping he would accidentally fall in the pool, or better yet, go back to Colorado or wherever he came from. I assumed Colorado, because that's where he had grown up and that's what his license plate said, but who knew. I for one didn't care, as long as it wasn't here.

"Kelli," he called out after me.

I continued to ignore him. We had nothing to say to each other. Well, I did have a diatribe I had been working on for years in case I ever saw him. It went something like, "If I could do it over again, I would have flunked calculus. Okay, maybe that's pushing it a bit far, I would have settled for a C. But I wouldn't have sat down at that library table. I wouldn't have looked past your boring clothes and offish manners to see what I found or thought it was that I found—a kind soul with a giving heart. It was all a lie. You were a lie."

I made it to my door and dropped my bags like they were hot potatoes so I could retrieve my key and punch in my security code like my life depended on it. Ian unfortunately had long legs and couldn't take a hint. He made it to me just as I was punching in my last number.

I looked over to him and scowled. "I feel like I keep saying this to you today. What are you doing here? Better yet, how do you even know I live here?"

He ran his fingers through his hair.

Lucky fingers, I thought. What was wrong with my subconscious? We didn't like him.

"You gave me no choice when you didn't answer your phone."

"Oh, you had a choice. You still do. I suggest you use it and leave, but first tell me how you know where I live." That kind of creeped me out.

"I have access to all the employee files."

I glared at him. "Well, I'm not an employee anymore." My stupid voice cracked.

He sighed heavily. "Come on, Kelli, can you give me a break here? It's been a long day."

"And I should care, why?" I smirked.

I could tell he was ready to lash back, but he stopped himself, took a breath, and thought before he spoke. "Kelli, I'd like to talk to you about rescinding your resignation. Please," he begged.

Wow. He sounded so downtrodden; I was curious why. "Fine, you have two minutes. Go."

His lip twitched like he was going to smile. "Can't I come in?"

That was a negative. "I don't let strangers, especially of the male variety, into my apartment."

He crossed his arms and narrowed his gorgeous brown eyes at me. "We are hardly strangers."

"Isn't it funny how sometimes the people we think we know the best are the ones we really don't know at all?"

He stood there and stared at me for a moment. I didn't budge. I was serious about not letting him into my apartment, and I was serious about not knowing him. After he broke up with me that was one of the hardest parts for me to reconcile. I thought I knew him so well, but in reality, I didn't know him at all, because my version of Ian may have freaked out a little bit about the whole love thing, but he would have never treated me so harshly.

He bravely stepped toward me and loosened his tie. "I have a feeling I'm going to need more than two minutes to convince you. Can I take you to dinner?"

I stared into his deep brown eyes. I noticed he had some subtle lines around them now, and I even noticed a gray hair or two in that dark hair of his. So much had changed in thirteen years. Thirteen years ago, I wouldn't have even given his invitation a second thought, but now I needed a third and even a fourth.

While I was mulling over his invitation, he smiled at me. "Will this impose on your belly dancing class?"

Before I could stop myself I half-smiled at the jerk. I was still so embarrassed about the look -at-my-butt incident this morning.

"Please," he whispered.

I involuntarily shivered. It was chilly out. Yes, that's what that was.

We stood and stared at each other some more while I thought. Looking for a new job sounded dreadful. But working for my ex sounded worse. Except, I loved my job. Maybe I could convince him to quit. "Fine, wait here."

He visibly relaxed.

I unlocked my door and hauled all my bags in before shutting it in his face. That gave me some satisfaction. I was greeted by my lazy tabby cat, Charlie, lying on the top of my couch waiting to be adored. I headed his way and stroked his head several times until he purred. He was such a diva. Afterward I freshened up a bit. I smiled to myself thinking of Ian standing out in the cold. Maybe that was rude, but the guy did break my heart once upon a time and he stole my job. And if memory served me correctly, he enjoyed cooler temps. After I took my own sweet time, I walked back out to meet him.

He was walking around the pool area looking around. When he saw me, he walked back my way. "Great, you're ready."

I wasn't sure I was *ready* to be alone with him, but I was curious to see how and why he was here living my dream. We proceeded to the parking lot. He tried to make small talk while I kept my distance. His scent still did things to me.

"This is a nice complex. Do you like living here?" Ian asked.

I shrugged. "For apartments they're great; a little pricey, but worth it."

"Hmm..." he responded.

Weird.

When we made it to the parking lot he asked, "Should I drive?"

Absolutely not. I knew the kind of things that happened in his car. I didn't need the reminder of the fond memories. "I was planning on following you in my car."

He raised his eyebrow at me. "You won't ride with me either?"

"You know what they say, stranger danger," I said without apology.

He tried to compose himself before he spoke. "I forgot how willful you are."

I smiled in mock delight. "So, where are we going?"

"Why don't I follow you, so you don't think I'm luring you anywhere?"

"Perfect."

He stared at me hard, mouth agape. I let him get in a few more looks before I walked away, smiling to myself for throwing him off his game. I honestly wasn't worried about Ian taking advantage of me. Heck, I had to practically throw myself at the guy when we first started dating. Our spark was undeniable, but boy did he try to fight it. Looking back, I suppose he was right to; I was pretty young at the time. But the heart wants what it wants, and did my heart ever want him.

He followed me to my favorite restaurant, Alicia's. I personally knew the owners, Alicia and her husband, Jose. They were my first client as a junior account manager at Chandler Media. That was seven years ago. They still used the logo and ad designs I created for them. The design used an old-world map of Mexico as the backdrop. I had offered several times over the years to touch it up or create a new one for them, but they'd become very attached to it.

Ian had no trouble keeping up with me. I kept wondering what he was thinking about as he followed me. I was surprised he was going to all the trouble. I thought he would've been happy to see me go. Funnily enough, my sister thought otherwise. She had predicted he would ask me to come back. She believed he had ulterior motives for coming to Chandler Media, but I'd told her she was crazy. "Crazy like a fox," she'd responded.

Alicia's parking lot was almost full; that was a good sight for me. Alicia and Jose deserved the continued success. I had never met harder working or kinder people, and their food was to die for, especially their smothered burritos. My mouth was watering just thinking about them.

Ian parked his car in the space next to mine. We met each other on the sidewalk. He looked up warily at the place. I forgot, this probably wasn't his style. He was more of the quiet café type, or at least he used to be. Oh well, if he wanted to talk to me, he was going to have to do it on my turf.

"I hope you like Mexican." I knew he did, but I was treating him as if I didn't know him at all. I could tell it bothered him, but I wasn't sure why.

He tilted his head. "Of course," he replied.

I led the way to the entrance. There was a bit of awkwardness when we got to the door; we both reached for it at the same time and our hands touched. Where the heck did those tingles come from? I backed off quickly and let him open it. I had no problem with men opening my door, and normally I assumed they would, but I was making no assumptions with Ian, now or ever.

"Um... Thank you."

"You're welcome." He waved me in.

As soon as we walked in, we were hit with the sound of their live salsa band. I had forgotten Fridays were their salsa night. I could tell it made Ian a little uncomfortable. Perfect. He deserved to squirm.

We didn't even make it to the seating hostess before Alicia accosted me. "Kelli!" she said as she squeezed me to death. She looked me over like a fine Mexican momma. "Eres hermosa."

Another reason to love this place, it was a great self-esteem booster. "Gracias, igualmente."

She kissed my cheek and then she noticed I brought company. "Ahh, who is this, Hermosa?"

I wanted to say, "Don't get your hopes up." She was constantly trying to set me up. "Alicia, this is Ian. He's the new Marketing Director at Chandler." You had no idea how hard that was to say.

She pressed her lips together and patted my arm. I probably shouldn't have told anyone I was hoping to fill that position. I could have done without the look of pity.

Ian took his cue and shook her hand. "It's a pleasure to meet you."

"You should know Kelli is muy talented." She dropped his hand and wrapped her arm around me.

Ian tugged on his collar. "I've heard that a lot today." He sounded sincere, but there seemed to be a hint of annoyance mixed in.

On that note, Alicia showed us to a booth toward the back. It was the farthest away from the band which pleased Ian. She took our drink order and kissed my cheek before she left to fill it.

Ian was fixedly staring at me.

"Do you want to know what's good here?" I asked.

"Sure." He grinned. "But I was wondering, does everyone in this town know you and love you?"

I laughed. "I think you've met most of my inner circle today."

"Yes, and it's been painful. I may be the most hated man in Nashville at the moment." He unfolded his napkin and placed it on his lap.

I couldn't help but grin and be delighted about that, but I kept my sarcastic comments to myself. It sounded like he'd had enough for the day. I may not like him, but I wasn't one to pour vinegar into open wounds, at least not all at once.

He leaned forward ever so slightly. "So, Kelli, I think we may have gotten off on the wrong foot today. I'd like to start over if we could."

"You think?" I responded.

He sat back and folded his arms. "How about this, let's not discuss business for now."

"Then whatever do we have to talk about?"

"Well, we haven't seen each other in almost thirteen years."

I took a chip from the bowl and dipped it in their homemade salsa. "Really? Has it been that long? I guess time flies when you're having fun."

Yeah, he didn't know what to do with me by the pained look on his handsome face. Of course, I knew how long it had been since I had last seen him. That memory, unfortunately, would be forever etched on my heart and time-stamped in my brain, but he didn't need to know that.

"I barely recognized you today when I first saw you."

I raised my eyebrow at him and practically choked on my chip. "Well, okay. Most men would lie and say, 'The years have been good to you, Kelli. You look great.' But I guess honesty is the best policy."

His face burned red.

To hide my embarrassment, I picked up my menu and began to read it even though I had it memorized, and I already knew what I was ordering. I had never had anyone point blank tell me I was unattractive or unrecognizable. I'll admit that stung coming from someone who used to call me beautiful on a regular basis.

He cleared his throat. "Kelli, I didn't mean to imply that you are anything but hermosa."

I looked over my menu. "Do you even know what that means?"

"Your belly dancing classes have definitely paid off." He smirked.

"Hmm…"

"Really, Kelli, I only meant to say you look grown up now."

I rolled my eyes at him. "Now you sound like my dad."

His eyes sparkled with delight. "I've heard that somewhere before."

I was supposed to be pretending like I didn't remember a thing from our relationship. *Darn it!*

"How is your dad?" he asked still grinning like a fool.

I set down my menu and placed my hands in my lap. "He passed away six years ago."

That wiped the grin right off his face. "Kelli, I had no idea. I'm sorry."

I shrugged my shoulders. "How would you have known?"

"I keep screwing up here, don't I?"

I almost felt bad for him, so I threw him a bone. "Tell me how your family is." I was honestly very interested in his answer. I adored his parents and sister. His parents lived on a cattle ranch outside of Glenwood Springs, nestled in a beautiful valley surrounded by the mountains of Colorado. I was so surprised the first time I met them; they were so different from Ian. I couldn't imagine Ian growing up on a ranch, but he had. I really enjoyed the time we spent out there, and I would have liked to have stayed longer, but Ian, at the time, was very busy, and I always kind of got the feeling that wasn't who he wanted to be. I don't think he was embarrassed of his parents, they were salt of the earth kind of people, but I think he always wanted more out of life. Being a rancher is back-breaking work, and sometimes for not a lot of pay. But I had never met happier people.

His sister, Noelle, and I really hit it off too. I met her during the one and only Thanksgiving I spent with them. She was home from school on break. At the time, she was attending the University of Texas as a junior. We had kept in touch for a while after Ian broke up with me. She thought he was the biggest prat ever for ending our relationship. I think she had even tried to talk some sense into him, but once Ian made his mind up, that was it. Over the years, I had thought about her and wished we had remained friends. She was even more sarcastic and feisty than me; we were quite the pair.

He looked at me thoughtfully.

I hoped they were all still alive.

"They're doing well. My parents still work too hard."

I smiled at the news. I couldn't imagine them being any other way.

"Noelle's married now and lives in Houston. She and her husband Sean have a two-year-old son named Jax."

"That's wonderful. I'm happy for her."

"She wanted me to tell you hi and that she would love to catch up with you," he nervously replied.

That was a pleasant surprise for me. "I'd like that," I said quietly, though I thought it was weird he would have talked to his sister about me.

Alicia returned with our drinks and was ready to take our order. "Are you having your usual tonight, Hermosa?"

"Yes, ma'am." I handed her back the menu with my design work on it.

Ian hadn't even cracked open his menu yet. "I'll have what the lady is having."

That was a very un-Ian like thing to do. Anytime we had ever been out to eat, which wasn't often since we both were short on cash at the time, he was picky about what he ordered. He would ask the server lots of questions anytime we had gone out. Everything from how fresh their produce was to what their health code rating was. But most of the meals we shared at the time were cooked at his place by him. I think he fed me dinner for an entire semester. The man could make an amazing lasagna. I inadvertently smiled at the old memory.

"What are you smiling about?" he inquired.

I quickly put on my I-have-no-idea-what-you're-talking-about face. He would not be getting access to my thoughts, especially any which placed him in a fond light. That was dangerous territory, and I needed to tread lightly there, or better yet, stay away completely. Honestly, I thought I had. We needed to switch gears ASAP. "So, tell me more about your first day at the office," I said with a lot of evil glee in my voice.

His brows raised while he thought about what to say. I could see the wheels spinning in those dark eyes of his. "We'll get there."

I didn't like him taking control of the conversation direction. *Hmm…* "Then what do you want to talk about?"

He acted as though he was reaching out to touch my hand, but he stopped short. That was a good thing, too, if he wanted to keep it. "Kelli, it's been a long time. Tell me about you."

"Didn't you read my personnel file today?"

"Come on, Kelli."

"Fine, what do you want to know?"

He knew he was getting on my nerves, and he seemed to take pleasure in it as he sat back and surveyed me. "Tell me about Vanderbilt."

So, he *had* read my file. I wasn't surprised. I was only surprised that he even cared. "I received my MBA at Vanderbilt around seven years ago."

He held his hand out waiting for me to elaborate. "And…?"

Fine, he was getting my life story in a nutshell. "I graduated top of my class. I started working for Chandler Media during grad school. I've been the Regional Manager for three years until today."

He flinched when I mentioned my job status, but that didn't stop me from giving him the very watered-down history of my life after him.

"When I'm not working, I'm either with my sister and her family, volunteering, or belly dancing, among other activities. Oh, and I have a cat named Charlie. Is that enough for you?"

"How's Amanda?"

I was taken aback that he remembered her name. It's not like they'd ever met. "She's perfect. She and Zane recently celebrated their fifteenth wedding anniversary, and they have two daughters. Courtney's ten and Samantha's seven."

"I thought you didn't like cats."

"Yeah, well, turns out I do." I didn't really, except for Charlie. My sister bought him for me on my thirtieth birthday. She said she would be buying me a new one every five years unless I got married. She was setting me up to be a spinster cat lady. At first, I told her to take him back, but he was so dang cute, I couldn't help but love him. I warned her though, no more.

"Husband? Kids?" Now he was teasing me.

"Really? Don't you think that would be the first thing I would have mentioned?"

That made him smile. What was up with him? He wasn't usually this emotive.

I folded my arms. "Are we done now?"

"Don't you want to know about me?"

"What more do I need to know?"

He leaned forward. "You're not curious at all about your new boss?"

"You're not my boss." Not to say I wasn't a little curious, but heck, I could google him. And believe me, I would.

"I forgot. I'm getting ahead of myself."

"Way," I responded.

"So, what's it going to take to win you back?"

My forehead scrunched. That was a very odd way of putting it.

He turned a tinge of red. "What can I do so you'll rescind your resignation?" he corrected himself.

"Quit," I said, with hope. Like a lot of hope. Like betting my last dollar kind.

His countenance dropped. "You can take that off the table."

"A girl can try."

"Kelli," his hand inched forward across the table. "I don't know if you remember or not, but we used to work well together. And I think if you gave this a chance, we could do great things for Chandler."

Before I could respond, Jose brought our smothered burritos out to us. He greeted me with a kiss on the cheek after setting down our plates.

I figured I should be polite and make introductions. "Jose, this is the new Marketing Director for Chandler, Ian Greyson." Those words tasted like one-hundred-year-old vinegar in my mouth. It was so bad it left an aftertaste.

Jose patted my cheeks, his eyes said how sorry he was.

Ian held out his hand. "It's nice to meet you."

Jose reluctantly held out his hand to shake Ian's. He was polite but quick about it, only mumbling a hello. Jose turned his attention quickly back to me. "You can't leave without dancing with me tonight, Bonita."

Now that was something to smile about. Jose and Alicia had been teaching me how to salsa. It was almost as fun as belly dancing. "I wouldn't dream of it."

"So, you salsa, too?" Ian asked after Jose left.

"On occasion."

"I see you still enjoy life and learning new things."

"Yes, I do."

"Can you please try this?" he practically begged, which was so unlike him.

I tossed my head from side to side. "Ian, why are you here?"

He responded by taking a large bite of food and chewing very slowly. He didn't verbally communicate, but his eyes were talking. They said he was in no hurry to answer me. Fine. I was starving, and the food smelled way too good to let it sit untouched any longer. Besides, I couldn't stand looking into those warm chocolate eyes; it brought back too many memories. Like lazy Sunday afternoons watching old movies in his arms. Stop, I told myself. It was a long time ago.

We ate in silence for several minutes, but there was this electric current that zinged between us. It was always present whenever we were together. I wished there was a way to pull the plug on it. I thought for sure after all this time it would have fizzled. But it was if my heartbeat had found its rhythm again. No. No. Ian and I were never going to be in sync again.

"The food is excellent," he interrupted the silence.

I set my fork on my plate. "Tell me something I don't know. Like why you're here?"

He thought for a moment. "I'm here to find...success."

"Because selling your own company for millions wasn't enough?"

He took a deep breath and exhaled loudly. "Kelli, the digital ad software you've helped develop is a very unique concept, and I believe, with the right feature enhancements and marketing, it could put Chandler Media on the map as the leader in digital marketing software."

"I still don't get it," I said exasperated. "You could have just started something on your own again."

"I like a challenge, and I have a feeling this will be my greatest challenge yet."

The way he said that and looked at me, I couldn't tell if he was only talking about my product. Okay, it wasn't only mine. It was my idea, but it was Matt, our software developer, who made it into reality. I was just the architect and the one who made it look pretty after Matt worked his magic.

"Fine, then why didn't you tell Gary you knew me?"

He wiped his mouth with his napkin before placing it back on his lap. "Why does that matter to you?"

Oh, the nerve of him. I grabbed my bag, retrieved some cash, and threw it on the table. It would more than cover my half of the meal. "Good night, Ian."

His eyes widened before he jumped up. He hesitated, then gently reached for my arm. "Please don't go."

I stood stunned for a moment. His touch felt right, but that was wrong. "Why does it matter to you?" I threw back at him. What was wrong with me? I wasn't usually this snotty. He was bringing out the worst in me. He didn't used to. In fact, he used to bring out the best in me, but in my defense I cried for months over him once upon a time, and now he stole my job.

He gazed down at me. I had forgotten how tall he was, or how short I was. I had also forgotten how much I loved the way his eyes darkened the closer I got to them, and how good he smelled.

"I'm sorry. Please sit down." His thumb glided over my skin. I don't think he meant to do that by the way he quickly let go of me and backed off. Oh, how I wish he hadn't. I felt too good.

He waited for me to sit down before he did the same. He picked up my money and handed it back to me. "I insist on paying for dinner."

"I can't let you do that."

"Why do you have to be so obstinate?"

"I don't need your charity," I was back to being snarky. "I may not be a multi-millionaire, but I've done well for myself, and I'll be fine without this job."

He rubbed his neck with his free hand. "Kelli, this isn't charity. I know you've done well for yourself. Look at it like two old friends catching up."

"Ian, if that's the case, you're the worst friend I've ever had." There was no malice in my words only the truth. He was the worst because he used to be the best and his leaving took a piece of my soul.

He lowered his eyes. "I suppose I deserve that." He took several deep breaths before he sat up taller, all business-like. "Kelli, professionally speaking, today is going down as one of the most unpleasant of my career. I apologize for not being as forthcoming as I should have been with Gary. I didn't realize the personal and professional relationship that existed between the two of you. Let's just say he wasn't very impressed when I told him how I knew you and that I hadn't disclosed it."

I pressed my lips together trying not to smile, but I failed, maybe on purpose.

"Honestly, I think if there wasn't an iron clad contract in place, he may have fired me today. I've never seen anyone so upset about losing an employee, and then there was the executive secretary."

"I think the word you're looking for is admin assistant, or you could just call her Delfia. She hates to be called a secretary."

"Thanks for the heads up, but she already detests me."

Yep, I smiled big at that.

"I'm sure you're going to assume that I only want you to come back to make my life easier, but honestly Kelli, I would be a fool to let such a talented employee go. I know what you bring to the table. I've been very impressed. So name your terms." After his groveling, or as close as he ever came to groveling, he sat back against the booth, crossed his arms, and dared me with his eyes to come back to Chandler.

As I thought about what to say and do, Jose came back and brought our check. He handed it to Ian. I pushed my money back over to him.

"I won't take your money, Kelli."

I reluctantly took it back.

"Are you ready to dance?" Jose asked.

I grabbed my bag and scooted out of the booth. "Yes." I took Jose's arm before turning toward Ian. "Thank you for dinner."

"Kelli, please come back?"

I swallowed hard. "I need the weekend to think about it."

Ian nodded. "I understand, but I hope you'll change your mind."

Chapter Four

ON MY DRIVE HOME, I couldn't get over the day I'd had. To think it had started off so hopeful, only to end with my ex-boyfriend and would-be boss staring at me on the dance floor. I thought he would have just left after he paid for dinner, but he stayed and watched me dance with Jose. I couldn't help but watch him too. I swore in his eyes I saw the memory of us slow dancing outside of his apartment in the first snow of the season during the year we were together. While I generally didn't care for the frosty white flakes, when I shared it with Ian it took on a new life, a magical one. Ugh. My brain needed to stop recalling every memory of him, except the one where he left me crying and wondering what I had done wrong. Or of all the phone calls that went unanswered. He ghosted me before it was even a term.

Tonight, Ian walked out on me again without saying a word, but this time it felt different. I didn't have the punch in the gut feel. It was more of a prick of my heart. Too many what ifs ran through my mind. I had no business wondering what if that fateful night thirteen years ago never happened? Or what if we had stayed together? It didn't help when Alicia remarked after he left, "He looks like a man who knows regret."

Don't we all know regret? Like me. I regretted going to work today, and a little of me regretted my snotty attitude. Just because Ian was a jerk didn't mean I had to be one. I felt so bad about it I called Amanda as soon as I got home. I needed her to make me feel better. I replayed the whole crazy dinner story for her. "Was I out of line?" I asked. "And why couldn't I control my snarkiness? I'm not used to being rattled."

She laughed. "Oh honey, don't be so hard on yourself. He's lucky you didn't punch him. It's his own fault for leaving you with so much pent up anger. He's the one who chose to walk away without giving you a reason."

"Manda, he didn't love me. End of story. What better reason is there than that?"

"Kelli, that's malarkey. Real men don't walk away and never speak to you again just because you say you love them. And they don't just show up out of the blue thirteen years later for no reason either."

"All right, wise one, what possible reason could there be?"

"Did you find out if he's married?"

It drove me nuts when she responded with a question not an answer. She did that more often than I liked. "I didn't ask, but he didn't have a ring on. Hold on, I want to google him. Let me put you on speaker." I set my phone down and typed in Ian Greyson on my laptop. The first listing was for an attractive actor who shared his name. Too bad I didn't have time to ogle handsome men online. I scrolled down the page and found an article about the sale of Ian's software company, IAG Inc. It sold for a cool thirty million. *Wow!* I scrolled a bit farther down as I listened to my sister bark commands at my nieces, who were balking at going to bed. One of them yelled, "Come save us, Aunt Kelli!"

I laughed.

"Just wait until you have your own," Amanda retorted.

"I can't wait." I tried to keep the longing out of my voice.

"Kelli, you're going to have your own."

I hope so.

A very interesting article popped up. Well, well, it looked like Ian married Denver socialite, Marissa Randall, eight years ago. I wasn't sure if I should feel relieved or, dare I say, jealous. *Wait.* I was definitely not jealous. Their engagement photo was pretty hoity-toity. Ian was in a black tuxedo and she was in some silver evening gown. She was what I would call a buxom blonde with overdone make-up and hair. I was just about ready to tell my sister he was married when another article caught my eye from two years ago.

Amanda was now yelling for Zane to come deal with his offspring.

"Hey, sis, it looks like he's divorced." I chimed in before she really raised her voice. "Or at least he was a couple of years ago."

"Does he have kids?"

I scrolled down the article. It was a gossip column from the *Denver Post*. I couldn't believe Ian was popular enough to get mentioned in the society pages. No wonder he looked like a runway model now. I honestly preferred the Clark Kent version. Don't get me wrong, he was easy on the eyes, but there was something sweet and innocent about the man I knew so long ago. Now he looked like he lived in a boardroom.

"There were no children from the union." I read out loud to Amanda. "So, no kids, at least not from Ms. I-May-Tip-Over-Because-My-Hair-And-Boobs-Are-So-Big."

"Send me a picture of her," Amanda requested.

I snapped a picture like a thirteen-year-old girl and texted it to her.

"My, my..." Amanda responded.

"I know, right?"

"You're way prettier."

"Thanks, sis, but I don't care."

"Sure you don't."

"Really, I don't. Why would I?"

"Every woman cares about who their ex-boyfriends end up with, even if there are no longer any feelings there."

"Well, I don't. It was a long time ago."

"Don't get your panties in a wad, Missy."

I set my laptop down and lay down on my couch. "Sorry, it's been a long day. I thought I would never see him again. It was something I had come to terms with. And now here he is, and not only that, I could be working for him. What do I do?"

"Honey, I think you need to be honest with yourself about why you don't want to work with him, and if you can come to terms with that, then I think you should go back and show him what Kelli Bryant's made of."

"What do you mean, be honest with myself?"

"I think you know. Good night, Kelli Jelly."

I think I knew too, but I didn't want to admit it. "If you say so. Good night, Manda Panda."

I set my phone down and sighed. Charlie took that as his invitation to come and pounce on me. For some reason, he loved lying on my abdomen. As I lazily stroked Charlie, I tried to process the day, especially what my sister had just said. At first, I lied to myself and told myself I had such a strong reaction to working with him because obviously, I wanted that job and felt I deserved it. But the truth wouldn't be ignored. My heart asked me what if someone besides Ian had gotten the job? The answer was I would be drowning myself in a hot fudge sundae now, but I wouldn't be unemployed. I would have put on my game face and kept doing my job the best I could. I would have done my best to welcome the new blood.

Speaking of hot fudge sundaes, I got up and traded my clothes for a night shirt before I made my way to my kitchen and pulled out my dad's old recipe for hot fudge. I needed my dad's lawyer mind, or just his arms. I missed him so much. His life had been cut too short by a brain aneurysm. We were told he died in a matter of minutes. Our only consolation was that he died doing what he loved, defending the weak and the innocent. My dad was my hero. He could have been a wealthy man if he had wanted to be. He was a brilliant attorney, but he only took paying cases so that he could take more pro bono ones. Don't get me wrong, we lived a good life, but we weren't spoiled, except in the ways that mattered most.

I stirred the hot fudge on the stove to the perfect consistency, all while trying to self-diagnose. I had come to terms a long time ago with the fact that Ian didn't love me. I knew when I told him, so many years ago, he probably wouldn't reciprocate. His favorite line was, "I'm crazy for you, Kelli," or sometimes, "You drive me crazy, Kelli." Sometimes he meant that endearingly, but I knew I did drive him crazy. We were very different people, but that was what I loved about our relationship. He helped me enjoy quiet, simple pleasures, like nature hikes and art museums. He even took me fishing once. And I managed to get him to be loud and crazy occasionally—like when I dragged him to the Festival of Colors, and we threw colored chalk at each other. Another time I pulled him up on one of the campus benches and made him slow dance with me for everyone to see, just because I liked the song playing on my iPod. He used to give me a look that said, "I can't believe I'm doing this," and then he would kiss me as if to say, "I'd do anything for you." Maybe that's why I thought he might return the sentiment.

We were happy together. I mean, truly happy together. As different as we were, we never fought, and there was never any drama. That's why it took me so long to get over him. When he walked away, I felt like someone had removed all the oxygen from the air. Foolishly, I thought he only needed to come to terms with it and he would realize it didn't change anything. I expected him to come back that night, or at least the next day, because surely he missed me like I missed him. But he didn't. He wouldn't even answer my phone calls or his door when I went to talk to him. He had removed me from his life permanently, with no thought at all.

With my large bowl of vanilla ice cream, topped with the best hot fudge sauce ever, I sat back down on the couch and did a little bit more digging into Ian's past. It probably wasn't a healthy thing to do. I had never had any desire to research old boyfriends, and I had tried very hard to never know anything more of Ian. That's why I let my relationship with his sister fade away. I'd always regretted that, though, because we really were like two peas in a pod. But I couldn't stand the reminder of Ian. Even if we didn't talk about him, she was a reminder of that pain. Oh, well, he was here now, so I guess it wasn't going to hurt to pry.

I started with IAG, Inc. I assumed that stood for his initials. His full name was Ian Anthony Greyson. His dad's name was Anthony too, but he went by Tony, because Anthony was too formal for a cattle rancher. It looked like Ian started IAG ten years ago. Initially it started with a free web-based project management tool. From the sounds of it, it became well used and garnered the attention of investors. Interestingly enough, Miles Randall, his ex-wife's daddy, was one of those investors. From there, it looked like IAG developed several web-based business solution products, ranging from project management to accounting and even marketing. I always knew he was borderline genius and would make it big.

I wondered if he'd met the socialite first or the daddy. I had to say, I really was surprised by his choice of wife. Of course, the timing was right on his schedule. He thought he should be married somewhere between twenty-eight and thirty. That was the optimal age in his mind. He figured he would be well enough into his career, but not too far in. That was important because he didn't want a woman who was only attracted to his paycheck. Looks like he got his wish as his ex-wife came from money. I used to laugh at him and tell him not to overthink things. I would also tease him that I would never marry him for his paycheck. He would always clear his throat when I said things like that, but he would never acknowledge it. I should have known then that he never thought I'd be the one he would marry.

I, on the other hand, thought it was perfect. When he was twenty-nine, I would have just graduated from college. He would have never had to worry about me marrying him for his money because I fell in love with him as a poor grad student. Too bad he wanted big boobs and a wealthy wife. I looked down at my smallish chest and lamented, "Thanks a lot, girls."

It looked like the only part of his plan that hadn't happened was children. He wanted two children, maybe three, and they were to be spaced two and half years apart; he read somewhere that was the most optimal time for the children and for the mother's health. He wanted to be done having children by the time he was forty.

I laughed at myself.

Why I remembered all this nonsense, I had no idea. Okay, I had an idea... It was because I had pictured myself so many times as Mrs. Ian Greyson, wife and mother extraordinaire. Obviously, I had been young and delusional.

As I kept scrolling through pages, I wondered why he got divorced. I couldn't find any additional information other than it was him that filed for divorce and cited the catch all: irreconcilable differences. The only thing I found of interest was Miss Boobs was already remarried to a guy named Timothy Oberman. I wondered if that bothered Ian and if he was still in love with his ex-wife. I don't know why I wondered.

I practically licked my bowl clean before I called it a night and turned off my laptop. It had been a very long and weird day. It felt very surreal as I lay in bed and waited for the sleep to come. All I could think about was Ian. The old Ian, the Ian I used to love. The Ian that made me study charts for finals and supplied me with Diet Pepsi during said finals, even though he thought it wasn't good for me. The Ian who would call me in the middle of the night because he had a brilliant idea and he had to share it with me. The Ian who had worked extra hours so he had enough money to buy me a birthday gift, an expensive perfume I adored. It was a small bottle, but I didn't care. I wouldn't have cared if he hadn't bought me anything at all. His homemade cupcakes alone were perfect.

I hadn't tortured myself like this in years. I was over him. So, so over him. I would be a fool to be anything but. You shouldn't hold a flame for a man who you hadn't seen in almost thirteen years. The fact that I'd never found anyone else that made me as happy as him didn't mean anything, right? It only meant that I had to keep looking. Surely, someone other than Ian Greyson could make me happy and would love me as much as I loved him. It wasn't that I hadn't had some nice relationships in the past ten years or so, but they'd never had that spark and the overwhelming "yes, this is it" feel. I wasn't going to settle for anything less than that.

Some would say, "At nineteen, how do you even know what 'this' is, or what love feels like, for that matter?" Maybe I didn't, but I knew I'd never been as happy with anyone else. I'd never felt the deep connection I'd had with Ian with another man. My only problem was choosing a man who didn't love me back. I suppose it wasn't my only problem, because now that man was back, and he wanted to be my boss.

So, I had to decide. Could I work with Ian or should I start polishing my résumé? Or should I be booking a trip? Door number three sounded fabulous. Maybe not the wisest thing to do, but hey, you only live once. Too bad I was so responsible. I would never do such a thing until I knew I had a job. I wouldn't be able to relax, so it would be pointless. Maybe that's what I would do—secure employment but tell them I couldn't start for two weeks. Then I would book a trip to somewhere warm with sandy beaches and hot single men. I laughed to myself. I was all talk. I hated the single scene, which might be the reason I was still single. Maybe I should hit the library, it worked the first time. Too bad hardly anyone went to the library anymore, and even if they did, I was too old for them now.

I lay in bed and thought and thought and thought some more. Then I dreamt about Ian. I hadn't dreamt about him in a long time, which was a good thing, because it usually was me crying, feeling hopeless and hollow. I would wake up and have to remind myself it was okay, and it was only a dream, even though I had felt that way for a long time after he broke up with me. It was a terrible feeling, but this dream, in a way, was worse. This dream reminded me of why I had loved him so long ago. It reminded me of what it felt like to be enfolded in his arms and warmly kissed. For a moment, when I awoke, I craved him and that feeling.

I sat up and threw my pillow. Why did he have to come back here and get into my head? I had kicked him out of it so long ago, or at least I thought I had.

I crawled out of bed, dead tired. That was the worst night's sleep I'd had in forever, and he was to blame. I was still no closer to knowing what I should do, so I got dressed and headed to the YMCA to workout.

They didn't offer belly dancing on Saturday mornings, but Zumba would suffice. I would take anything that made me sweat profusely and helped me not to think about Ian for just a bit.

On the way to the Y, Holly Chandler called. "Honey, Gary and I are so worried about you. Are you okay?"

"I'm fine." That was mostly true.

"Are you sure?" She knew me too well.

I took in a deep breath. "Yes, I'm sure."

"Well, I'm here if you need to talk."

"Thanks, Holly. Tell Boss not to worry about me."

"Why don't you tell him yourself when you come over for dinner tonight? Are you free?"

I would never dream of missing dinner at their house. "What time should I be there?"

Holly and Gary had been so good to me. Holly had been Amanda's and my surrogate mother. She was the one who talked to us about periods and boys. She even helped us shop for prom dresses. She was my dad's equivalent to a superhero.

I could have been their daughter for real. I dated their son, Luke, while I was in grad school. He was a few years older than me, but he could never seem to get his act together. I was thankful his parents didn't hate me when I broke up with him. They knew Luke had issues. I honestly only stayed with him so long because of his parents and part of me wanted it to work out. I loved the Chandlers, but I never loved Luke in that way. Luke wasn't happy at all when I broke it off, but it was one of the best decisions I'd ever made. Luke was now a beach bum in Florida, working as little as he possibly could, and getting in trouble on a regular basis. He'd never really grown up and caused his parents a lot of heartache. Gary even had to fire him. He was nothing like his brother, Ethan, who was a successful accountant and owned his own firm in Atlanta. Ethan was married to the sweetest woman, Bethany, and they had three adorable kids, two boys and a girl.

I knew once Gary retired, he and Holly would be spending the majority of their time in Atlanta. Holly loved being a nana more than breathing. I was going to miss them, but they deserved any and all happiness that came their way. I was truly blessed to know them. Thinking about them made me more in favor of going back to Chandler, even if I wasn't the Director. I would still have influence, and I could make sure Mr. Hot Shot didn't screw anything up. If only I didn't have to work with Mr. Hot Shot. I was so confused.

Zumba gave me a much-needed endorphin boost. On top of that the forecast was going to be sunny and seventy degrees! That improved my mood by leaps and bounds. I knew the warmth wouldn't last, but I would take what I could get until spring officially sprung. In honor of the warm temps, I decided to procrastinate doing Saturday chores and instead headed to Amanda's to grab my nieces. We were going to the park and then out to lunch and whatever else they could talk me into.

My sister and Zane were more than happy to have a childless day. I hoped someday, after fifteen years of marriage, I would be sappily in love with my husband. I knew they didn't have a perfect marriage. They argued like normal couples, but they still had it for each other. Court and Sam were ecstatic because I got them out of *their* Saturday chores too. What were aunts for, anyway?

As I watched my nieces play along with what seemed like every other kid in the suburbs of Nashville, I couldn't help but think of Ian. We had many dates at the park near campus. They were cheap dates, but was there anything more romantic than your boyfriend pushing you on a swing or stroking your hair as you lay your head in his lap while he studied macroeconomics? In my book there wasn't. I missed those kinds of simple dates. Most men thought they needed to spend a lot of money and take you somewhere exclusive, but I wished for someone who would take me to the park. I wanted to walk barefoot with him in the cool grass. Or have him push me on a swing or feed me peanut butter and jam sandwiches while we watched the clouds in the sky. I also wished I had never fallen in love with Ian Greyson.

After the park, the girls and I made our way to the new pizzeria in town that made great pizza but even better gyros. Their gelato was pretty good too. I loved being with my nieces. They reminded me so much of their mother and me, except Court was fair and blonde like her daddy. Sam, though, could have been mine. We shared the same dark hair and the blue-green eyes that we inherited from my dad. The girls were the best of friends and the worst of enemies, just like Manda and I had been growing up. Now we were only the best of friends. I knew Court and Sam would eventually get there too. Honestly, I enjoyed watching their little tiffs. It drove my sister nuts, but I didn't live with it day in and day out, so for me it was entertaining. Court had my sister's personality, sweet and a little snarky. Sam was like me, more snarky than sweet. Her nickname "Sassafras" suited her well.

We rounded out our day together at Build-a-Bear, because I'm a sucker when it comes to them and I had no one else to spoil. I knew my sister wouldn't love me for it. That's why I would be dropping them off and waving to my sister from the car. She could reprimand me by phone later, and I'm sure she would.

When I got home, I showered quickly and did something I hadn't done in years while I waited for my hair to dry. I figured it was about time, and maybe it would help me solve my little issue. My dad had encouraged me and my sister to keep a journal for every year of our life. Some years I was better than others, but I had one for every year since I was sixteen, even though some of them were spotty. Each journal was filled with my thoughts and sometimes random everyday happenings. Interspersed between some of the pages were pictures, awards, and cards from friends, or anything else I found of value. Whenever I reminisced, there were always two journals I skipped over, my eighteen- and nineteen-year-old ones, for obvious reasons, but today they were going to see the light of day. Several times over the years I almost ripped out the pages that contained anything to do with Ian, but I thought someday I would regret that. I hoped someday I would be able to look back and not cry because it was over, but smile because it happened, just like Dr. Seuss said. That day had never come.

As I sat on my bed, I reverently cracked open the pages of journal eighteen. And, before I changed my mind, I skipped to the pages that contained Ian. The first entry I came to was about the first time I had met him. I had to smile at my stupid young self, writing about whether I would be able to concentrate around my new calculus tutor because he was hot. I also made fun of him because he was so serious. There were several more entries of me rambling on about how much I liked him, and I thought maybe he liked me too. I read about the 'A' I received on my first calculus test after Ian had started tutoring me and how happy I was about it. I kissed him spontaneously at the next tutoring session. I wrote about his confused reaction. I knew he liked it, and he even reciprocated, but he left in a hurry and told me we shouldn't do that again. But I was persistent, and after several weeks, he finally gave in and said he was done resisting me. I could feel the joy leap off the pages as I read about us becoming an "official" couple. There were several pictures of us together. I particularly loved the Thanksgiving pictures. It was my first holiday away from home, but Ian and his family kept me from being homesick. It was one of my most favorite Thanksgivings. There were pictures of us building snowmen, making snow angels, and of the canned food drive I helped head up on campus. I'd made Ian help too. He was right, we had worked well together. That was the school's most successful drive to date, as far as I knew.

I flipped through page after page of happy memories, then one particular passage jumped out at me dated February 10. It read:

Today I asked my dad how he knew he loved my mom and she was the one, or did he know she was the one. I mean, she did leave us. He got quiet on the other end of the phone, but then he said, Kelli, you just know when you know. It will be the most undeniable, peaceful, all-encompassing feeling. It will feel like drowning in pure intelligence. He told me that he did feel that way about my mom. He said sometimes, just because something is right, doesn't mean it will work out, especially when other people's choices are involved. He said my mom made her choice, but he would never regret marrying her because he still loved her. It made me cry. I told him that I was in love with Ian. I thought he might laugh at me or maybe even be upset, but all he said was, I'm happy for you, but don't get too carried away, you're young. I promised him I would try, but I had been drowning in that pure intelligence for some time now. I haven't told Ian because he frequently worries about our age difference and I've been hoping he would say it first. I hope I can hold it in. I've almost told him on several occasions. Anyway, it's late and I should probably go to bed, I have a big biology exam in the morning.

The tears started to fall softly down my cheeks. My sister was right. That was my problem. I had known, with every fiber of my being, I was meant to be with Ian. I knew at eighteen years of age, but he had made his choice, and there was nothing I could do, no matter how right I knew we were for each other. How do you come to terms with someone who robbed you of such a thing, especially when you've never been able to find it again?

I flipped through the rest of eighteen and the first part of nineteen. I stopped before I got to the breaking-up part. It was still gut-wrenching for me. I could still remember that hollow feeling in the pit of my stomach that lasted for days. Admittedly, some of it still existed.

I stood and wiped away my tears. I'd had enough. I packed the journals away in an out-of-place spot in my closet. I didn't want to see them anymore. Anger and determination filled me. I wasn't going to allow Ian to rob me of anything else. I loved my job at Chandler, and I belonged there, whether he was there or not.

Chapter Five

As I drove to the Chandlers' I tried to remove all thoughts of Ian from my mind, but that was proving to be a difficult task. I thought I had mastered that skill long ago, but now that he was back, I found myself out of practice and very unskilled. I knew I was going to have to think about him as we were going to be working together, but I needed to forget the past. I didn't know this Ian, and maybe I never knew him. No, that wasn't true. In my heart, I knew that I had once known the real Ian, I just didn't understand why he did what he did to us. I remember his mom telling me once that Ian was his best self with me. "I was really worried about your age difference, but once I saw the two of you together, those thoughts vanished. You're a perfect match," she said. I had thought so too.

By the time I arrived at the Chandlers', I wasn't in the best of moods, but seeing their home had a calming effect. In a way, it was like coming home. Their home reminded me of late-night talks, holidays, and shoulders to cry on. It felt warm and instilled a sense of belonging. The best part of dating Luke had been the extra time I got to spend at his parents' home.

I looked up at the pristine, white, two-story home with black shutters and smiled. I reminded myself of the blessed life I led, and that Ian was only a road bump. The thought of running him over made me smile even more. With that lovely thought still in mind, I walked myself up the stone path that led to the wrap-around porch that was a gateway to a piece of happiness. I eagerly knocked on the door and was soon greeted by Boss.

Without a second thought, Boss pulled me to him for a big bear hug. "How are you, kiddo?"

"I'm looking forward to that raise you promised me," I uttered against his chest.

He laughed and let me go. "That's my girl."

I could hear the relief in his voice. He wrapped his arm around me, and we walked back to the kitchen. Holly was putting dinner, which looked like some cheesy pasta dish, into the oven. That was out of character for her. Dinner at the Chandlers' home was normally served promptly when guests arrived.

An uncomfortable look passed between Boss and Holly when we entered the kitchen.

"Is something wrong?" I asked.

Boss cleared his throat. "Not at all, we're expecting another guest, but we wanted you to come early so we could talk to you before he arrives."

"He? This isn't like a blind date or something is it?" I laughed nervously.

Holly waved her hand in the air. "No, we would never dream of doing such a thing."

"Okay, do I know this 'He'?"

Boss's forehead began to perspire. He was doing that a lot lately. Ugh. He didn't even need to say his name.

"It's Ian, isn't it?" I grabbed onto their kitchen island for support.

"Now, before you leave or get upset, hear me out," Boss pled.

I gripped the island tighter. Why would they do this to me? Their home was one of my safe havens. It ranked right up there with Amanda's and my own place, and now they'd invited *him* here.

"First off, Kelli, I had no idea you and Ian had dated," Boss said.

"I know that."

He breathed a small sigh of relief, but he shifted his feet.

Holly joined his side and put her arm around him as if to show her support. She kept looking at me with those motherly eyes of hers.

"I'm not exactly sure what happened between the two of you, but I take it, it didn't go well by your response yesterday. But, honey, I can't do anything about it now unless I want to hire a team of lawyers and spend my life savings trying to get out of his employment contract."

I reached out and touched his arm. "I would never ask you to do that."

"Honey, we don't want to lose you." He patted my hand. "I meant what I said about you being the best employee I've ever had. And you know how Holly and I feel about you personally. We couldn't love you more than if we shared last names."

I began to tear up. That immediately brought Holly to my side. She wrapped me up in her gentle, loving arms. I had found myself in her arms many times over the years. As soon as she began to rub my back, the emotions brought on from the last couple of days made my eyes spring a massive leak. Ian being here brought back more memories than I cared to remember, especially because so many of them were so sweet that it was painful. I also missed having a mother, and Holly had this way of making me feel so loved.

"Is he the man you met your first year at school?" she asked.

I couldn't speak, so I nodded my head against her shoulder. The only people I had really opened up to about Ian were my Dad and Amanda, but Holly knew I had gotten my heart broken in Colorado. She had always tried to get me to talk about it, even though her true desire was for me to marry Luke. At least it had been. She knew in her heart that it wasn't right for me or even fair to me.

"Hmm... That's what I thought," she said with all the tenderness of a real mother.

"Kelli, I really am sorry," Boss said.

I lifted my head. "It's not your fault. How could you have known?"

He rubbed his neck. "I don't know. He did seem very interested in you, but I assumed it was because I had mentioned several times that you were the heart of the office, and let's be honest, even the brains."

That earned him a smile.

"Of course, there's your profile picture and bio on our website, and what man wouldn't be interested in you?" he added.

I shook my head and laughed through my now intermittent tears. The Chandlers were always too kind. They thought everyone loved me. Love can be blind.

"All that being said, Ian is a brilliant businessman and I wouldn't have hired him if I didn't think he was the right person for the job. I've had background checks run on him and the whole caboodle."

"Boss, I'm not worried about Ian being a predator. He's not interested in me that way anyway. And believe me, I know how smart he is."

"Of course he's interested in you that way. Who wouldn't be?" Holly smoothed my cheek.

Remember what I said about love being blind? I wiped my eyes. "No. He's not, and it's okay. I came to terms with that a long time ago. He's here because, like you said, he's a brilliant businessman and he likes a challenge."

Holly rubbed her lips together. "So...how do you feel about him?" Holly hesitated to ask.

"I won't lie, I loved him," my voice cracked. "But now my feelings are quite the opposite." They both tensed, so I added in, "Don't worry, I won't let it get in the way of me giving my job 110 percent."

"I would never worry about you doing your job well, kiddo."

"Do you want to tell us what happened between the two of you, sweetheart?" Holly asked. She loved a little intrigue.

"Not really. Honestly, I wish I could forget." I meant it too. Sure, it was mostly amazing, but that was the problem. It was amazing and right, and apparently, it could never be duplicated. As much as I never tried to compare my relationship with Ian to any others I had, I still did.

The standard had been set, and I wanted nothing less. Unfortunately, I'd never even come close, and man had I tried. Well, not lately, but you can only try so many times before it feels like a lost cause.

I could tell my unwillingness to talk about Ian's and my past disappointed them, but the less everyone knew the better. Especially since Ian was coming over. It was bad enough that I knew, and of course, that Ian knew. I wished I could forget how distasteful it was for him to know that I loved him. But that's something a girl doesn't ever forget. And it's not really something you want other people to know. It was still embarrassing, but I guessed I was going to have to get over it if I wanted to keep working at Chandler.

"We understand, honey." Holly gave Boss a squeeze.

"Can I ask why you invited him for dinner?"

Holly headed for the refrigerator, leaving that question for Boss to answer.

Boss became interested in the hot pad left on the island and picked it up, blankly staring at it. "We…"

Holly turned around and gave him the eye.

"Okay, I thought it would be a good idea if you two got reacquainted outside the office," he admitted. "I thought perhaps I could smooth things over."

"So, this is a therapy session?" I joked.

Boss dropped the hot pad. "Kelli, this isn't going to work without you on board, and I feel terrible about the situation I've placed you in. I need to know you're going to be all right. The company is secondary to you in this situation."

I walked over and hugged Boss. "I love you. You don't need to worry about me. He's only a man after all."

Boss squeezed me tight. "Yeah, well, I know men, Kelli. And I know you, and I've never seen you react like you did yesterday."

I tried to wave off his concern. "I was caught off guard, that's all."

I don't think either he or Holly believed that, but it was the best I could do. I couldn't bring myself to tell the whole truth and nothing but the truth when it came to Ian. If I had to work with him, I needed to pretend like we never knew each other. I wasn't sure how I was going to accomplish that, but not talking about it was a good place to start. Maybe I shouldn't have told Amanda. Too late now.

"Again, had I known Kelli…"

I looked Boss straight in the eye. "You would have made the same decision. You're a businessman, too. And I respect that."

He gave me another good squeeze. "Someday that office will be yours," he paused, "that is… unless you find something else that makes you happier."

I let go of him and tilted my head. The way he'd said that was interesting. He winked at me and then asked Holly what he could do to help. I pitched in as well. It was like old times, except that I was fretting on the inside worrying about Ian showing up. For Boss's and Holly's sake, I needed to put on my game face. I didn't want them worrying about me or their company when they should be relaxing and enjoying retirement and their family. I could be a big girl about this. I just needed to act as if the best year of my life never happened. Easy, right?

Just as we finished setting the table, the doorbell rang. It made me jump. I flexed my hands trying to relax and get my head in the game.

While Boss went to answer the door, Holly joined me at the table and took my hand. "Life has a way of giving us what we need, not always what we want; but, if we're smart, we'll realize that's what we wanted all along."

I didn't have time to respond to her curious advice because Boss walked back with Ian. I closed my eyes for a split second, breathed in deeply, and put on a counterfeit smile that would pass for the real deal any day.

Ian immediately zeroed in on me with a tentative smile. In fact, everyone was looking at me and smiling. I could tell though that Boss didn't quite buy my smile, but what could he say now?

After the greeting pleasantries, we were seated. Ian and I ended up next to each other, whether by design or accident I couldn't tell; but, no matter, I was concealing not feeling. I smiled inwardly at my *Frozen* reference. I couldn't wait to tell Amanda. She was so tired of hearing the girls sing the songs from that film. Now I could tell her about the real-life application and give her a laugh.

Dinner started a little awkward. I'm not sure anyone knew what to say right off.

Holly, though, was a gracious hostess. "Ian, tell us how you like Nashville so far. Have you found a place to settle yet?"

He lowered his glass "It's been interesting, but I'm looking forward to getting to know the city better. And for the interim I'm staying at the Westin. I have an idea of where I'd like to land, but I'm not quite sure yet."

I wondered if he was in one of the penthouses the Westin offered. It was hard to imagine Ian in a penthouse. I had always known he would be successful, but when I knew him, he lived in a small basement apartment with an untidy roommate named Jeff. Ian only put up with him because he paid half the rent.

"I would be happy to put you in touch with a friend of mine that's a realtor," Holly offered.

"Thank you, but I don't think that will be necessary."

Maybe that meant he wasn't planning on staying long. I tried not to get my hopes up too high.

Holly and Boss went on to tell Ian all of the great places he needed to go and where the best neighborhoods were. I stayed mostly quiet, unless I was asked a question. I knew Holly and Boss were trying to engage me because they talked about some of my favorite places, like Cheekwood the nearby botanical garden, and the Grand Ole Opry. All I offered up was my agreement that they were worth visiting. Ian kept glancing my way, obviously hoping for more engagement. I would flash him my fake smile. It was better than crying or screaming, because that's what I really wanted to do. I wanted to know why he couldn't have loved me. And why did he have to look so darn good? And why, oh why, did he have to come here?

Then things got really interesting. "So, will your family be joining you soon? This is a great place to raise a family." Holly winked at me.

From our earlier conversation in the kitchen, I got the feeling she already knew he didn't have a family. What was she playing at?

Ian set his fork down and cleared his throat. "I'm sure it is, but I'm single."

She placed her hand across her heart. "Oh, I'm sorry. I thought Gary had mentioned a wife?"

Holly looked to Gary, and Gary and Ian both looked at me. I'm not sure why.

Ian was definitely uncomfortable. His skin even pinked a little. I tried to be unfazed by it. I was thankful I had googled him last night and already knew his marital status. Ian spoke to Holly, but his eyes were on me. I avoided looking directly into his deep dark optical pools. Unfortunately, that meant getting a good view of his five o'clock shadow that was begging to have some hands on it. Holy crap, where did that thought come from? *Um hello*, my brain said, *we have firsthand experience. Remember how amazing it felt.* My brain and I were having words later.

"No need to apologize. I'm divorced," Ian hesitated to admit.

"Well, I'm sorry to hear that," Holly said, but she didn't look sorry at all. Her smile was so wide it showcased all her capped teeth.

"It was for the best," he said it so matter-of-factly, I couldn't tell if he was upset by it or not. Not like I cared. Right?

Not only did I need a change of subject, but I needed him to quit looking at me. "Holly, Boss said you got some new pictures of your grandbabies."

That did the trick. Holly jumped right up and went to retrieve the pictures in the living room. Boss gave me a strained look that said he knew what I was doing.

Ian turned his attention to Boss. "How many grandkids do you have?"

Boss's face lit up like the Times Square's Christmas tree. He was ever the proud grandpa. "Three." He went on to brag, and rightly so, about his babies, Sara, Ethan Jr., and Camden.

Holly rejoined us, passed out the pictures, and bragged along with Gary. Camden was just starting to walk, Ethan was the star pupil in kindergarten, and Sara, the eight-year-old, played the piano, just to name a few of their many wonderful qualities. I oohed and ahhed at the adorable pictures, and fortunately the grandkids took us all the way through dinner.

As soon as dinner was over I jumped up. "Please, let me clean up."

"I've got it, honey." Holly stood. "Why don't you just relax?" Holly picked up one of the serving dishes.

I wasn't taking no for an answer. I would be more relaxed at my annual gynecologist appointment than I would be sitting there with Ian. My limit for concealing had almost expired for the evening. I hoped the longer I was around Ian, the easier it would get to completely hide my true feelings around him.

While in the kitchen, Holly sidled up to me. "Wow is he handsome. Did he look like that when you knew him?"

"He's a better dresser now, and he used to wear glasses, but he's always looked nice."

Nice was an understatement. He looked like he stepped out of the pages of GQ. Tonight he was wearing designer jeans, a perfectly pressed shirt, and a canvas jacket that looked tailored to fit him. He was definitely eye candy, but like I said before, I missed the boring khakis and polos, and even the glasses. I had to quit thinking of the past. I didn't know the man who was impeccably dressed. The man who was now my boss. The thought made me want to cry. Why did he have to be the new director?

"No wonder you were attracted to him." Holly placed a plate in the dishwasher. "He seems nice, too."

"Uh-huh." He was nice—or at least he used to be—it was one of the reasons I fell for him. He could have made me feel like a real idiot when he tutored me, because, for some reason, calculus was difficult for me to understand. But he was patient and took the time to explain it until I got it, even if it took several times.

"Are you okay, sweetie?" Holly took the plate from me I'd just rinsed off.

I came out of my memory. "Who, me? Of course."

"You were awfully quiet at dinner."

"That's because that pasta dish was so amazing. I need the recipe."

She laughed. "You've always been a terrible liar."

"I'm just trying to adjust. But, seriously, I want that recipe."

She tapped my nose. "I'll give you the recipe, but you know I'm here if you need to talk."

"I know." Too bad it couldn't have worked out with their son. They would have been the best in-laws ever. And pictures of my cuties would be on their fridge too. If only Luke could have gotten his act together, he would have been the director. It was Boss's hope to turn over his company to his son someday, but Luke, unfortunately, was the poster boy for substance abuse.

Holly and I put dessert together: strawberry shortcake. When it was ready and plated, we each took two and brought them out to the dining room. Holly served Gary. That left me to serve Ian.

Ian touched my hand when I set down his dessert in front of him. "Thank you."

"You're welcome," I whispered. My hand tingled, and I felt a tad warm from the touch. I took a breath and reminded myself to conceal, not feel.

As soon as I sat down, Ian turned toward me. "Gary told me the good news. You've rescinded your resignation." He sounded more than pleased.

I gave him a close-lipped smile.

Gary raised his glass of water to me. "To our girl." He looked between Ian and me. "May this be the beginning of the most successful chapter Chandler Media has ever known. I'm expecting great things from this partnership."

Ian raised his glass to me. "I second that."

I ignored him and raised my own glass. "To Gary—the best boss a girl could ever ask for." And that's where I slipped. A single tear escaped. I wiped it away, but not before Ian noticed. I wasted no time in turning to my dessert for comfort. I tried not to focus on the conversation going on around me. I was ready to go home, and it wasn't too long after dessert that I made my move to do exactly that. Unfortunately, Ian had the same idea. We ended up walking out at the same time.

His car was parked behind mine, so he followed me. "We should celebrate. Let's go get a drink," he suggested.

Was he for real? "I'm not a big social drinker." I reached for my door.

He walked toward me grinning. "I didn't say it had to involve alcohol."

"Hmm . . . Thanks for the offer, but I don't think it's a good idea."

He stepped closer.

It made me all sorts of uncomfortable. My senses were drawn to him. And the way his cologne lingered in the air was my undoing.

"Why not, Kelli?"

I bit my lip. "Because you're going to be my boss." Okay, so I lied.

"I just saw you kiss and hug your current one goodbye."

"He's like a father to me."

"I remember someone telling me once or twice that I sounded like her dad."

I forced myself not to smile at the memories. "I don't know who you're talking about."

His smile faded. "Why can't you acknowledge we knew each other and that we share a past?"

"In my experience, it's not good to dwell on the past. Good night, Ian." I opened my door.

He gently grabbed my arm before I could get in. "So, you're saying you don't remember anything?"

I pulled my arm away from him. "No. I'm saying I remember everything."

Chapter Six

"**G**ARY AND HOLLY REALLY INVITED you both over for dinner?" Amanda asked.

I had called her as soon as I got home. I was a little thrown off by the evening, and all I could do was lie on the couch and stroke my lazy cat. My head was spinning, and I felt nauseous. "Yes, can I just say, awkward?"

"But you've decided to go back to Chandler?" There was a fair amount of hope in her voice.

"I'm sure I'll regret it, but yes."

"How did your new boss take the news?"

"He seemed genuinely happy about it. He even asked me to go out after and celebrate."

"Well, that's certainly interesting. What did you say?"

"Amanda, please keep your conjecturing out of this. He's not interested in me that way. And I'm certainly not interested in him. He's going to be my boss, for goodness' sake."

"You are so naïve sometimes, Kelli."

I laughed at her. "Really? This coming from the woman who thought Sam's soccer coach was only being friendly."

"Hey, how was I supposed to know? The guy knew I was married."

"Thanks for proving my point, sis."

"You are such a brat, Kelli Jelly. And you're naïve if you think this guy doesn't have ulterior motives that involve *you*."

I was really getting tired of her saying that. "That doesn't make any sense at all. I haven't seen the guy in almost thirteen years, and the last time I did see him, he made it clear he wanted nothing to do with me ever again." I started to cry. It was such a stupid thing to do over such a stupid man.

"Honey, don't cry."

"Why did he have to come back into my life? Everything was going so well."

"I don't know, but I know it wasn't by accident. Just be careful."

"What do you mean?"

"I don't think you've ever really gotten over this guy."

"That's ridiculous, Amanda. Of course, I have. Don't you remember? I almost got married."

"Kelli," she sighed. "You didn't almost get married. Yes, Luke asked you, but there was never any chance of you saying yes."

"That had nothing to do with Ian."

"No one's saying Luke didn't have issues, but you didn't love him or anyone else that's come your way."

"I've tried. I really have."

"I know you have."

"And I don't love Ian." I don't know why, but I needed to say that out loud.

"Maybe not, but you've got to admit, that relationship has affected all others."

"That makes me sound pathetic."

"No, it makes you sound human. Kelli, look at your life, it's not like you've closed yourself off. You're successful, beautiful, and no one puts their heart into anything the way you do. You are the best aunt, sister, friend, employee, coworker—you name it. I'm not saying you've sat around and pined for this guy. I'm just saying there may be some underlying feelings that have never been resolved. And he obviously has the same issue."

"Amanda, you know I love you more than my cat, and you're hands down the best sister and friend ever, but Ian's here for business. Period."

"Okay. Keep telling yourself that." She was trying to placate me. "Good night."

"Good night, sis."

She was killing me. She was supposed to make me feel better. Now I was more confused, and my head hurt. I wasn't going to lie, I was still physically attracted to Ian, but any woman would be. He had the whole tall, dark, and handsome thing going for him, and to top it off, he had this mysterious, brooding air to him. But the attraction meant nothing, because I was attracted to him before, so why would that change? His attitude and mannerisms were mostly the same, too, except I seemed to frustrate him more, and not in the fun, cute way I used to. Like tonight, he seemed legitimately upset by my refusal to acknowledge our previous relationship, which was weird. I could also tell at dinner he was expecting more from me, and he was bothered when I didn't rise to the occasion. Then he stormed off without a word after I told him I remembered every- thing. I still couldn't believe I was agreeing to work with him. I had a feeling there was going to be lots of turbulence and frequent warnings to put my seatbelt on.

Typically, I reveled in the weekend, but I was happy to have this one over and done. I needed to get away from myself and my thoughts. I needed to work, even though working meant seeing Ian. Hopefully our contact would be limited. I mean it wasn't like Boss and I worked together constantly. In fact, he ran his accounts and I ran mine. In addi- tion, I took care of the running of the office. Boss and I met weekly, and sometimes we collaborated, but it wasn't an everyday thing. I was sure Ian would want to collaborate even less. He was the type who hated group projects. That thought made me feel much better.

I got up super early on Monday and dressed with a purpose. My sister was right; I was going to show him what he'd missed out on. I wore a nude pencil skirt that left no question I was a woman, a very feminine yet chic red wrap-around blouse, and beige suede peep-toe pumps. I may not have been the new boss, but I was going to do my best to look like it. The red lipstick was even coming out again. If I had been one to take selfies, this would've been the morning for it. I pulled my hair up in a messy yet sexy bun, made my lunch, and was out the door with a spring in my step.

I was hoping to be the first one there, but I was disappointed when I saw the Infiniti with Colorado license plates. *Dang it.* Delfia wasn't even there. No matter, I was a big girl. I just needed to remember to treat him like I had never known him before. I was going to be professional. I proudly walked into the empty foyer and made my way up the stairs. I took a deep breath before I opened the door. It felt right. I belonged here, no matter who the director was. I smiled to myself as I opened the door to the executive level.

I heard Ian before I saw him. It sounded like he was still using the conference room, which made sense. Boss was still going to be working here this week while he turned everything over to Ian. I think he also wanted to be here just in case he needed to referee. But I planned to be on my best behavior, or basically employ a simple strategy of avoidance, if I could get away with it. That plan didn't work so well when I tried to scoot past the conference room unnoticed.

It was as if he was waiting for me, like a cheetah ready to pounce on its prey. Ian met me at the conference room door as I passed. "Good morning," he said.

I wanted to say it *was* a good morning until that moment, but I acted professional. "Good morning. Did you have a nice weekend?" That was professional, right?

He thought for a second and pressed his lips together. I also noticed that his eyes drifted over me. "It was interesting. How was yours?"

"Fabulous."

His forehead scrunched. He knew I was being sarcastic.

We both stood silent for a moment.

"Well, okay. Have a good day." I walked off, criticizing myself for sounding so stupid. I was supposed to sound professional, not like an awkward ex-girlfriend.

"I'd like to meet with you later today to discuss the digital ad software. Let me know what your schedule looks like," he called out after me.

I took a deep breath, and before I turned around I reminded myself to treat him like I would any colleague, even though he was already getting on my nerves. "I'll send you a copy of my schedule, and you can let me know what works best for you."

"Thank you, Ms. Bryant."

I had already begun to turn around, but I stopped dead in my tracks and turned back toward him. "Did you just call me, Ms. Bryant?"

"Yes." He stood tall and proud. "I feel it's important to maintain professional boundaries with my employees within the office."

I wanted to say what a pompous twit he was, but I kept it together. "I see, Mr. Greyson."

He opened his mouth like he was going to respond, but he thought the better of it and turned and went back to the conference room.

I headed straight to my office and shut the door harder than I intended to. I sat at my desk and stewed. What was all this bull about professional boundaries? If he thought he was treating me like just another employee, he had another thing coming. Boss said this was a partnership, and Boss had treated me like a partner. Seriously, Ms. Bryant? What an idiot!

As soon as my laptop booted up, I immediately began to fill my schedule for the day. I smiled to myself. Looks like I wouldn't have much time for that meeting with Mr. Greyson after all. I almost laughed, thinking about his formality. It shouldn't have surprised me, but seriously, this wasn't the 1950s, and I wasn't some little girl who took orders. With more than a little glee, I emailed him my packed schedule. With a wicked smile on my face, I went to work catching up on all the emails I had missed on Friday.

Halfway through me playing catch up, Delfia came in and gave me a big hug. "You don't know how afraid I was you weren't coming back."

"I'm sorry I didn't call you back and made you worry. I needed to . . . sort some things out."

She waved away my apology. "All is forgiven, just tell me what's up with you and the new boss?"

I knew I needed to proceed with caution. I had no desire for the whole office to know that Mr. Greyson and I once dated. Or worse, that I had been more than smitten with him. I loved Delfia, but she was the queen of office gossip.

"What do you mean?" I asked innocently, or as innocently as you can get when you're lying.

She playfully smacked my arm. "Oh, honey. There's definitely a history between the two of you."

I tried to answer honestly without telling the whole truth. "He was my calculus tutor my freshman year in college." That was the truth.

She tapped her finger against her lip. "Why do I get the feeling those were private lessons?"

"Delfia!"

"Fine, you don't have to tell me, but I have a feeling it's going to get really interesting around here."

I didn't even bother with a rebuttal. I let her walk out, laughing to herself. She was right, though, things were going to get really interesting. In fact, "interesting" only took a few minutes. Mr. Professional Boundaries decided to grace my office doorway with his presence, and here I thought I wouldn't see him all day.

"Can I help you, Mr. Greyson?" I tried to keep the derision out of my voice, but my nineteen-year-old self begged for it to come out. I mean, for heaven's sake, this man used to wrap me up in his arms and kiss me until I saw stars, and then he would whisper in my ear, "Kelli, I'm crazy about you." Now here he was expecting me to call him, "Mr. Greyson."

He raised his brow at me. "Do you have a problem with calling me Mr. Greyson?"

I saluted him. "No sir." So much for being professional. I looked at the time. That had lasted all of about forty-five minutes.

"Kel—"

I smirked at him

"Ms. Bryant, in my experience, it's important for someone in my position to set the proper expectations. I'm not here to make friends."

I so badly wanted to comment. I had the best comeback on the tip of my tongue; it took everything I had not to say what I so desperately wanted to. I wondered if Boss knew what an arrogant jerk he had hired to take his place. We were going from the man who was everyone's friend to a man who apparently wanted to be an island.

I held in my comment, but it was really hard.

"Do you have something to say?" He knew me too well.

I shook my head no, but he waited several seconds before he spoke again. It was like he was daring me to say it. I almost did, but in this battle of wills, I planned on being the victor. When he realized I wouldn't be rising to the sarcastic occasion, he invited himself all the way into my office, came around, and stood behind me at my desk. I thought it was odd.

He leaned down and looked over my shoulder, pointing to my screen. "Would you mind pulling up your schedule?"

Oh, he smelled good. He was still wearing the same cologne he had so many years ago. It was a warm, spicy scent. It drove me crazy, and when I looked over to him, our faces were too close for comfort. I quickly turned away and complied with his request, trying to ignore my rapid heartbeat. This was ridiculous.

When my schedule popped up, he reached over my shoulder and began touching the screen, asking about each appointment and if it could be rescheduled. Each time I replied in the negative. He was becoming increasingly frustrated with me. That delighted me more than it should.

"How about a working lunch?" he suggested.

"Hmm ... I had wanted to run some errands."

"Kel— I mean, Ms. Bryant."

I loved how he couldn't even stick with his own dumb rules.

"It's important that we meet. I would be happy to have Ms. King, order something in for us. Or if you would like, we can go out somewhere together."

I pinched the bridge of my nose. Everyone else called her Delfia, it had taken me a moment to figure out who Ms. King was. He was giving me a headache. I really didn't want to meet with him, but I knew I couldn't keep avoiding it. The more I put it off, the worse it would be. "I brought my lunch," I huffed. "I'll meet you in the conference room at noon."

He stood up straight. "That wasn't so hard now was it, Ms. Bryant?"

I swiveled in my chair to face him. "Is that all, Mr. Greyson? As you can see, I'm busy."

His chest rose and fell. "I look forward to meeting with you." He turned and walked out.

Yeah, well that made one of us! I crumpled up a piece of paper and threw it at the opened door.

I peeked out my office door to see Delfia trying to hold back her laughter. I shook my head in disgust, threw my earbuds in, and went to work. I had emails and proposals that needed my attention.

The only interruption I welcomed was Boss coming in to wish me a good morning. "You look good in this office, kiddo," he said.

I wanted to say I would look even better in the adjoining office, but I left it alone. What's done is done.

The morning unfortunately flew by between catching up on email, sending out two proposals, and having a conference call with a demo. As noon approached, I headed to my private bathroom and touched up my make-up. I knew it could have seemed like I wanted to impress my new boss, but I would have done it for anyone, and mostly for myself.

I pulled up the roadmap for the product on my laptop before I undocked it and grabbed my lunch. I made my way over to the conference room. Delfia wagged her brows at me as I walked by. I rolled my eyes at her.

"By the way, you look sizzling today," she whispered.

I laughed and kept on walking. I loved her.

I walked in to find Ian, I mean, you know who, set up with two laptops running, surrounded by a myriad of files. It also looked like he had ordered in sushi. Yuck. When he noticed me, he stood and pulled out the chair next to him. Ugh, I was planning on sitting across from him. Once again, he thwarted my plans.

I begrudgingly took the seat next to him. "Thank you," I said somewhat politely. I almost added in that it was probably crossing a professional boundary for him to pull out my chair, but I decided to keep that to myself and get this meeting over with.

"Would you like some sushi?" he asked as soon as I was situated.

"Uh, no thanks. We like our fish fried here in the South."

He chuckled. "You might like it."

"I don't think so." I pulled out my crunchy peanut butter and plum jam on whole wheat bread sandwich.

Before I took a bite, he stared at my sandwich. "Remember that day in the park when . . ."

I whipped my head toward him. Our eyes locked. For a brief moment, I saw the old Ian. It was a little disconcerting. Then just like that, it was gone.

He shook his head. "I can't believe you still eat those."

I had probably eaten more peanut butter and jam sandwiches than I could count, but I still loved them. They were a reminder of childhood and happy times. Some of those happy times included Ian. I wondered what day in the park he remembered, because there were several to choose from. It was our favorite place to study and engage in other activities.

I shrugged my shoulders. "Well, I can't believe people eat raw fish."

He held up a sushi roll and downed it.

I went back to my plain sandwich. "So, what did you want to discuss?" I asked after a few bites.

He wiped his mouth with a napkin and pulled up a file on the laptop closest to him. "I wanted to discuss the direction of the product, new feature enhancements, branding, etc."

"Great, I've been working on a roadmap…"

He didn't even let me finish my sentence before he began showing me mockups of a totally revamped product. It looked nothing like the original. It was overly sleek and slightly complicated in my opinion.

"Have you ever worked with banks and credit unions before?" I interrupted him after several minutes.

"A few," he responded.

"Okay. Then did you know that most marketing departments, especially in smaller financial institutions, don't have access to IT departments, and most of them lack high tech skills?"

"This product doesn't only have to be utilized by financial clients."

"I agree, and I would like to branch out to other verticals, but I don't want to alienate our current clientele in the meantime. I believe the roadmap I've created addresses both issues."

He sat back in his chair and folded his arms. "Show me what you have." It was like he was daring me to dazzle him.

No problem. I pulled up my roadmap that included a presentation outlining what I believed to be key feature enhancements, like an expanded ad library and tools to create your own ads with the ability to add branding and logos. I discussed my idea for tier levels of features and support with varying price points. I also mapped out a free version with a limited feature set that was just enough to water the mouths of potential clients in the hopes of turning them into paying customers. Between speaking I would glance at Mr. Greyson. He was engrossed in the presentation. When I was done, I let out a deep breath and turned toward him.

He grinned and nodded his head. "I'm impressed."

"You sound surprised."

"I am," he said bluntly.

I couldn't help it, I rolled my eyes. "What did you expect?"

He touched my hand, but quickly seemed to realize that was crossing professional boundaries. He pulled it back, but it was too late. My hand was saying, *Hey, I remember that touch.* And unfortunately, it liked it. Dumb hand.

"You're taking that wrong."

"Oh really, how *should* I take it?"

He leaned forward. "Are you going to be sensitive about everything I say?"

I leaned in closer, getting right in his face. "Do you plan on being continually condescending, Mr. Greyson?"

We both stared hard at one another for several moments. Boss walked in and caught us in our staring contest. We both jumped and sat up straight. I smoothed out my blouse. Boss looked between the two of us. I could feel my cheeks redden out of embarrassment and anger.

"Great, I'm glad to find you both together," Boss said uneasily.

"Ms. Bryant was just showing me her roadmap," Ian, or whoever he was, informed Boss.

Boss smiled at me like a proud father. "Impressive, isn't it?"

"Very," you-know-who replied, but then he ruined it. "I would like to add in a few more feature enhancements like more variability and ordering control. I would also like to bring in a graphic designer to update the interface."

I whipped my head toward him. "What's wrong with the current design?"

"It's busy and outdated."

I looked to Boss for support. That was my design, and we had carefully gone through several versions until we got it right. We had even sent it out to several potential clients for feedback.

Boss tugged on his collar. "Kelli, maybe this is a good time to turn over the design work to someone else, so you can focus more on marketing and selling the product."

My shoulders dropped. How could Boss take his side?

"I didn't realize the design was yours," Ian said.

I glared at him. I wanted to say it wouldn't have made a difference, he still would have said the same thing, but all I could manage was, "Is our meeting over, Mr. Greyson?"

"What's with all the formality between you two?" Boss asked.

I stood up without Ian's answer. I was declaring the meeting over. "Mr. Greyson feels it sets the proper boundaries between himself and his employees." I almost said lowly subjects, but that would have been going too far. I walked toward the door but turned back before marching out. I caught a glimpse of Boss's confused face and Ian's stunned one. "Excuse me, I have an appointment." There was no need to say it was with me, myself, and I.

I headed straight for my office to put on my walking shoes and grab a jacket. I needed to walk around the lake to clear my head and possibly reevaluate my decision to work for Mr. Pain in My Backside. As I walked back past the conference room, I could see Boss and Ian deep in discussion through the window of the now-closed door. I'm sure my name was being brought up.

When I hit the cool air, I breathed in deeply. I felt so out of control. I couldn't, in recent memory, remember feeling so out of sorts. I needed to get it together, but for some reason I couldn't seem to, no matter how hard I tried. As I walked, I tried to focus on my breathing. I tried not to think about the idiot who occupied the conference room and ate sushi. Okay, I may have thought of him, but it was to pray that his sushi was tainted. He deserved a good case of food poisoning. How dare he be surprised that I actually have talent. And how dare he call my designs outdated. I worked hard on those. I researched the best color schemes, patterns, and placements for ease of use and aesthetics.

So, I wasn't doing well in not trying to think about him. Stupid, good-smelling, handsome man.

After thirty minutes of walking I felt a little better, but I knew I couldn't stay out there forever. Good news though, the trees around the lake were beginning to bud. Spring was just around the corner. Thank goodness. More good news, when I made it back upstairs to my office, the conference room was devoid of people. I walked back to my office in peace and finished the rest of my day on the phone with potential clients. I was more than ready to leave when five rolled around. I walked out to an empty reception area. Delfia had gone home for the day as had Boss. I didn't think he planned on working full days for the remainder of the week. It seemed like his brain was already set on retirement.

With high hopes, I approached the conference room, but it seemed where Ian was concerned, my hopes would always be dashed. There he was, still working away. I planned to walk on by and not say anything. Yes, that was unprofessional, but I think where he was concerned, the less I had to do with him, probably the better for both of us. He, unfortunately, had other ideas.

"Do you have a few moments?" he said as I walked by.

Reluctantly, I stopped and leaned against the door frame. I gave him a look that said sure, whatever.

He set down the file he'd been going through. "I hope I didn't give you the impression that I'm anything but impressed with your work and vision. You're very talented."

"Thank you. Have a nice evening," I said dully.

The way he pinched the bridge of his nose said he was disappointed in my lackluster response. "Good evening," he replied.

I took that as my cue to skip out of there.

There were a few account managers left on the lower floor finishing up their day. I said my goodbyes to them. A couple of them expressed their wishes that I had been made the new director. I wasn't sure how to respond other than to thank them and lie by telling them Boss knew what he was doing, and I was sure Mr. Greyson was beyond capable. That wasn't a total lie, I had no doubt he was capable, I just didn't like his methods thus far.

It was a little depressing thinking about the could-have-beens as I walked out to my car. Oh well, I got a raise out of it, right? It didn't help much; money wasn't the most important thing to me. I had learned more money didn't equal more happiness. But it did buy trips to the Virgin Islands, and that could make me happy. On that cheerful note, I threw my satchel in the car.

"Kelli," Ian called my name.

Really? I turned around to face him. "Don't you mean, Ms. Bryant?" I mocked.

"No. We're off the clock," he said it like it should be obvious.

"You can't have it both ways," I countered.

He grinned. "Sure I can."

"Well, Mr. Greyson, it's either one or the other for me. Do you want to be Ian or Mr. Greyson?"

He stepped closer. "How about we discuss it over dinner?"

Why does he keep asking me to eat or drink with him? And why is he so pleasant outside of the office? I didn't know whether to make heads or tails of him, so I took a moment, my brow furrowed.

He, on the other hand, kept smiling like a fool. "Kelli?"

"Tell me who you are first. Ian or Mr. Greyson?"

"I'm both."

"That doesn't work for me."

He frowned. "Why do you have to complicate things?"

Oh. That phrase. My hand flew to my heart as if that would protect it. That was his response when I had told him I loved him. It was a complication to him. I knew it shouldn't have affected me, but hearing him say those words to me again triggered my emotions. All of the pain and confusion I'd felt came rushing back, overwhelming me. "I guess it's just something I'm good at, isn't it? Good night, Mr. Greyson." I jumped in my car. At least I was the one who got to walk away this time.

"Dammit," I heard him say before I shut my door.

In my rearview mirror I watched him stand there in the parking lot running a hand over his hair, looking as if he'd lost his best friend. I knew the feeling.

Chapter Seven

A FTER THAT FUN FIRST DAY, the rest of the week was less interesting, thank goodness. Mr. Greyson and I didn't avoid each other, but we both seemed to make it a point to spend as little time together as possible, which was A-Okay in my book. When we did have to be in each other's presence, it was filled with that forced politeness that makes everyone uncomfortable. I could tell this worried Boss, but I assured him it would all get ironed out as we got used to one another. It was a big fat fib, but I wanted Boss to be able to enjoy retirement.

To help Boss feel better, I took my licks, in a matter of speaking, and then nursed my wounds at home. And there seemed to be plenty every day. Mr. Greyson had suggestions for everything from my PowerPoints to the way I formatted my proposals. They weren't really suggestions; he expected them to be to his liking and specifications. I think he kept looking for me to fight back, and believe me I wanted to, but I figured what good would it do?

When Friday rolled around, Boss moved all his personal belongings out of the big office and Mr. Greyson moved in. I couldn't help it, I cried. I was losing my mentor and champion. I felt like an idiot crying in the office for the world to see, but it had been a rough week, and now reality was really setting in. As Boss held me, Delfia and Mr. Greyson looked on, concerned.

Boss kissed my head. "Make me proud, kiddo."

I sniffled and nodded.

"You always have." He gave me a good squeeze.

More tears came. Would it be shameful if I grabbed onto his legs and begged him not to leave?

Boss let me go, turned toward Mr. Greyson, and shook his hand. "Well Ian, I trust I'm leaving my company in good hands. I expect nothing less than greatness and high profit margins." Boss looked between him and me, before sternly saying to Mr. Greyson, "Ian, don't forget our earlier conversation."

Mr. Greyson focused on me. "You have my word."

I wondered what that cryptic conversation was about. Delfia looked perplexed too.

Boss hugged me one more time. "Well, I guess I'm off." He waved to everyone. "See you all next weekend." He and Holly were leaving the next morning for Cancun, but they were coming back next weekend for his retirement party.

As soon as Boss was out of sight, I went to my office, closed the door, and cried a little more. I was terrible with change, and this had been a week of nothing but change, and not the good kind either.

Amid my mourning, there was a knock on the shared door. No one ever knocked on that door. Boss and I had an open-door policy. I wiped away the last straggling tears. "Come in," I called out.

Mr. Greyson took a moment to look at me before he spoke. His eyes were softer than I had seen them in days. "Would you join me in my office? I would like to get your opinion on the new company logo," he asked kindly.

"You want my opinion?"

"Why does that surprise you?"

"Is that a trick question?"

"Ms. Bryant, please."

I stood and walked toward his office. He smiled with lips pressed together as I neared him. He waited for me at the door and held it open. When I passed him, he touched my shoulder and I stopped.

"I know this is a difficult transition for you and I'm sorry."

I half smiled and shrugged my shoulders. It was a nice gesture. I hadn't been this close to him in years. I got another glimpse of my Ian, but this time it lasted more than just a few seconds. Neither of us moved as we searched each other's eyes. He kept his hand on my shoulder. The feel of it wasn't lost on me. My body said, *Ahhh, isn't this nice*, but my head said, *Girl, get your head in the game.*

"Are you ready to show me the prototypes?" I asked, once out of my brief stupor.

He dropped his hand slowly and cleared his throat. "Please, have a seat."

He had already changed the office around. Boss's desk used to face the adjoining door, like mine. But Ian had it facing the door toward the reception area. He also added some pictures of the Colorado landscape. They were breathtaking. As I looked at them, I thought someday I really should go back and visit that place. I had loved living there. The Colorado mountain scenery was second to none. One picture particularly caught my attention. It was of the hot springs near his parents' home. I had fond memories of that place. During Thanksgiving break, Mr. Greyson, aka Ian, had taken me there. We spent a very enjoyable day in each other's arms with the steam rising all around us and the snow lightly falling down. Just the thought made me blush. I had needed some hefty amounts of Chapstick and lotion after that day, but it had been well worth it. The man was a master kisser. His kisses always conveyed what mood he was in. That day had been one of those rare Ian moments where his mind wasn't wrapped around fifty different things. He had let go that day and only let *us* occupy his thoughts. I think it was the first day he finally gave himself permission to really let me in and see the real him. It was the day he said to heck with what everyone would say about our age difference; he wanted to be with me, and so he was going to be.

I came out of my memory to find Mr. Greyson smiling at me. I nervously tucked my hair behind my ear. "Nice pictures," I said lamely before I took my seat.

He looked to his right at the picture I had just been admiring. "That's my favorite."

I wanted to say, "Mine too," but that was ridiculous. He probably didn't even remember that day, and if he did, I didn't want him to know I remembered it. I'm sure it was his favorite because it reminded him of his home.

"Ok, so logos," I said.

"Yes, logos." He took his seat.

He turned his monitor toward me and showed me three different designs. Right away I abhorred two of them. I wasn't sure who had done the design, but tacky was putting it nicely. The third design had some promise. I honed in on that one. "I think the C in Chandler should be more prominent, and it would look better if the letters were more rounded and in lower case. And personally, I would increase the font size by two," I suggested. "Those changes would make it feel cleaner and more modern. It would encompass the new direction of our company."

He looked at me thoughtfully when I finished my suggestions.

I raised my left brow. "Surprised again?"

"As always, when it comes to you."

"I'll let that slide."

"I meant it as a compliment."

I stood. "You might want to work on that." I smiled at him before I could stop myself.

I walked back to my office and downed my bottle of water while I thought of all the reasons I disliked my new boss, because it was better than picturing him shirtless, with my arms around him, kissing him until my lips threw up a white flag and surrendered. And what was I doing using my flirty voice there at the end of our conversation? I think it was time for me to go home.

It was my plan to take the weekend and unwind. I was thinking a marathon weekend of cheesy Netflix movies and ordering-in was the ticket. That seemed to work well on Friday night, but I got up on

Saturday feeling crappy about stuffing myself the night before and lying lazily on the couch with Charlie, so I figured I better get my butt to the Y and maybe do some grocery shopping.

Walking outside reminded me it was March, and boy was it coming in like a lion. The rain was coming down in sheets. As I ran to my car, I noticed a moving truck. I felt sorry for whoever had to move in this weather.

After hitting it hard at the Y, I was feeling less like a slug and more like myself. It helped me make better choices when I went to the grocery store. Well, mostly, I needed some chocolate after the week I'd had.

When I returned to my complex, the rain was still coming down. My sister's words rang in my head, "You could have an attached garage if you would only buy a home." Yeah, but how lonely would a big empty house be with only Charlie and me?

I took heroic efforts to carry all my grocery bags in at once, even for-going my umbrella. I figured I was showering when I got home anyway. On my walk in, I noticed the moving truck was still there, along with two soaked movers. I hoped they were getting a good tip. As someone was moving in, the gate was open. Gratefully I didn't have to maneuver it with full arms and hands, but I quickly became ungrateful as I literally ran into him. You know, the *him* who was causing regular disruption in my life as of late. Yeah, that *him*.

I stood there stunned, staring at him, rain dripping down my face. "Mr. Greyson, at the risk of becoming redundant, what are you doing here?"

He flashed me a sly grin before sharing his large umbrella with me. I had to admit that was gentlemanly. He was even more of a gentleman when he reached for my bags. "Let me help you with those."

I instinctively pulled away from him. "No, thank you." I repeated my question, "Why are you here?" Then a terrible realization hit me before he even spoke.

"Kelli, as of today, I live here."

I shook my head no. "No, you don't," I stuttered.

His brown eyes danced with amusement.

"Please tell me you're kidding," I begged.

He wouldn't say it. All he did was continue to smile at me. Why wouldn't he say this was some kind of sick prank? I began walking toward my apartment in a zombie like trance. How could this be happening?

Ian followed me, keeping the rain off of me as I went.

I couldn't speak, but if I could have, I would have told him to hit the road. There were also a bunch of other things I would have liked to say, too, but they may have burned my own ears off.

I dropped my bags when we made it to my door and fished my key out of my pocket. "Thank you, Mr. Greyson. I've got it from here."

"Are you ever going to call me Ian again?"

"Nope. I think Mr. Greyson fits you."

He frowned and pressed his lips together. "Kelli..."

I opened my door and pushed it open as quick as I could, trying to ignore the shiver it gave me when he said my name so tenderly. I grabbed a few bags, hoping Mr. Greyson would get the hint and skedaddle.

That was wishful thinking. He picked up the remainder of them with ease.

"I've got it," I snapped more than I meant to.

"I'm sure you do." He, on the other hand, was kinder than me. That was until he came right into my apartment uninvited. His audacity was stunning.

"I told you I don't invite men into my apartment."

"No, you said you didn't invite in strangers, and we both know I'm not one and this isn't the first time I've been in one of your apartments." He looked around and grinned. "But this one is a lot nicer than the last one."

I stared at him with my mouth wide open, not sure what to say. Two weeks ago, I would have never in a million years imagined this could ever happen. I finally managed to find my words again. "Did you just wake up one morning and think, 'I haven't tortured Kelli Bryant in years, I need to get on that?'"

"You got me," he said as he walked past me toward my kitchen. He set the grocery bags on my counter, turned around and strutted right back toward me.

All I could do was stand by my door and watch him.

He stopped to the side of me, leaned in close and whispered in my ear, "Or maybe this has nothing to do with you at all."

Goose bumps erupted all over my body. Curse him.

On that note, he walked out my door laughing. He turned, though, before fully exiting. "I'm in 211B, just in case you wanted to know. And by the way, I welcome women into my apartment."

I dropped the bags I had been iron gripping. Who was this man? I was torn between chucking something at his head or giving him a house-warming kiss.

Chapter Eight

CHARLIE RUBBING AGAINST MY LEGS begging for attention pulled me out of my Mr. Greyson stupor. The man was infiltrating every space of my life, and his whole "this has nothing to do with you" comment kept running through my head. Of course it wasn't about me, but still.

After putting my groceries away, I called Amanda. She was probably sick of all the calls this week, but I knew she would want to hear about this turn of events. At least I wasn't crying this time.

"Whaaaat!" she exclaimed.

"You heard me right."

"I knew it."

"You knew what?"

"He still has feelings for you."

I adamantly disagreed with her for the hundredth time on the subject and told her about his "nothing to do with me" comment.

She snickered. "Yep, he's got it bad for you."

"Did you hear what I said?"

"Loud and clear, my dear sister. Hold on, I want to tell Zane."

I could hear Zane laughing in the background as she told him. He asked if he should come over and talk to the guy.

"Tell Zane that's not necessary."

"Well, I think I'm going to come over. I want to see this guy for myself."

"Amanda, you will do no such thing. Plus, you can meet him at the retirement party. And I expect you to keep your incorrect conjectures to yourself."

"Oh honey, I'm not the wrong one here. Even Zane agrees with me."

"Well then, *that* makes it all true."

"So snarky this morning, Kelli Jelly."

"Yeah, after the week I've had, snarky is the nicest of my emotions right now."

She paused for a minute. "You know, I think this is good for you."

"Really? Because I was thinking more along the lines of so freaking *not* good."

"You needed a shakeup," she sounded overtly motherly. "You've been working too hard, and when was the last time you even went on a date?"

I thought for a moment. "It's been a while, but FYI, I'm not going to be dating my boss, who just happens to be my ex-boyfriend, who just happens not to want to date me, and oh yeah, I can't stand him."

"Ooh, I don't know, I think I'm sensing some serious tension between the two of you and dating the boss could have its perks."

"Get your head out of those romance novels you hide under your bed."

"Come on, some stolen kisses in the copy room—it could work. And by the way, I download those books on my e-reader now."

"Well on that note, I'm going to go take a shower."

I stayed in the shower until the water began to run lukewarm, planning on how to avoid Mr. 211B. Maybe it was time to go house hunting, or husband hunting. Though there didn't seem to be a large herd of single, available men that were good husband material. Sure, I shot a few that were nice boyfriends, but no one who made me want to spend forever with them. Well, there had been one. But we're not talking about him. Besides, Ian no longer existed; now there was only Mr. Greyson.

When I got out of the shower, I decided to write a list of qualities I wanted in a husband. Like that would help. But I'd read that until you wrote a goal down it was only a wish.

Top Ten Husband Qualities

1. Gainfully employed.
2. Good kisser.
3. Must want children.
4. A non-yes man.
5. Handsome and well groomed.
6. Must adore me.
7. Challenges me to be better.
8. Preferably never married.
9. Minimal baggage. See number 8.
10. Above all, faithful to me.

That was a good starting place, I thought. Now if I could just find a man who met all of them. I didn't want perfection, I only wanted someone perfect for me. I took a magnet and pinned the list to the refrigerator. Maybe if I looked at it enough, he would magically appear. Uh-huh.

I spent the rest of the weekend hiding out in my apartment, except on Sunday I snuck out to go to church. I probably looked like a fool as I tried to covertly exit and enter my apartment complex without being seen. Not like he was looking for me, but I didn't want to run into him. It was bad enough I had to see him every day at work, now we were practically neighbors, too. He lived across the courtyard in the higher priced buildings. From the apartment number, it sounded like he had one of the two-story apartments that came with large lofts. I don't know why he would choose to live in an apartment when he clearly had plenty of money. I guess I had plenty of money not to live here either, though.

I counted my lucky stars that I didn't see him again for the rest of the weekend, but I woke up on Monday knowing that was all going to change. At least the sun was back out and it was going to be warm. The sound of birds chirping was like music to my ears as I got ready. I threw on some fabulously fitting jeans, a white dress shirt, and a tan jacket. I accessorized my ensemble with turquoise jewelry and some sexy heels. I even curled my hair and added some volume.

I walked into the office feeling pretty good about myself. Per usual, Delfia and Mr. Greyson were already there. Mr. Greyson was giving directions to Ms. King on how he liked his appointments scheduled. He was OCD about spacing. I couldn't help but smile a little. I had never met anyone who had given more thought to every aspect of his life than he had.

Delfia looked relieved to see me. "Good morning," she said with a hint of exasperation.

"Good morning, Delfia…Mr. Greyson."

He looked at me from top to bottom and did a double take. He didn't return the greeting; in fact, he grimaced. "Jeans?"

I didn't give him the satisfaction of a reply, but I could see Delfia's eyes widen as I stalked off. Now he was the fashion police? I bet he was going to send out a memo about the dress code. He had already sent out several dealing with tardiness, proper break room etiquette, expense accounts, etc. I stewed about his comment while my laptop came up, drumming my fingers against my desk. This was not the way I had wanted to start Monday morning. I was tired of taking my licks from him. As soon as I heard him walk back into his own office, I marched myself right over to the adjoining door and threw it open.

He jolted a bit, startled by my sweeping entrance.

I started right in. "Do you have a problem with what I'm wearing today, Mr. Greyson?"

He set down the file he had in his hand on the desk. He took a few seconds to respond, exhaling loudly as his eyes swept over me. "Ms. Bryant, as an executive in this organization you need to set the proper example."

"We're not in 1950s."

"Jeans convey a lackadaisical approach to one's job, no matter what time period," he said without apology.

"Is that the impression I've given you about how I approach my job?"

"Not at all."

"Then I would appreciate it if you would keep your opinions about how I dress to yourself. And just for the record, I never wear jeans when I meet with clients. Oh, and next time you want to let me know how displeased you are with me, don't do it front of Delfia or anyone else for that matter." In a huff, I turned toward my office.

"Ms. Bryant, note the way that door swings. I expect you to use my main door, and I expect you to knock," he called out.

I didn't even bother looking at him. "Duly noted, sir!" I slammed the door. Welcome to Monday morning. I threw myself in my chair, stared coldly at the adjoining door, and mocked his words in my head. "Note the way that door swings." Well, if he thought he could use that door to walk into my office, he had another thing coming to him. I decided it was time to do some rearranging of the furniture in my office. I eyed the credenza to the right of the door. Perfect. I took off all of my awards that graced the top and emptied the contents so it would be easier to move. I began pushing it over, but that wasn't working so well. I way underestimated how heavy it was.

After several minutes of pushing and only moving it an inch, I peeked out my door and thankfully found Delfia by herself at her desk. I silently motioned for her to come into my office. She scrunched her brow but honored my request.

I quietly closed my door. "I need you to help me move my credenza over," I whispered.

I'm pretty sure she thought I had lost my mind, but she agreed. It took our combined strength, but we finally did it. Now it sat centered right in front of the door.

I stepped back and admired our handiwork. "Thank you."

She started laughing and shaking her head. "You know it's the kids that suffer when the parents fight."

I rolled my eyes at her. "We're not fighting."

"Oh, you just raise your voice now when you talk to the boss and slam doors? And you decided on a whim to move your credenza?"

"Thank you, Delfia," I said as I showed her out my door.

"Yep, it's going to get interesting around here." She chuckled on her way out.

That was an understatement, I thought as I placed everything back on the credenza. By the time I got to answering email, I was exhausted. Stupid man. I was so tempted to pull up my résumé and begin polishing it, but I hated to see all the hard work I had put into the marketing software get turned over to him. I had a feeling if I left, others would leave too, and I didn't want Boss to worry about his company. It was only 8:30, and I had a headache. I popped some Tylenol and rubbed my temples. My sister was so wrong, this wasn't good for me at all.

I didn't have to see him until that afternoon when we had a meeting with our account managers. About an hour before the meeting, I heard a knock on the adjoining door. I looked up and grinned as I saw the doorknob twist, and twist some more. It made my day for at least a minute or two. It didn't take too long, though, before there was a knock on my other door. I sighed. I knew who it was, but I had no choice but to say, "Come on in."

He stepped in. "Ms. Bryant, there seems to be something wrong with the door. It wouldn't . . ." He looked over.

"Looks good to me," I said cheerily.

He turned back toward me, and before he could say a word, I cut him off at the pass. "I did some rearranging today, do you like it?"

"Not particularly." He frowned.

I shrugged my shoulders. "I guess you can add it to the ever-growing list of things you don't like about me or how I do things. Anyway, what can I help you with, Mr. Greyson?"

"Kel— Ms. Bryant, I don't have time to address that comment at this moment, but believe me I will. Right now, we need to go over the agenda for the managers meeting, and I need to get some sales numbers from you."

I motioned for him to have a seat, and we discussed the agenda. We only disagreed on a few points. He kept pinching the bridge of his nose.

Apparently, I gave him a headache like he gave me one. I almost offered him some Tylenol, but then I thought he deserved to suffer. When we went over sales numbers and goals it got a little contentious as we haggled about where those numbers should be, but we eventually ended up on the same page as we each gave in a little.

"It's important we show a united front and convey we're a team, Ms. Bryant." He stood ready to leave for the meeting.

"I guess you want to be team captain."

He offered me a sincere smile. "That's what I've been hired to do."

"I suppose so."

On that note, we walked down together to face the troops.

He stopped me on the landing. "I couldn't have asked for a better co-captain, Ms. Bryant."

"I don't know whether to believe you or not, but thank you."

He tilted his head. "I've never lied to you."

"Hmm." Maybe he hadn't ever really lied to me, but when you tell someone daily how much you're crazy for her and then all of a sudden you stop for no real reason, it kind of seems like a lie. But that was ancient history, right?

"What?" he seemed confused.

I sighed. "Nothing, let's just get this meeting over with."

He took a moment to peer into my eyes as if he were desperate to know all my thoughts. I refused to allow him access. I turned with a loud exhale and walked down the stairs.

The meeting went better than I expected. I tried my best to soften Mr. Greyson's rigid, no-nonsense way of putting things. I was proud that I did it without once contradicting him. Instead, I used humor and charm to get our point across. Honestly, I agreed with a lot of his ideas and plans, I only hated his delivery. His brilliance was masked by his seriousness. I kept hoping he would lighten up just a little, but that thought made me sad because I used to make it my job to get him to do just that.

I was exhausted by the time I got home. I had a hunch I would be feeling that way a lot now. Working with Mr. Greyson was emotionally taxing, and if I had to keep moving furniture, it was going to be physically taxing as well. I laughed to myself thinking about him trying to open that door.

But no matter how tired I was, I was going to belly dancing class. I needed some happy endorphins. It worked marvelously too. I loved our little instructor, Roslyn, from Panama. Her favorite phrases were, "Sexy ladies, show your body who is boss," "Pop that booty," and my favorite, "Check those inhibitions at the door." I loved that for an hour I could pretend that I was some exotic, graceful dancer, all while burning calories. It was a win-win situation.

Just as I was feeling fabulous from the full effects of the endorphins, I was reminded why I had so desperately needed them. As I was walking out of the Y, *he* was walking in. *Of course he is.* He had already invaded every other place in my life, why not here, my happy endorphin place? We both stopped on the sidewalk near the entrance. He was smiling mischievously as his eyes roved over my form fitting tank top and exercise pants. Not something I really wanted him to see me in, but oh well. At least he couldn't tell me it was unbecoming of an executive.

"Mr. Greyson, let me guess, you have a membership at the Y, too."

"I have to work out somewhere."

I rolled my eyes. "Yeah, well, enjoy your workout."

I walked away without another word but turned back to catch another glimpse of him in his tight-fitting tee and shorts. Was he ever easy on the eyes, but unfortunately, he was watching me. He smirked at me, and I quickly turned around and hurried my pace. Stupid man.

When I walked in my apartment door, Charlie looked up at me lazily as if to say, *You silly woman.* I walked over and scratched his head. "You're right Charlie, I am a silly woman." He purred in agreement. I showered quickly, threw on some sweatpants and a tee. I sat cross-legged on my couch, turned on some mindless television, and enjoyed some warmed-up stew from the night before. My sister called and we chatted about my fun day. I had a feeling she was only calling me now for pure entertainment purposes, and honestly, as I recounted my day to her, I sounded ridiculous, moving furniture to block doors. What was I thinking?

As I was saying good night to my nieces, there was a knock on my door. I figured it was my neighbor, Faith, who I liked, but she used me as her second pantry. She probably needed an egg or something. I finished making kissing sounds and told Court and Sam I loved them before heading for my door. I opened it to find I should have ignored it. There stood Mr. Greyson, with a pint of chocolate fudge brownie ice cream along with two spoons, grinning like a fool in well-fitting dark jeans and a handsome button-up shirt.

"Mr. Greyson, do I dare even ask what you are doing here?"

"Kelli, please call me Ian."

"At the office, too?"

He thought for a moment, a battle raging in his eyes.

"Mr. Greyson it is then."

He sighed and held up the ice cream, which happened to be my favorite ice cream ever. "I brought a peace offering."

I bit my lip and carefully weighed my decision on whether I should let him in or not. "How about just the ice cream stays?"

He pulled the ice cream back. "No deal."

"Fine, come in." I could use a chocolate binge after the day I had. I motioned toward my couch. "Have a seat, I'll get some bowls."

He held up the two spoons. "Bowls aren't necessary."

"Are you sure you want to share ice cream with me? That seems a little too unsanitary for you." He had worried about those types of things when I previously knew him.

He surprised me with a wink. "I've already been inoculated against you."

I felt a little heat in my cheeks. What a thing to say. Not that it wasn't true, we had swapped plenty of germs in our day, but that was ages ago. Sharing food still didn't bother me, so I joined him on my cocoa-colored chenille couch. I sat close, but not too close, with my legs cross-legged, facing him.

He handed me a spoon and opened up the carton. "Ladies first, or is it beauty before age?"

I took the spoon and scooped up a large spoonful as I eyed him warily. "Either works," I responded before I indulged in heaven.

He watched me as I ate the first bite. His sweet and gentle grin had me feeling a little off.

I nervously ran my fingers through my still damp hair. "What?"

"I was just thinking about the last time we had ice cream together. You were in a similar outfit, but we were sitting outside."

I wished he would quit talking about the past. It both bothered and delighted me that he remembered such details. I decided to ignore the memory part. "Do you have something against this attire too?"

"Not at all."

"Hmm … then maybe I'll wear something similar to the office tomorrow," I said with a very wicked grin.

He hung his head. "I didn't mean to offend you or demoralize you today."

"Wow, you weren't even trying. You're good."

He let out a deep breath and gave me his *what am I going to do with you* look. I had seen it before. "Kelli, I just want this company to succeed."

"You realize we want the same thing then, right?" I took another large bite of ice cream.

He still hadn't eaten any.

"I do realize that," he responded.

I pointed with my spoon toward the carton. "I hope you realize too, that I may eat this whole pint."

He dived right in with his spoon. He'd seen me down an entire container before.

While he was eating, I took advantage of his silence. "You know, you really need to lighten up. First of all, you're taking over an already-successful company with good, hardworking people. Secondly, you're in the South, and we like friendly people down here. And lastly, life is too short to be so serious all the time, even at work."

He stuck his spoon in the ice cream and scooted closer.

I almost scooted back, but I held firm.

"That sounds like a speech I've heard a few times before."

"And did you listen to it?" I whispered.

"I don't know, did I, Kelli?"

I nervously ran my fingers through my hair. That was Ian talking, but Mr. Greyson was in front of me. Boy did he look like Ian and boy did I like it. *He's your boss, Kelli, and remember he left you with no thought at all.* "Um, well, the question is if you are listening to it now."

His chest rose and fell dramatically. "Someday Kelli... we're going to talk about the past."

I shrugged my shoulders and took another large bite of ice cream. That was a dangerous and painful road. I wasn't sure I was ready to take that road with him, now or ever.

"Kelli, I understand what you're telling me now, but believe me, it's not that simple. I had to learn the hard way not to mix my professional life with my personal life."

"But you ended up with a very successful company," I countered.

"After lots of mistakes and at great cost."

I hesitated to ask, but I was so curious. "Is that why you're divorced?"

He was about to take another bite of ice cream, but he slowly lowered his spoon and placed it back in the carton, gazing into my eyes. I got the feeling he didn't like me mentioning he was divorced.

"I'm sorry, your personal life is none of my business."

"Don't apologize. Let's just say I married for all the wrong reasons, business being one of them."

I cocked my head. What an odd reason, but I left it at that. I honestly didn't like to think of him married. It reminded me that I once hoped to marry him, and he rejected me.

"So…Kelli, can we call a truce at the office?"

I tossed my head back and forth as I thought about his request. "I guess so, Mr. Greyson, but I hold out my right to reserve a break in said truce when I feel it necessary."

His eyes sparkled in all their rich deliciousness. "I would expect nothing less of you."

Chapter Nine

THE REST OF THE WEEK had considerably fewer fireworks and blow-ups. I didn't move the credenza, which I could tell irked him, but I wasn't ready to completely give into him—maybe after a few months, if things went well. I wore jeans to work on Thursday just to test the waters.

He raised his eyebrow at me. "Please don't wear those to our meeting tomorrow."

"You don't need to tell me that," I not so politely responded.

I was actually a little taken aback that he wanted me to attend this particular meeting. It was with the largest health insurance provider in the state of Tennessee. They were interested in doing a pilot program using our ad software. Boss usually handled clients this large, so I was pleased that Mr. Greyson asked me to join him. In fact, he insisted I do the presentation. Of course, he gave me pointers and he meticulously went through my PowerPoint and notes. He wanted me to script out everything I was going to say, but I told him I didn't work that way. I always worked with an outline that gave me room to adjust depend-ing on the mood and interaction of those in attendance. "I need to be organic when I present. Just trust me, I'm good at reading people," I informed him.

I could tell he didn't like it, but he reluctantly gave in. I'm sure he had a backup plan in place, in case I screwed up.

When I arrived on Friday, I was dressed to kill. I pulled out the red pumps and a black dress that said, *Hello.* Mr. Greyson's red and irritated eyes said just that when he saw me. Yep, he did a double take.

"I know it isn't jeans, but I hope this works for you." I smiled wickedly, leaning against Delfia's desk. She had gone to make some copies.

He cleared his throat. "It's very appropriate."

"Remember when I said you need to work on your complimenting skills?"

"To properly compliment how you look would be inappropriate for the office."

His response totally caught me off guard. "Why thank you."

His eyes started watering.

"What's wrong with your eyes? You look terrible."

"Thank you, Ms. Bryant, for that observation. I'm having a terrible time with allergies. I've never had problems before. I even had to take my contacts out."

"Welcome to the South," I replied.

"Are you ready to go?" he asked.

I nodded. "Just let me get my laptop."

He offered to drive to our meeting and I reluctantly agreed. It was kind of weird for me. It brought back a lot of memories. I didn't have a car my freshman year, and he was my main source of transportation. I kept reminding myself that memory was of Ian, and I tried to pretend Ian didn't exist—only Mr. Greyson.

We walked down together and out to his car. To my discomfort he followed me to the passenger side.

"Um . . . this isn't a date."

"Sorry, old habit." His ears pinked.

Yeah, this is why I didn't want to drive with him, but he opened my door anyway. When he opened his own door, he looked at his hands. "What in the world is all this yellow stuff on everything?"

I laughed at him until he got in and reached up to rub his eyes. I instantly grabbed his hand without a second thought. He stiffened at my touch, not sure how to react. I tried not to react other than to say, "Believe me, you don't want to touch your eyes. That yellow stuff is pollen." Only southerners would understand. Back West, pollen didn't manifest itself this way.

I let go of his hand and reached into my satchel to pull out some wet wipes. "Here, wipe your hands off."

He took the wipe from me and wiped his hands. When he was done, I handed him an allergy tablet. I stocked up on them this time of year. "This will dissolve in your mouth. It should help with your itchy eyes."

"Will this make me drowsy?" he asked.

"I think what you meant to say was, 'Thank you, Ms. Bryant.' Because Ms. Bryant isn't fool enough to give someone medication that would make him an unsafe driver, especially when she's a passenger."

"Thank you, Ms. Bryant."

"You're welcome, Mr. Greyson."

After taking the medicine, he flipped down his visor and pulled out a pair of glasses. When he put them on, I found myself involuntarily smiling at him. There was my Ian.

"I know, I hate them, but I can't drive without them with my contacts out."

"I like the glasses," I said quietly. I probably shouldn't have, but it slipped out.

He narrowed his eyes as if I was being insincere.

"Really, I do." And unfortunately, I really did. I turned from him and looked forward, putting on my own sunglasses. We hadn't even gone anywhere, and I was ready to be out of his car. I kept repeating, *this is Mr. Greyson, glasses or no glasses.* I also tried not to remember the marathon make-out sessions that had occurred in his old Toyota Corolla. Boy did I miss that car.

He brought me back to reality when he asked me to run through my notes with him again. I normally would have declined, but under the circumstances, I was grateful to think about something other than him. He threw in some last-minute suggestions, but I assured him I had this.

"You need to trust me. And you can always jump in if you need to. This isn't only my show, we're a team." That sounded so weird to say.

He briefly glanced my way. "I like the sound of that."

I stared out the window. "Yeah," I mumbled.

The ride was mostly quiet after that, which was fine with me. It confused me when he was nice to me.

He was super tense as we walked across the parking lot.

"Is this your status quo?" I asked.

"It helps me stay focused."

"Okay, but at least smile."

He flashed me a smoldering smile before opening the glass door.

I swallowed hard, trying not to be affected by it. "See, that wasn't so hard. Remember, you're in the South now." I inadvertently winked at him. Stupid Kelli. He would probably send me an email later telling me that was unprofessional.

Together we walked in and headed toward the receptionist desk. "We're here to see Lorelai Duchane," Mr. Greyson informed the receptionist. Lorelai Duchane was the CEO and President.

"They're ready for you in conference room one," said the receptionist, who could hardly take her eyes off my boss. When we followed her back to the conference room, she kept glancing back at him, hoping he was enjoying her backside. It was nice and perky. But Mr. Greyson was all business and kept his eyes forward and to himself.

We entered the conference room to find three others besides Lorelai. I scanned the room quickly to pick up any cues from my audience. I always tried to hone in on who I really had to sell because it wasn't always the big boss. It didn't take long for me to see that was the case here. I needed to sell the hotshot in the corner, Nicholas Price who was the Executive Vice President. His stiff posture said he was only waiting to say no. I loved a challenge.

Without being too obvious, I directed my presentation to him and put on some subtle charm. I inserted Nicholas's name whenever I could instead of saying things like when Customer A logs in. It worked quite nicely. He began to playfully banter with me during the presentation. By the end, I had him eating out of my hands, and he was selling it to Lorelai for me.

Mr. Greyson had, surprisingly, let me do my job. He said maybe two words the entire time, and they were at appropriate times and blended well with the direction of the conversation. After the presentation, I let him take over and discuss the finer points of implementation and the mechanics of launching it on their site. He also addressed any security issues they had. We really were a good team; I had better people skills, but his technical knowledge gave people confidence that their data was safe with us.

I could tell that Mr. Greyson was pleased with the way things had gone when he smiled at me between questions and more requests for information. That was always a good sign. Mr. Greyson wasn't the only man smiling at me. Nicholas Price kept flashing his blinding white teeth at me and trying to engage me in conversation that was unrelated to our product or presentation. I might have paid a little too much attention to him.

At the end of the meeting, Nicholas handed each of us his card, but he didn't let go when I took it. "My personal number is on the back," he said, like out of one of those bar scenes in a movie. I almost expected him to call me baby or something. He also held onto my hand longer than appropriate when shaking it. I gently tried to extricate it without appearing rude, even though he was in the wrong. I could tell his overt advances bothered my ever-proper boss. To be honest, they bothered me too. Mr. Greyson was pressing his lips together, his face reddening from probably holding back his comments. I'm sure he wanted to school Nicholas in proper workplace behavior.

As we walked out into the parking lot, I thought Mr. Greyson would be happy, or at least pleased, but he seemed agitated. His shoulders were twitching.

"I think that went very well," I said cheerfully.

"Maybe too well," he muttered.

"How is that even possible? What's wrong?"

He stopped and took a breath. Some of the tension lines in his forehead relaxed. "You did a great job."

"Thank you?"

"Really, you did. We should go to lunch and celebrate."

"That would be nice," came flying out of my mouth. I covered said mouth, wanting to smack myself.

His eyes widened, astounded I said yes. No one was more astounded than me. I think it was the glasses. I saw too much of Ian in him. And, it wasn't like this was an unusual request. Boss and I had been to lunch several times over the years to celebrate, or just to have lunch together. I guess it was appropriate for Mr. Greyson and me to have the same type of post-presentation lunch. Of course, he would never be a Boss, but like it or not, he was my boss.

He behaved like Ian again, opening my door. When I grimaced, his unrelenting posture said I could deal with it. Honestly, though, I was having a hard time dealing with the Ian-Mr. Greyson whiplash. How he could be so different on and off the clock was almost impressive. I wondered what happened at his company to make him behave so rigidly in the office. Or should I say even more rigid than he naturally was?

While Ian seemed pleased I agreed to have lunch with him, he was obviously still bothered by something that happened in our meeting. I could still read him. He kept tapping the steering wheel or clenching and rubbing it. He was also silent, working through something in his thoughts. He should be happy. I had no doubt those guys were signing on the dotted line.

I was trying to think of something to say to break the uncomfortable silence. I finally came up with, "Do you have any other ideas or contacts in other verticals we could approach? Because I was thinking we could go after—"

"Are you going to call that guy?" he abruptly interrupted me. "Because I don't think that would be a good idea until we close this deal."

I paused and took a second to make sure I heard him right. Yes. Yes, I had. "I'm not sure that's any of your concern. In fact, I know it's not; but no, I have no intention of calling him."

His shoulders relaxed and he quit tapping on the steering wheel. He also slowed down considerably. He drove fast when he was stressed. I didn't understand why this was such a stressor.

He briefly glanced over my way. "Why aren't you going to call him?"

"Is that a real question?"

"Yes," he said matter-of-factly. "I think he is what most women would find attractive, and I guarantee his position there pays at least triple what you make."

"And that should mean something to me why?" I asked.

"Money's not important to you?"

"Not in that way, no. I don't care about the size of a man's paycheck, as long as he's a hard worker and a decent person."

He pursed his lips, skeptical.

"I'm telling the truth."

He nodded, like sure you are.

That ticked me off, so I went off on him. "A good portion of the men that have meant the most to me in my life have made very little money. And just for the record, I wouldn't date someone like Nicholas because I know his type, and no amount of money would compensate for it." I turned and looked out my window at the cars passing us by. For some reason I had the urge to cry. "Maybe we should just go back to the office," I muttered.

I felt the slightest touch on my knee, but I didn't react to it. I kept staring out the window.

"Kelli, I'm sorry."

"Don't you mean, Ms. Bryant?"

"No."

"Apology accepted, Mr. Greyson."

"Do you have any suggestions for where you would like to eat?" His tone was repentant.

I thought for a moment. "Sure, there's a great little café near the river walk." I spouted out directions to him.

"So, just for the record, what type of man is Mr. Price?" he asked bravely, or maybe stupidly.

I wasn't sure why he wanted to keep on this line of questioning. You would think he would have left well enough alone, but fine, I decided to play along for a bit. "He's all about the flash, there's nothing real about him. A date with him would mean an exclusive, overpriced restaurant. The food would be awful, and the conversation would be worse, as it would center completely on him. Then he would probably have tickets to a sold-out show, and he would congratulate himself all evening for scoring said tickets. To top it off, he would expect to be paid back for showing you such a good time by some physical means. Of course, when that didn't happen, he would be disgruntled, but he would play it off because now you just became a challenge and he likes the chase. But eventually he'd get tired of the chase and realize there were easier women out there, and he'd never call again."

He pulled into the café parking lot, turned the car off, and faced me. "You got all of that from one meeting?"

I unclicked my seatbelt. "I can read people very well, men in particular. And I've had the unfortunate pleasure to know a Nicholas or two in my day."

His forehead crinkled. Not sure why that bothered him.

I exited the vehicle and took a moment to let the sun shine on my face. It was such a beautiful day, I felt like it shouldn't be wasted inside. "Would it bother your allergies too much if we ate outside?"

"The allergy medicine seems to be working well." He briefly took a moment to look around at our surroundings. "I think eating outside is a great idea."

I wasn't sure if he was being sincere or just trying to please me, but I accepted it. I was hoping we would be lucky and there would be some struggling musicians playing out by the river. This was Nashville after all.

Ian asked the hostess for a table for two outside, and we were immediately seated.

"They serve breakfast here all day and everything is fabulous." I plucked my menu out of the stand on the table. I pulled that baby in front of my face, to give myself a moment's reprieve. Staring at his gorgeous face for long periods of time was making me do dumb things, like go to lunch with him. Who knew what else might happen? Obviously, nothing, right? Right. We were keeping it strictly professional.

I decided on the Denver Omelet, full of ham and cheesy goodness. I never understood why Denver was its namesake. He decided on their bleu cheeseburger with sweet potato fries. Of course he asked what temperature they cooked the burger to. I had to stop myself from laughing. It was a very Ian-like thing to do. The poor waitress had no idea, she had to ask someone.

Once the flustered waitress left there was no way I could keep staring at my menu. It also meant Mr. Greyson only had eyes for me now. "Do you miss Colorado?" he asked.

I shrugged my shoulders. "Sometimes. I've been thinking I should take a vacation there someday. How about you? Are you homesick?"

"Men don't get homesick."

"If you say so."

He leaned in closer across the small round table. "I find I'm liking Nashville more and more."

I leaned back, trying to keep up the boundaries I needed to stay in place. "Nashville's great, but it lacks the mountain scenery."

He looked out toward the river and then back to me, capturing my gaze. "I'd say Nashville has some pretty great scenery of its own."

I cleared my throat. Surely, he didn't mean me. I was thankful when our sweet little waitress returned with the waters we had ordered. It was getting awfully warm.

Mr. Greyson skimmed the rim of his glass. "I'm curious, you say you can read men well. What is your summation of me?"

"Ha! I don't think you want to know."

His shoulders sank, but he quickly recovered, sitting up even taller than before. "Say you just met me today and I gave you my number. What would you think?"

"Oh, so now we're pretending. Fine." I studied him for a moment or two, trying to keep my unflattering opinions of him out of it and think as if I had never met him. I knew what I thought of him the first time I ever met him, but that was Ian, not Mr. Greyson; however, I knew I would think the same thing, *Oh my, he's attractive.* Yeah, I wouldn't be saying that out loud.

He sipped his water, eagerly waiting for my reply.

"Well... First of all, I would think it was out of character for you to hand me your number. You look like somebody who likes to be in control—you would want my number instead. That way you could control the variables and timing."

He brought his hands together and rested his elbows on the table. "Very good."

"I told you." I sat back and congratulated myself silently.

"You can't end it there. You didn't say whether you would give me your number or not."

"No," I said quickly.

"Just like that?" He sounded offended... no, maybe disappointed?

"No, not just like that."

"Then why?"

I leaned forward and lowered my voice. "Because you look troubled, like there's a woman. I'm guessing an ex-wife, that's still under your skin, and you can't get over her. You want to and you've tried, but to no avail. I don't like that kind of competition, Mr. Greyson. But it doesn't really matter because this is all pretend."

He leaned forward too, entering my personal space. We were so close I could see my reflection in his lenses. His soulful eyes were penetrating my own, making me forget to breathe.

"You're right, Kelli, there is a woman, but it's not my ex-wife. And I did try to get over her, but I discovered that's where I went wrong." He sat back.

I took a deep gulp of air before taking a long drink of my ice water. This conversation was much more than I had bargained for. I wondered who the woman was, and for a brief second, I was jealous of her. I wanted a man to speak of me in such hushed and reverent tones. Not just any man, I wanted Ian to. What she had that I didn't, I knew I'd never know—except for Ian's heart.

"Will you excuse me for a moment?" I stood and walked to the ladies' room as fast as I could, reminding myself I was over Ian, that Mr. Greyson was my boss, and that I should never eat lunch with him again.

Chapter Ten

HAD NEVER BEEN HAPPIER TO see a weekend come. I needed some Mr. Greyson-free zone. I mean, I knew I would see him on Saturday at Boss's retirement party, but I could avoid him there. My plan was to stick close to Boss and Holly. I missed them something terrible. It felt like it had been an eternity since I'd seen them, when in reality it was only several days. I told Holly I would come early to cook or clean, or whatever else they needed. She laughed and said they were having it catered, but that I should come early anyway.

I dressed up in my newly acquired cyan-colored wrap dress. The hues made my eyes pop. I put some loose curls in my hair and let it fall and frame my face. It was weird when I looked in the mirror; I almost didn't recognize myself; not in a bad way, but there was an unfamiliar aura to my reflection. Maybe I really had snapped. I felt like it wouldn't be too long before I did, working for Mr. Greyson.

I arrived two hours before the actual party began. I noticed the addition of two cars in the driveway, one with Georgia plates and one with Florida plates. It looked like Luke was coming after all. Last I'd heard he'd told his parents he couldn't make it. I was relieved to hear it. Now I was anxious. I bet Holly and Boss had to send him the money so he could afford to come. I took a deep breath to prepare myself for having to see him. He had a way of making things awkward. I was one in a long list of people he blamed for his problems. He was convinced if I had married him, his life would be perfect now and he would magically be someone else. I wished he hadn't been able to come; it was a selfish wish I know. I should be happy for Boss and Holly that their whole family could be here to celebrate such a wonderful occasion. Who knew, maybe Luke would be on his best behavior.

I eagerly rang the doorbell, and it didn't take too long before I was greeted by Sara, their granddaughter. "Aunt Kelli's here," she yelled. I loved that they thought of me as their aunt. Sara ran straight into my arms.

"You're beautiful. I can't believe how tall you've grown," I said as I hugged the life out of her.

Within seconds, I was joined by practically the whole Chandler clan. Even Luke came out to greet me. Looking at him made me wish things could have been different, that *he* could have been different. He was two different people. There was the sweet charming person he was most of the time, and then there was the mean-spirited and sometimes downright vile person. For the first part of our relationship, he was very sweet and charming, but then he started drinking and a monster was unleashed. I tried to help him through it, but I refused to be an emotional punching bag. Luke stood there looking as handsome as ever with his sandy blonde hair that laid perfectly against his head with his flawless swooped bangs. His sun-kissed skin didn't hurt either or that smile of his with one dimple. But his once bright blue eyes were dimmed by the alcohol and drugs. Even tonight I could see they were bloodshot.

There was a line of hugs. Holly was first. "You look absolutely beautiful, but there is something different about you," she whispered in my ear.

It made me feel better. At least I wasn't crazy thinking the same thing.

"I can't put my finger on it, but it suits you," she said.

Boss was next and held on extra-long. "How's my girl?"

"I'm great." Tonight that wasn't a lie.

Luke was at the end of the line. He hugged me tighter than I would have liked. "Hi gorgeous," he whispered low in my ear before he kissed my cheek. The smell of tequila tickled my nose. I backed away as quick as I could.

"Thank you." I tried to convey in my tone that his advances wouldn't be welcome. By the look in his eye, he didn't get it. One more man to avoid tonight. I focused back on Holly and Boss and asked them to tell me about their trip. I also had plenty to catch up on with Ethan and Bethany, but I didn't get a lot of info as they were busy chasing kids.

Boss and Holly were anxious to hear about how things were going at the office. I gave them a glowing report. I didn't want to give them any reason to worry, especially not tonight. Boss was particularly pleased to hear about the meeting we had the day before. I noticed Luke listening intently; I'm sure he was still bitter his Dad fired him, but he only had himself to blame. Thankfully, he decided our conversation wasn't to his liking and he left. From there I enjoyed pictures of Cancun and playing with baby Camden. He was an adorable, curly haired redhead that had the most addicting giggle. I wanted one.

Before too long, guests began to arrive. I think I knew everyone, from clients, to employees, to the people we all went to church with. I was happy that Amanda and Zane showed up before my new boss. I wanted to make sure they were going to be on their best behavior and not embarrass me. They had been teasing me all week about what they were going to say to Mr. Greyson when they met him tonight. It ranged from the absurd all the way to the blush-worthy inappropriate.

As soon as they got there, I cornered them, but it did no good. They had evil glints in their eyes. I didn't like it one bit. "Please don't embarrass me. Remember what I told you yesterday. He's in love with some other woman. And he's my boss. And I don't like him." They weren't buying it.

"I'm telling you, Kelli, the woman he was talking about at lunch is you," Zane said.

My sister nodded in agreement.

"You both have lost your ever-living minds." I walked away from them and toward the patio, knowing it was a lost cause. I prayed the good Lord would have mercy on me and Mr. Greyson wouldn't come. But just as I thought it, he appeared. It was eerie.

"Kelli." He tapped my shoulder.

I sighed and turned around. "Mr. Greyson."

He cocked his head to the side. "I almost think you call me that just for enjoyment now."

"Now, Mr. Greyson, why would you think such a thing?"

He moved closer and lowered his voice. "I, too, can read people."

"Oh really?" I placed my finger on my temple. "So, what am I thinking now then?"

He stepped even closer. "You're thinking, 'How come he hasn't complimented me yet on how amazing I look.'"

My eyes popped and I dropped my hand.

He smiled.

"Um…" I bit my lip. "Not even close."

"Oh, well I tried."

Wow, was it getting warmer? It was then my sister and Zane decided to grace us with their presence.

"Kelli, who is this?" Amanda sing-songed. Oh my gosh, like she didn't know. I was going to kill her later.

"Mr. Greyson, let me introduce my sister, Amanda, and my brother-in-law, Dr. Zane Culver."

Ian shook both of their hands. "Please call me Ian." His eyes pled with me to do the same.

I shook my head no.

My sister and brother-in-law looked to be enjoying the show by the way their heads ping-ponged between us.

"You're a doctor? What is your field of medicine?" Mr. Greyson asked Zane.

"I can't believe you didn't mention already that I was the best dentist in Nashville," Zane teased me.

I faux bowed. "My apologies, oh great one."

"Bryant women are so sassy." Zane nudged me.

"Tell me about it," Mr. Greyson said.

My sister playfully smacked her husband, but I puffed out my chest proud of the characterization. Zane and Mr. Greyson seemed to hit it off immediately. I wasn't sure what to make of that, or how to feel about it. While they chatted like old college buddies, my sister pulled me over to the side. "Whoa Kelli, how do you get any work done with him around?" she whispered.

"It's easy, I ignore him."

"Why would you want to? Look at him."

I did look at him, and he looked great. He was wearing some brown dress slacks paired with an off-white shirt and vest. I tore my eyes away before I imagined kissing him in the copy room. He was my boss, end of story. "So, he's good looking. So what?"

"You're not fooling anyone, Kelli, and neither is he. I saw the way you two were looking at each other when we walked out here."

"You got the whole loathing vibe then?"

She squeezed my shoulder and laughed.

I rested my head against hers briefly. For some reason, I needed the comfort only she could give. I wasn't sure why I needed it at that particular moment, but it felt nice. The feeling of peace that it brought only lasted for a moment as Delfia and Matt, our in-house developer, joined us. They looked like they were together. I thought there might be a little something going on between the two of them. I had noticed the stolen glances between them when Matt came up to work with me. I was pretty sure he was like ten years younger than her, but they looked great together.

Delfia was nibbling on her bottom lip, which was unlike her. I'd never seen her nervous before. Matt too seemed nervous, walking close to Delfia, but not too close. Amanda knew both already from our monthly lunch dates, so there was no need for introductions. I didn't say anything about them being together since they were acting so unsure, but it only took me a minute to wish I had brought up my suspicions about them. My sister and Delfia started talking about me and my boss, who, at the moment, was engrossed in conversation with my brother-in-law. While Amanda was trying to extricate any juicy details from her on what went on in the office, she spilled the beans.

"Did you know that Kelli and Ian dated when she was a freshman in college? She had it bad for him." Amanda fanned herself.

"Amanda." I was infuriated she let that little detail drop out of thin air like an atomic bomb. She ignored me.

Delfia's entire face lit up. "I knew there was a past there. You should see the fireworks in the office."

Matt gave me a strained smile, obviously uncomfortable with the direction of the conversation. Him and me both.

I finally couldn't take it anymore. "I'm off to find Boss and Holly." No one cared that I left; they were enjoying their gossip fest. I walked past Zane and Mr. Greyson on my way back in, they were now sitting and talking like two old men on a front porch. It made me nervous. I didn't want him to be friends with my family, and where was the family loyalty, for crying out loud? I glared at both men as I walked by. Zane laughed, but Mr. Greyson acted like he was going to stand and follow me until Zane grabbed his attention with some more business talk. I didn't expect that, but I should have because ever since he walked back into my life, it had been nothing but unpredictable.

Unfortunately, there was one thing I could predict tonight. And that was Luke. He didn't disappoint. When I walked into the house, he was coming out. He reeked of alcohol, even more than before, like he had taken a bath in it while I was on the patio.

"Baby doll, I've been looking for you."

I hated when he called me that, but I ignored it. The last thing I wanted was for him to blow up at his parents' party, and when he drank you never knew what would set him off.

"Do you know where your parents are?" I tried to distract him.

He shook his head no while perusing every inch of me. The sinister gleam in his eyes gave me the willies. I couldn't believe this was the Luke I used to know. He grabbed my hand and tried to pull me back outside. I pulled back, but for a drunken guy, he was still well in control of his body, and he sure didn't lack strength.

"Luke, please let go."

"Come on, baby."

He drew closer, and I almost puked from the smell.

"Luke, knock it off," I tried to keep my voice down, not wanting to cause a scene. He refused to let go, and now he was disgustingly licking his lips. That was it. I yanked as hard as I could. That did the trick, but it set him off.

He reached for me again. "Baby, don't play innocent with me. You know you want me. It's why you dressed like a whore tonight."

He might as well have slapped me. I'd never been called such a thing. I held my stomach, stunned. That gave Luke another shot at me. He gripped my arm like a vice. Thankfully, Mr. Greyson and Zane were alerted.

Mr. Greyson grabbed his hand while Zane grabbed the back of his shirt.

"I suggest if you want to keep that hand you let go of her immediately," Mr. Greyson growled. I had never seen him look so furious. His eyes blazed with hatred toward Luke.

Luke let go, and Zane directed him forcefully out the door. Luke kept spouting out more vile words. "You ruined my life, tramp. I'm glad I never married you," he spewed.

All the guests on the patio or near the door were now staring at me. It was dead silent. I was hot with embarrassment, trying to hold back my tears. I managed to say, "Thank you," to a livid Mr. Greyson before I darted off as fast as I could. I wove my way through a crowd of people and out the front door. I made it as far as the porch swing before I lost it. No matter whether you believe what a person says about you, it still hurts.

I clung to the swing's chain, tears pouring down my cheeks, silently fall-ing on my new dress.

It wasn't long before a harried Mr. Greyson was running out the door. He almost ran past me until he heard me sniffle. "There you are," the concern in his voice made me cry harder.

He rushed over to me.

I tried to wipe at the tears furiously, but to no avail—they kept coming.

"May I join you?" he asked. He looked so sweet. He looked like my Ian.

I nodded my reply.

He sat right next to me and handed me a tissue.

I gladly accepted the tissue. "Thank you. Where did you get this?"

"Your sister thought you would need one."

She knew me so well, but I wondered why she hadn't come to find me as I dabbed my eyes and cheeks. "Did Luke leave?" I asked.

"He won't be bothering you anymore."

That didn't really answer the question, but it made me feel better. I didn't want his parents' party to be spoiled. "Do Gary and Holly know?"

He gently picked up my arm and began carefully pulling up my sleeve. "Quit worrying about everyone else right now. Are you all right?" He lightly touched the finger marks left by Luke. "Does that hurt?"

I shook my head no.

He delicately placed my hand back in my lap. He reached up and brushed a few tears away.

"Doesn't this cross some professional boundaries?" I sniffled.

He brushed my cheek one more time. "I guess it's a good thing we're not in the office."

Without thinking, I reached up and grabbed his hand as he touched my face. It was so natural. It was an old habit, and my heart leapt. For a moment our eyes locked, and there I saw... "Ian."

His lips curled up. He took my hand and held it between his own, caressing it as if it was a treasure.

Oh, that felt good. Too good. I pulled my hand away. "I meant, Mr. Greyson... Thank you. We should probably get back to the party now."

His shoulders dropped, and he sighed. "Someday, Kelli."

"Someday, what?"

He tucked some of my hair behind my ear. "Just someday."

I popped up and smoothed out my dress. His touch was killing me. "Do I look like a mess?"

"After everything that just happened, that's what you're worried about?"

"I don't want to worry Boss and Holly. Plus, a girl never knows when Mr. Right will pop up."

He shook his head at me and stood.

I gazed up at his beautiful face wishing... No, I couldn't ever risk that wish again.

"You still look amazing, but—"

"But?"

He leaned in like he was going to do far more than answer my question.

Oh, good heavens, his lips looked inviting.

"But... the question is, will you ever call Mr. Right by his first name?"

What a weird response. It was good though. It helped me forget that I wanted to plant my lips on his. "Unless his name is Mr. Darcy." I thought that was a clever response.

"You still love that book?"

"Doesn't every available woman in her thirties?"

"That I wouldn't know," he responded.

I headed for the door. We needed to be around people.

He didn't follow. "I need to take off."

I turned around. "So soon?" Why did I sound disappointed?

"I have an early flight tomorrow."

"Oh."

"I'm heading to Colorado. Some personal things have come up that I need to take care of."

"How long will you be gone?" Not like I really cared.

"A week, maybe two. But don't worry, I'll be checking in every day."

"Oh, thank you, you don't know how worried I was there."

He chuckled. "Good night, Kelli. I'll call you."

Wow that sounded familiar. It made me catch my breath. "Good night, Mr. Greyson."

He walked off muttering, "Someday, Kelli, someday..."

I watched him walk off, and I felt a tiny tug in my chest. I chalked it up to heartburn.

Chapter Eleven

FELT LIKE I KEPT SAYING this lately, but that did not go how I had anticipated it. All I had wanted was a nice evening with family and friends
to celebrate one of life's milestones with one of the greatest men on earth,
but instead I ended up being manhandled, to put it nicely. That led to
kind of a moment on the porch with my boss, which caused all sorts
of confusion, and to top it off, Mr. Greyson was now my brother-in-
law's new BFF. They were even going golfing when he returned from
Colorado. Oh yeah, and now the office would know that I had a thing
with Mr. Greyson, and if that wasn't enough, Mr. Greyson now knew
about my history with Luke. It was like my life was coming undone
stitch by stitch. My sister said this was a good thing, because I needed a
change of wardrobe.

Mr. Greyson was her favorite now, too, since he played hero. I admit
I was truly grateful for that. Not like Luke could have really done any-
thing, even if he had got me outside, but I appreciated Mr. Greyson and
Zane remedying the situation quickly.

As I lay there in bed thinking about the weirdness that had become
my life, my phone rang. I picked it up and was surprised by the name
that appeared and by the lateness of the hour. I was intrigued by why
he would call so late, so I answered it. "Mr. Greyson, let me guess, you
already have a list of directives for me to follow while you're gone."

"Funny, Kelli, but no."

"Darn it. And here I was hoping you would finally tell me how to properly dispose of the used coffee filters at the office."

He laughed. "Well, I see I don't need to ask if you're okay."

"Don't tell me you were worried about me."

He cleared his throat. "I was."

"Oh. Well…thank you."

"Luke didn't come back, did he?" he asked.

"No, I think he knew better."

"Kelli?" I could hear his hesitation. "What happened between you and him?"

I was taken aback by the inquiry and not exactly sure I wanted to talk about it with him. I didn't respond for several seconds as I was mulling over what I should or shouldn't say.

"Kelli?"

"I'm here." I wasn't sure why I still was. I wasn't sure it was professional behavior to be talking to your boss about your love life on a Saturday night near midnight, and in particular, this boss. I took a deep breath and lost my head. "I dated Luke during grad school when he worked for his dad."

"He used to work for Chandler?"

"Yep. His dad fired him not long after I started working there."

"Did he do something to you?" The concern in his voice was apparent and confusing.

"No, his termination had nothing to do with me. He let alcohol and drugs consume his life, and his dad caught him stealing funds from the company."

"Ouch."

"That's putting it mildly. His parents were devastated."

"How about you?"

"If you're asking if I was devastated by Luke, the answer is no. I was hurt, but by that point, I knew Luke and I didn't belong together. But as you know from tonight, he disagreed, and he didn't take it well."

"I'm sorry, Kelli."

I sat up in bed. "Why are *you* sorry?"

It was his turn to pause. I wasn't sure why; it seemed like a straight-forward question.

"You deserve better," he finally answered.

"Something we agree on," I replied.

"Do my ears deceive me?" I could hear the smile in his voice.

"Good night, Mr. Greyson."

All I could hear him say as I went to hit the end button was, "Some-day, Kelli."

I set down the phone and rubbed my face. What a bizarre night, from the beginning to the end. There was a time when him calling me in the middle of the night was expected and even looked forward to, but now it was just plain unnerving. Mr. Greyson needed to quit acting like Ian.

I snuggled down under my blanket and let the sleep I needed take me over.

I woke up early on Sunday and got ready for church. When I left, I had a surprise taped to my door. It was an envelope. I recognized the handwriting immediately. I snatched it and opened it right away. In it I found instructions on how to properly dispose of used coffee filters. I couldn't help it—I laughed. I didn't remember him being playful like that, I wasn't sure what had gotten into him. That note was definitely not written by Mr. Greyson, and where Ian had been thoughtful, he was never one to really joke.

I drove to church with the note in my passenger seat. I wasn't sure why, but I kept looking over at it. It was like it held some mysterious power over me. Even in my head that sounded dumb, but it was true. I even folded it up and put it in my purse before I headed into church. Then I did something really dumb: I texted the fool who wrote it. *Only you could have made up ten steps for such a simple task.*

I was surprised he texted right back. I wondered if he was at the air-port or already in Colorado. *I could have added at least five more.*

I had no doubt. I smiled at the phone as I walked into the chapel area. I looked up to find my sister and her family waving me over. I made my way over to sit in the pew we had been sitting in for at least the last twenty years. Before I sat down, I turned off my phone and threw it in my purse next to the note. I sat in-between my nieces, who both looked very pretty in pink today. The pastels were a sure sign that spring had arrived.

"What were you smiling about?" Amanda asked.

"Nothing."

She eyed me warily.

I ignored her and turned my attention to Sam and Court, who were now fighting over who rightly owned the purple marker. Court had it in her hand. It was funny until they both started reaching over me and grabbing each other. The argument was short lived. All Zane had to do was look their way and they ceased and desisted, but true to form, Sam made a very sassy under-her-breath comment. I tried not to crack a smile.

Zane leaned over Amanda. "You should've brought Ian over earlier. He's the first guy you've dated that I like," he spoke in hushed tones.

I felt my eyeballs dilate. "I'm not dating Mr. Greyson, Zane."

"Yet," he laughed.

Louder than I should have in church, and of course just as the pastor stood up, out of complete frustration I blurted out, "I think you mean when hell freezes over."

The pastor looked my way, as did most everyone. Amanda lost it and began shaking uncontrollably, trying not to laugh out loud. Zane was grinning like an idiot, and Sam and Court put the final nail in the coffin. "Ohhh, you said hell in church," they said in stereo.

That did it. Amanda lost it for reals, and so did I. We both had to leave to the stares of our fellow church goers. I'm sure they all thought we had lost our minds, and in my case they were correct. Once in the foyer, we laughed so hard it hurt. We were going to hell for sure.

Our little indiscretion at church was played over and over at the Culver dinner table that night. Maybe it was sacrilegious, but I needed the laugh after the month I had been having. To make up for it, I would put a hefty donation in the plate next week at church. Annoyingly, another thing that was overplayed that night at dinner was Amanda and Zane's obsession with Mr. Greyson, whom they called Ian. They were both convinced he had it bad for me and it was just a matter of time before we rekindled our romance. I adamantly disagreed and left early.

Monday dawned and I thought I would be happy that I had a Mr. Greyson-free week or two to look forward to, but oddly I didn't feel that way. I found myself poring over that stupid note again. I should have just chucked it, but for some reason I couldn't. I did wear jeans though, just for spite.

I rushed into the office, hoping to head Delfia off at the pass. I hoped she hadn't already started to blab about the news my traitorous sister shared with her at the retirement party. My hopes rose as I noticed hers was the only car in the parking lot. I jogged in as best I could in heels and raced up to the executive level. There I found her as usual; busy as a bee, typing away, but as soon as she heard me, she turned to face me. A Cheshire grin broke out across her face. I shook my head at her, and she laughed.

"I knew you and Mr. Greyson had a thing."

I placed my hands on my hips. "I could say the same thing about you and Matt."

She blushed. I don't think I had ever seen her do that. "I know he's kind of young."

I walked toward her and touched her arm. "I think it's great, and he's a lucky guy," but I had to throw in, "you cougar."

She chuckled a little. "We kind of want to keep it quiet. Well, at least Matt does. He's not a big fan of interoffice dating."

Perfect. "Well... I'll keep your secret if you keep mine."

She held out her hand. "Deal, my friend."

Inwardly, I took a big sigh of relief while shaking her hand.

"But," she said, "I want details."

I laughed as I walked away toward my office. There would be no divulging of details. When I walked into my office, I shut my door. It was weird that had become a habit. Before Mr. Greyson, I never really shut that door, but now it was commonplace. I wondered if it would ever be different. Would I ever become comfortable with him being my boss?

I found myself staring at my credenza that remained in front of the adjoining door, and I found myself wondering why he had to go back to Colorado so soon. He said it was personal. I wondered if it was the woman who he had tried to get over. Then I wondered why I wondered before I told myself to enjoy my Mr. Greyson-free zone and to get to work.

I took the time while he was gone to work on the graphics for the new release of my marketing software. I knew he wanted to hire that out, but I had a feeling he was going to use whoever designed the logo concepts, and those were basically terrible except for the one, and even that needed my help. Of course, I didn't think we needed a new interface, but as he did, I decided to do some more research. I felt like I had come up with a perfect blend of what he called sexy and what I knew was practical and intuitive. It was my plan to wow him when he came back.

Around ten, while I was in deep design mode, my phone rang, and for some reason I smiled when I looked at the caller ID. "Good morning, Mr. Greyson."

"You sound chipper, Ms. Bryant."

I guess since it was working hours, I was Ms. Bryant. He really was annoying.

"Of course, I am. My boss is out of town."

"Don't get used to it," he quipped.

"So, are you calling to see if I put your coffee filter instructions to good use this morning?"

That made him chuckle. "No, but did you?"

"I framed them and put them up in the break room."

"Kel—" He cleared his throat. "Ms. Bryant," he corrected himself in his this-isn't-the-time-to-be-humorous-after-all-it's-business-hours tone.

"Yes, Mr. Greyson?"

"Lorelai Duchane emailed me and would like us to email her a proposal. Do you think you can work on that?"

"I think I can manage that."

"Send it to me to look over before you email it to her."

"I think I heard a please in there somewhere."

"Please, Ms. Bryant."

I could hear the exasperation in his voice. It filled me with pride. "Mr. Greyson, I would be happy to do that for you." I almost gagged on my own words. It was then I heard a woman's voice in the background.

"Hey Kel— I mean Ms. Bryant, I need to go, but I'll call later." He sounded flustered.

I again began to wonder.

While I worked, my mind wandered frequently, and it frequently landed on someone it shouldn't. By lunch, I decided I needed a distraction. I ditched my sack lunch and headed out. I decided to go to a travel agency and check out some vacation packages. My sister and Zane had invited me to go to Disney World with them in a few weeks during the girls' spring break. I had thought about saying yes, but I think they did it because they felt sorry for me and because Zane and Amanda wanted kid-free time to do what married couples do, so I politely declined. Besides, theme parks weren't my idea of a good vacation. I would rather be lying out on the beach or scuba diving and snorkeling than waiting in never-ending lines.

As I perused the brochures, it was just another glaring reminder that I was single. They all showed happy couples and families. It wasn't quite the distraction I was looking for, but I still took several brochures for the Virgin Islands, various cruises, and even London. I could see myself on a double-decker bus, visiting Jane Austen's homeland. Maybe I would even get to meet my own Mr. Darcy. I laughed at my stupidity.

By the time I got home for the day, I was melancholy. All I did for the first half hour was lay on the couch and stroke Charlie's back. He was a purring machine by the time I was done. I asked him what he thought of riding a double-decker bus. I think he may have rolled his eyes and said, *Be quiet silly woman, you missed a spot.* I needed a life. At least I had belly dancing to look forward to.

On my way to the Y, I saw something to lighten my mood. There was a sign informing the residents that the pool would open on the first day of spring this year. That was only a week away! With that news and a killer workout, I was in much better spirits when I arrived back home. After I showered and made dinner, I settled myself on the couch, while listening to some smooth jazz. I was feeling relaxed and content when my phone rang. It probably shouldn't have surprised me, yet it still did.

"Hello."

"Kelli."

He sounded Ian-like, so I said, "Mr. Greyson."

I heard him sigh. It never got old.

"You know, I could still be at work, and you just crossed professional boundaries by using my first name."

"Are you at work?" he inquired.

I didn't answer.

"That's what I thought." I could hear the grin.

"So, what can I help you with, Mr. Greyson?"

"I called to see how your day was?"

"Um . . . I'm just about finished with the proposal for Lorelai and—"

"I didn't call to talk about work," he interrupted.

"This is a social call?" I asked because I really needed the clarification. I mean, why would he call just to call?

"In a manner of speaking," he responded.

"Huh," was all I could say.

"So, how was your day?" he repeated.

"It was fabulous," I exaggerated, because I didn't want him getting the wrong idea. "So . . . how was your day?"

"Not as good as yours, apparently."

I laughed because he probably did have a better day than me. He probably spent it with his "personal matters."

"Well, you know I'm living the glamorous life over here." I looked down at my sweatpants and t-shirt.

He chuckled. "Is that right?"

"Yep."

It was silent for a moment. Like the awkward kind.

He cleared his throat. He did that a lot now I noticed. "It's snowing here."

"Then I'm glad I'm not there."

"Still not a fan of the snow?"

"Not really."

"Do you remember when I tried to teach you how to drive in the snow when we visited my parents for Thanksgiving?"

Oh, did I ever. My heart began to race at the thought. There were too many good memories wrapped up in that trip. That being one of them. As always, he had been patient with me, even when I got his car stuck in a ditch. He didn't get bent out of shape, instead he kissed me and kept me warm until his dad could come haul the car out. I sighed out loud.

"Kelli?"

"Yeah."

"Do you remember?"

"Mr. Greyson, I don't think we should talk about it."

"Why?"

"Because I can't."

"Kelli..."

I waited for several seconds.

"Kelli, I need to explain to you what happened back then."

"No, you don't, Mr. Greyson." I responded firmly.

"Will you please call me Ian?"

"I can't."

"I'll call you tomorrow," he said before he hung up hastily.

I lay down on my couch and tried to process what had just happened. I wasn't sure what to make of it. All I knew was my heart ached and I felt that hollow feeling in the pit of my stomach. Why did he have to bring up such things? And what good was his explanation going to do after all these years? He didn't love me. What else was there to know?

The next day he called me again while I was at the office to bark orders at me. Okay, maybe not bark, but he was kind of demanding. I was glad he didn't bring up the night before. We had left things in a weird place. I figured that was the end of the social calls, but again I was wrong.

That night I was making myself a pasta salad for dinner when my phone rang. I almost didn't answer it, but I admit I was curious. "Mr. Greyson, to what do I owe the pleasure?"

"I was calling to see how your day was, *Kelli.*"

Emphasizing my first name was not going to get me to call him by his. "Well, let's see. I totally rocked it at work today, in jeans no less." I waited for him to respond.

"Hmm…"

"Yes, Mr. Greyson?"

"Sounds like a good day."

I could tell he had to swallow down what he really wanted to say. "I can't complain. How was your day?" I asked.

"Long."

"That was insightful."

He chuckled on his end. "Seen any good movies lately?"

"That was an abrupt and odd change of subject."

"So, no?"

I couldn't believe the change in direction, or why he even cared. "Not really. I have this new demanding boss, so I haven't had a lot of free time." I laughed at my own wit.

"I don't remember asking you to work any weekends."

"I'm sure it's coming."

"I'm not a big fan of working on the weekends."

"Really?"

"I'm sure that surprises you."

"You could say that."

"All right, so no new movies. Favorite movie in the last ten years?"

This conversation was getting more and more odd. "Uh...I don't know. I guess anything with Sandra Bullock in it. Maybe *The Blind Side*."

"Is that because it was made in Tennessee?"

"Maybe. How about you?"

"I really liked the new Star Trek remakes."

"I actually liked those too, or maybe it was Chris Pine. I was happy to see that they picked a handsome Captain Kirk this go around."

"I think William Shatner would be offended."

"He's like eighty years old now."

"Someday Chris Pine will be eighty, too."

"Yes, but he'll still have startling blue eyes."

"You want a man with blue eyes?"

That did not go where I wanted it to, and the answer was no. I was somewhat partial to the Hershey chocolate ones. "Um, I'm an equal opportunity eye color enthusiast."

"I like bluish eyes," he replied.

That's what he used to call mine. "Oh, that's nice," I said like I had never heard the term before. It was a totally lame response, but I wasn't sure how to respond. His "personal matters" probably had bluish eyes.

"How is your family?" he asked at the lull in conversation.

"They're doing well. Well, except my niece, Sam, is sick."

"I'm sorry to hear that."

"It's only a little cold. She's still as sassy as ever, so she must not be too sick."

"Takes after her aunt, huh?"

"You could say that."

"I need to go, but I'll call you tomorrow."

"Do you mean during the day or night?"

"Both. Good night, Kelli."

"Good night, Mr. Greyson."

This pattern went on for the two weeks he was gone. I almost found myself looking forward to the nightly calls. We never talked about the past, though he skirted the issue a few times. He seemed almost desperate to talk about it, which I couldn't understand. One thing he would never talk about was why he was in Colorado. All he would say was he was working things out and he would get back to Nashville as soon as he could.

Every night he had a new question for me. One night it was, "What was the best concert you've seen in the last ten years?" Every question centered on the ten-year mark. The answer to that was easy, Jake Owen. Now there was a fine-looking man. So that night we talked about music. He admitted to me that his favorite concert was Kenny G. I laughed so hard at him, but he wasn't ashamed. He was impressed with a man who could hold a note for forty-five minutes. That was impressive.

Then there was the best vacation and my favorite restaurant. It was weird, but our conversations gave me hope that maybe when he came back, things wouldn't be so tense in the office. I figured that was why he was calling me "socially." He wanted a better working environment.

I was still curious, though, about what was keeping him away, but let's just say I know why they say curiosity killed the cat. I thought after almost two weeks of phone calls, that all would be better when he came back. I drove in the Monday of his return looking forward to the week ahead after a glorious weekend of basking in the sun by the pool, and swimming with Court and Sam. I even smiled when I saw the white Infiniti in the parking lot on my way in. I knew he had gotten in late the night before.

I looked at my reflection in the glass door before I entered and thought, *not bad*. My skin was glowing from being sun-kissed all weekend, and my peach dress looked like at least half a million bucks on me, so I was feeling pretty darn good about myself as I walked up those stairs. That, however, all came to a crashing halt.

I walked through the executive level entrance door to find Delfia in a dither, which was completely uncharacteristic. She was throwing papers around her desk and muttering to herself. I looked around trying to find the source of her agitation, but all I noticed was Mr. Greyson's door was closed. I could hear voices, which was odd, considering I only saw his car and Delfia's in the parking lot.

Delfia finally noticed me and in hushed tones she spoke, "Heads up, Mr. Greyson..."

She didn't get to finish her thought. Mr. Greyson came out of his office. He was smiling, and he was wearing something, or rather, *someone* on his arm.

Chapter Twelve

"Kel— I mean Ms. Bryant." Mr. Greyson looked surprised to see me, though I'm not sure why. I did work there after all. Maybe he was disappointed I interrupted his interlude with his arm accessory. Wow, did he like women with voluptuous chests and painted on faces. I think this one may have done her makeup in the dark, it was awfully thick. He definitely had a type, and it wasn't me.

"Mr. Greyson," was all I could manage. In fact, I turned back to Delfia, flustered by the scene in front of me. "Um...Delfia can you please pull the Bergman file for me?"

Delfia nodded and went straight to the file cabinet.

"Thank you," I said quietly as I turned to walk to my office.

"Ms. Bryant," he called. "I want to introduce you to..."

I took a deep breath without trying to make it look like I was taking a deep breath and turned around with the fakest smile I had ever conjured up plastered on my face.

"This is Alexa Manselle." He shook her off him.

I put out my hand to shake hers.

She took mine, but hers felt like a limp noodle.

I couldn't stand people who couldn't give a good, firm handshake. I tried not to roll my eyes.

"Alexa," he called her, "this is Ms. Bryant. She's the Regional Manager."

She let out a high-pitched noise before saying, "Oh, of course."

I resisted putting my finger to my ear to stop the ringing. Who squealed like that?

She took ahold of his arm. "Ian told me I would be redoing your graphic designs."

I didn't even hear what she said after that. My head flew up and met Mr. Greyson's wide eyes and beet-red face. He pulled away from her grasp and stepped forward.

I stood my ground.

"Ms. Bryant," he stammered, "Alexa worked for me at IAG, and I've contracted with her to help us revamp the interface. She was the one who designed our new logo."

I was stunned. I didn't know what to say. Not only was she a terrible designer, but she completely lacked any professionalism. She grabbed Mr. Greyson's arm again, and it all made perfect sense. She was his "personal matters" and who he had mixed pleasure and business with at IAG. I thought he said that was a mistake, but yet here she stood in all of her buxom, blonde glory.

I spun on my heels, marched to my office, and slammed the door. I figured if he was no longer following professional boundaries, why should I?

Alexa? I kept thinking. He called her Alexa, not Ms. Manselle. Probably because she was going to be the next Mrs. Greyson. Suddenly, I felt nauseous. I sank into my chair. I even forgot to turn on my computer. I only came out of my stupor because Delfia knocked on my door, and before I could say come in, she was in and the door was closing behind her.

She sat on one of the leather chairs in front of my desk and threw the Bergman file on my desk, seething.

"What's wrong?" I inquired.

She kept shaking her head, and with every turn, her face turned a darker shade of red.

"Delfia?"

"That woman!" she finally spat out.

"What?" I asked.

"She came in here, all over Mr. Greyson, and with hardly an introduction, she began giving me orders. Everything from the kind of bottled water she likes stocked to the temperature the conference room needed to be every day. And then she started spouting off how atrocious all the office furniture was and how we really needed an update. Then she and Mr. Greyson disappeared into his office to do heaven knows what."

I put my hand up to stop her. I didn't even want to think about what heaven knew about.

"I'll talk to Mr. Greyson. She's not an employee, and I still manage this office. She has no authority over you."

Delfia gave me a half smile.

"Thank you for the file."

A calmer Delfia walked out the door.

I finally managed to get my laptop on, and the first thing I pulled up were my new designs for the interface. They were amazing, and apparently absolutely useless. I closed out the file with a tear in my eye. I gazed at the adjoining door. The conversations we'd had over the last two weeks had made me think that maybe I should move the credenza and that maybe, just maybe, we could have the working relationship that would allow for open doors. Now I was thinking of hiring a contractor to permanently remove the door and make it a wall with no access.

It didn't take too long before I had another visitor. He looked tentative when he walked in. To say he was stepping on eggshells was an understatement; landmines was more like it.

I didn't stand on ceremony. "Am I still the manager of this office, Mr. Greyson?"

He stopped in front of my desk. "Of course."

"So why is it that an independent contractor was hired without my knowledge or consent?"

He stood tall. "As Director, I don't have to run that by you."

I think my mouth may have dropped to the floor. I guess the whole team thing was big fat lie. "Fine! But you can tell your little plaything, I mean designer…"

His eyes widened to the size of saucers. "What did you just call her?"

"You heard me."

"I believe, Ms. Bryant, you're under the wrong impression," he spluttered back.

I smirked and interrupted him. "Please, Mr. Greyson, don't insult my intelligence. Just tell her that, as an independent contractor, she has no say about what goes on in this office beyond the purview of what she was hired to do, and that Delfia is not her personal assistant."

I turned back to my laptop and ignored him as he continued to stand there. I had nothing more to say to him. He must have stood there for a good minute. I still didn't look up. He finally stalked off and slammed my door. I heard his door slam a few seconds later.

Welcome to Monday. A tiny tear escaped and ran down my cheek. What was wrong with me?

I didn't know, but I needed my sister. I called her and begged her to meet me for lunch. She readily agreed. She tried to get me to tell her what was wrong over the phone, but I told her I couldn't talk about it. I bided my time until noon, and then I rushed out of my office. I couldn't help but notice the two lovebirds together in the conference room looking at a monitor.

Mr. Greyson called out my name as I passed by.

"I'm late for an appointment." I didn't even stop, or pass go, I just hurried down the stairs.

I drove like I was auditioning for *The Fast and the Furious* to Amanda's and my favorite little deli down by the river walk. The entire drive over, all I could see was Alexa's face. Sure, her makeup was way over done, but she was attractive, and she obviously fit his type, except she didn't have bluish eyes, they were more hazel. She reminded me a lot of how his ex-wife looked. I had to say, I was perplexed in his choice of women.

They didn't seem to fit him, but why should I even care? He was only my boss.

"I hate my boss." Those were the first words out of my mouth when I sat down at our favorite booth in Carl's Deli.

Amanda started to smile, but then I think she realized I was serious. "What happened?" she asked.

I rested my head on what I hoped was a clean table. "Alexa Manselle, that's what happened."

Amanda stroked my hair. "Who's Alexa Manselle?"

"Mr. Greyson's vixen who he hired to redo all of my graphics for my software and who knows what else."

"So, he has a girlfriend?" she sounded so surprised.

"I told you there was a woman and it wasn't me." I sat up. "And now Mr. Professional Boundaries has brought her into my office, and she's prancing around like she owns the place, and she can't keep her hands off him. It's absolutely disgusting. Oh…and to top it off, she's a horrible designer. But I guess when you're sleeping with the boss, it doesn't matter."

She grabbed my hands and cracked a smile. "You wouldn't be jealous, would you?"

"Of course not. I wasn't planning on sleeping with him." That was kind of my dirty—or maybe angelic secret. Not even Amanda knew that I was still, you know, a virgin. I think she just assumed I wasn't, because really who was anymore? At least, not a lot of people my age. It wasn't like I planned on being the only thirty something around to never have had sex, but here I was. I wasn't ashamed. There was nothing wrong with waiting for someone you loved and were undeniably and irrevocably committed to. I had seriously planned on that happening a long time ago. It was actually something that bothered Ian. He hadn't care that I was a virgin. In fact, he admired it, but he was afraid of stripping me of my innocence, as he called it. He made sure to never cross the line with me. It was weird how he'd been the only man I'd ever imagined giving the honor to. The only man I'd dated that I could see myself married to. That's how much I had loved him. But that was a long time ago.

"Honey, I know you're smart enough not to sleep with your boss," she interrupted my thoughts, "unless, you know—"

"Unless what?"

She paused. "Never mind. What I meant was, do you wish you were his girlfriend?"

"How many times do we have to go through this? No! It's just, I thought maybe things were going to be okay between us." I divulged the details of my two weeks of phone calls with Mr. Greyson.

She couldn't smile wide enough at the news. "And you're sure this woman is his girlfriend?"

"Yes." I threw my hands in the air. "It all makes sense. He said he had personal matters to take care of in Colorado, and he told me he had mixed business with pleasure at his own company, and guess what, she worked for him at IAG, and now she's here, and he's calling her by her first name, and she literally can't keep her hands off him."

She leaned back in the booth and folded her arms. "Well, that's surprising. I guess Zane and I were wrong."

"Thank you," I said smugly. "And you know what the worst part is?"

She waited patiently for me to answer.

"I redesigned the interface and was planning on showing him today when he got back. I think it was my best work, and now it was for nothing."

"You should still show him," she suggested.

"No. He didn't want me working on it anyway."

"I'm sorry."

I was sorry too.

We spent the rest of our lunch talking about their upcoming vacation. She followed me back to my office because she wanted to see Alexa Manselle for herself. Since it wasn't unusual for my sister to visit me at the office, I agreed to let her come up and take a peek. This way, she could see for herself that she and Zane were wrong. I hoped this meant they would, once and for all, quit implying that Mr. Greyson and I were supposed to end up together.

I stopped her on the landing on our way upstairs. "Don't say anything to embarrass me," I whispered.

She smacked my arm playfully. "Oh, Kelli Jelly, I would never."

"Ha!" I responded.

At least she made me smile.

We walked past the conference room, and there they were. Still together, sitting cozily, eating lunch. How quaint.

Mr. Greyson noticed us. "Amanda," he called out.

I'm surprised he didn't call her Mrs. Culver.

"Ian," Amanda sounded happy to see him.

"Ms. Bryant." Mr. Greyson swallowed hard, not quite meeting my eyes.

I didn't respond, other than to kind of grimace. That made him frown.

"So how was your trip to Colorado?" Amanda asked. She was laying it on thick, but I could see what she was doing. She wanted to get a good long look at his girlfriend, who from the looks of it needed some floss. She was picking at her teeth. Gross.

"It was long," Mr. Greyson responded.

That was an odd response considering he was probably with his human flosser there.

"Well…" Amanda said, "Kelli loved Colorado. I keep telling Zane we really should take a vacation there."

I nudged her to let her know she was pushing it.

It was then his little plaything got tired of being ignored. She stood and grabbed his arm. "You really should visit, it's like the best place in the world."

I took Amanda's hand, because I could see she was about to burst out laughing at the Barbie doll wannabe.

Mr. Greyson cleared his throat. "Amanda, this is Alexa Manselle, she'll be working here for a few weeks."

A few weeks. Someone please shoot me now.

She playfully smacked him. "Or longer, silly."

Did she just call him silly and say she'd work here longer?

That was it. I could see Amanda starting to shake. I pulled her toward my office.

"It was nice to see you, Amanda," Mr. Greyson called out.

She couldn't return the sentiment because she was about ready to burst into laughter, and she did as soon as we entered my office.

"Well isn't she special," she said once she got her laughter under control.

"Very," I agreed.

"Are you sure they're together? They don't seem to fit."

I shrugged my shoulders. "No, they don't, but doesn't she remind you a lot of his ex-wife?"

Dawning illuminated her face. "You're right."

"Wow! I'm right twice in one day?"

She gave me a wry smile. "Well, I guess I better get back to my domesticated life."

I sighed. Not because I didn't love working, but was it so bad to want it all? Career, husband, and kids?

She gave me a knowing look. "Someday you and I will be domestic divas together, but for now, you continue to be Chandler's rock star."

I hugged her tight. "I love you, Manda Panda."

She squeezed back. "I know, Kelli Jelly."

She left me, and I went back to work feeling a little better. I really did love that girl. The rest of the day flew by as I focused on doing what I'd always done, and that was my best. I reminded myself it had been a mistake to think that Mr. Greyson and I could be friends. I needed, once again, to separate him from the man I once knew. It was clear that man didn't exist anymore, and even if he did, I needed to remember that he left me with no thought at all.

Chapter Thirteen

RIGHT BEFORE I WAS READY to leave for the day, there was a knock on my door. I figured it was Delfia saying goodbye, so I said come in. It wasn't her. I sighed in exasperation. "What can I do for you?"

He leaned against the doorframe, taking a moment before he walked in. "Lorelai is ready to sign the proposal you sent her."

"That's great news," I said dryly.

"But she would like us to demo the product for her sales team before she signs on the dotted line. Are you available on Wednesday morning?"

I pulled up my calendar and glanced at it. "Looks like I'm available. What time?"

"Ten."

I put it on my calendar and said, "Okay." I figured that was it, so I hit the power button on my computer to shut it down, but he didn't leave like I expected him to.

"Ms. Bryant."

I kept putting things away, getting ready to leave. I didn't even look up at him when I responded, "Yes?"

"I apologize for not giving you notice that I had hired a contractor."

I shrugged my shoulders and closed my laptop. "You're the boss, right?"

"Ms. Bryant, please."

I shot him a cold glance. "Good night, Mr. Greyson." I grabbed my satchel and walked out, leaving him there staring after me. I ran straight into Alexa.

"Do you know where Ian is? I'm so ready to leave," she whined.

I pointed to my office and continued to walk away, thanking my lucky stars I wouldn't have to see her again until tomorrow, even though that was way too soon. Actually, forever was too soon for my taste, but at least I had belly dancing to look forward to, I needed a serious endorphin boost.

I needed one so bad, I only went home to change and drop off my laptop. I headed straight to the Y and ran on the track before my class. I was in such a mood, I kind of overdid it and dragged a little in my class, but it was well worth it. I was tired when I left, but it was the good kind of tired. Unfortunately, it wasn't the kind that could carry me through the scene I had waiting for me at my apartment complex. I returned just in time to see Mr. Greyson carrying what looked like Alexa's designer luggage from his apartment across the courtyard. He froze when he saw me, and for some reason, I froze too.

Alexa looked between the two of us and grinned wickedly. "Thanks for letting me stay the night last night," she announced loudly.

I smirked at them both and walked away. I already figured she was sleeping with the boss, but why she thought that would bother me I found interesting. I was happy to disappoint her. I didn't even bother looking at my idiot boss's reaction. He was the world's biggest hypocrite. It made me wonder what I ever saw in him. I used to think he was such a stand-up guy.

I walked into my apartment, and immediately my phone rang. It was the hypocritical idiot, so I ignored it. I was off the clock, and I didn't want to be friends with someone like him. I thought maybe we could after the last two weeks, but I was dead wrong.

I decided the next day that I would start getting to work extra early, even before Delfia; this way I could be safely in my office with the door closed before anyone else showed up. My target time was ten minutes until seven. I didn't think anyone got there before 7:15 usually, but I was hedging my bets. It paid off.

It was such a relief to walk into a quiet office, devoid of those who were now making my professional life hellish. It was so sad to think that it wasn't that long ago that I was happy to come into work every day. Now I felt on edge, and even slightly uncomfortable. Maybe I was being spoofed and any day now someone would say, "Just kidding," and I could go back to the way it was before Mr. Greyson showed up.

I reveled in the quiet as I responded to email and polished up my presentation for the next day. Delfia got there thirty minutes after me. She walked in my office and we took turns bashing our new "contractor." Apparently, I'd missed most of the action as I stayed behind closed doors. I guess she followed Mr. Greyson around everywhere and complained constantly. The complaints ranged from the humidity to how long lunch took to arrive. Delfia perfectly imitated her squeaky little voice, and we both broke out into hysterical laughter. I knew it wasn't kind, and it was quite unprofessional, but I needed the comic relief. At that point, it was either laugh or cry. I was proud of myself as I refrained from sharing my little news about them spending the night together. They were consenting adults and what they did in private should stay private as far as I was concerned.

I had a pleasant morning with just myself for company. It allowed me to get a ton done. If I weren't the manager, I would consider working from home, which reminded me, I really did need to come out of my sanctuary and go talk to the troops below. I freshened up, psyched myself up, and emerged to a smiling Delfia. "Is the coast clear?" I whispered.

She looked both ways for me and whispered, "Hurry."

This was so ridiculous.

I scooted out toward the stairs, but it was like he knew. As soon as I passed his door, he opened it. "Ms. Bryant, could I please speak to you?"

I hung my head in resignation and sighed. I'm pretty sure I heard Delfia laugh, that was until Mr. Greyson glanced her way.

He looked back to me, pleasantly smiled, and invited me into his office. I entered silently, and he closed the door behind us. I looked around and wished for Boss.

"Please have a seat," he said while motioning to the chairs in front of his desk.

He sat next to me instead of behind his desk and studied me for a moment. He rubbed his hands together. "I think we need to clear some things up. I know how things appeared last night."

I put my hand up. "Mr. Greyson, you owe me no explanation. Your personal life is just that, personal. But, I find your and your girlfriend's behavior in the office to be highly unprofessional."

"Girlfriend? Alexa's not my girlfriend," he spluttered.

"Oh please, I don't care what you call her, except I do find it hypocritical that you call her Alexa instead of Ms. Manselle. I guess professional boundaries are merely guidelines for you."

"Ms. Bryant, Alexa is not an employee, and I've known her for years."

"Like maybe thirteen or fourteen." I didn't add in that's how long we had known each other, but by the drop in his face, I knew he got it.

"No...not that long," he admitted. "But regardless, she's not an employee."

I stood. "I need to go. I have an office to run."

He stood too. He hesitantly reached out and touched my arm. "Ms. Bryant, please."

"Please what?" I peered up into those chocolate eyes of his.

"I thought that when I got back things would be...different."

I did too, but I didn't repeat the sentiment.

Alexa came barging in without knocking.

Mr. Greyson dropped his hand, and I took that as my cue to leave.

"Oh, did I interrupt something?" She batted her fake eyelashes.

I wasn't buying her faux sincerity. "Not at all, Ms. Manselle."

"Oh haha. Call me Alexa, silly."

I threw Mr. Greyson a look that said, *this is the best you could do,* before I stalked off. I heard her ask, "So where are we going to lunch?" before I closed the door.

Delfia was shaking her head, tsking when I walked out. That's all I felt like doing too. *Why her?* I kept thinking.

I was able to spend the rest of my day working with our account managers and going over sales goals. I actually waited for Mr. Greyson to leave before I went back upstairs. I ended up being the last one there. It was one very long day, so much so it was take-out, PJ's, and remote in hand for the rest of the night.

Again, I was the first one there the next morning. If I kept this up, I would be more than caught up on all my work for the next month at least.

Around a quarter after nine, Mr. Greyson opened my door. "Are you ready to leave?"

I barely looked up. "Yes, I'll meet you there."

"We're not driving together?" he asked.

I set down my pen. "No. I know where I'm going."

He stood still as if I might change my mind.

I was happy to disappoint him. "I'll see you there," I said, like that settled it.

He shut my door harder than was necessary. I smiled to myself. Irritating him was my new hobby. I walked out to find Alexa asking if she should go and present her mockups. If she was going, there was no way I was. I hadn't even seen the mockups, and neither had Matt.

I had to throw in my two cents, I didn't care who the boss was. "We shouldn't be showing our clients mockups until they have gone through an extensive internal review process."

I think she *tchted* at me. My eyes widened. How old was she?

Mr. Greyson surprisingly agreed with me. As she continued her whining, I walked away. I didn't need this, and it was getting to the point that I would be demanding she work somewhere else. As a contractor, she didn't need to be in-house, especially my house.

Mr. Greyson caught up to me on the stairs. "Are you sure you don't want to drive together?"

"Positive."

"How about lunch afterward?"

I laughed.

"What?"

"No thanks. I could only imagine how that would make your girl-friend whine."

"Ms. Bryant, I told you, she's not my girlfriend."

I rolled my eyes. "Well whatever your arrangement is, the answer is still no."

"Why?"

I stopped at the bottom of the steps. He was still on the last step, so he hovered over me a bit. "Aren't you the one who said you weren't here to make friends?" Then I amended, "But I guess that is unless they're 'contractors.'"

He wickedly grinned. "You really don't like her, do you?"

"Oh, you can read people after all." I threw open the door and marched out to my car.

The whole drive over I reproved myself for my own unprofessional-ism. It was like I was suddenly back in high school or transported into a really bad soap opera. I pulled into the parking lot and tried to expunge my mind of Alexa and Mr. Greyson. I needed to be on my A game. This account was a big deal, and I didn't want to be the one to blow it. I took a deep breath in and let it out slowly. It was show time.

Mr. Greyson met me at my car door and opened it for me. "Are you ready?"

I nodded.

He began spouting off pointers, and I let him. It was weird, but I needed that. That was normal.

We walked into a large conference room that was filled to capac-ity. Lorelai and Nicholas greeted us warmly at the entrance. I would say Nicholas' greeting was overly warm as he spoke to me. I could tell it annoyed my boss. He was such a hypocrite. To my regret, I let that thought take hold and responded too warmly in return.

They were running on a tight schedule, so we had to begin right away. This was one of my favorite parts of the job, and where I shined. Today was no exception. Mr. Greyson didn't even jump in once. When I finished, the chatter and commentary was extremely positive. I could tell their sales team was salivating at the possibilities our software afforded. There was no doubt we were leaving with a signature on the dotted line.

"Well done, Ms. Bryant," Mr. Greyson whispered as I was packing away my laptop.

"Thanks." I smiled.

After their sales staff left, it was just Mr. Greyson, myself, Lorelai, and Nicholas. We met at one end of the large conference table and finalized the deal. As I watched Lorelai sign, I reminded myself this was why I hadn't quit again. My baby had barely begun to see the light of day, and I wanted to see it through, even if it meant I had to put up with nonsense.

As we walked out, I could tell I wasn't the only one elated. Mr. Greyson's eyes sparkled. That was until someone called out after me.

I turned to find it was Nicholas. "Kelli, wait up."

I wasn't the only one to stop.

Nicholas looked between Mr. Greyson and myself, shrugged his shoulders, and ignored my boss. "How about dinner tonight to celebrate?"

Oh. This was awkward. I had never been asked out in front of my boss before. Where was Boss when I needed him? I bit my lip as I looked into his deep blue eyes and dimpled face. He really was a handsome guy, but I also knew his type. Then I thought, *Am I sure?* Maybe that was my problem: I judged too quickly. What if I kept missing out on Mr. Right?

He grinned as he watched me hesitate. "How about Pierre's at seven?" he tried to sweeten the deal.

"Sounds good, but I'll meet you there." I was serious about not letting strange men into my apartment or letting them know where I lived.

Nicholas touched my arm gently. "See you then, gorgeous."

I think I was blushing. I sure felt warm all of a sudden.

Someone else looked like they were warm too. When Nicholas left, I noticed Mr. Greyson's face was furiously red. I wasn't sure why. The deal was signed, so having dinner with him would have no effect on the sale positively or negatively.

"I'll see you at the office." It was all I could think of to say. I turned to leave.

Mr. Greyson followed, and as soon as we were outside, he tugged on my jacket. "I thought you said you wouldn't date someone like him?"

"It's only dinner," I replied in my defense.

"The guy is hoping for more than dinner."

I narrowed my eyes at him. "Why do you care?"

He opened his mouth several times to say something, but nothing ever came out.

I waited patiently for a reply.

"You did well. I'll see you in the office." He walked off, seemingly frustrated.

"Thanks," I called out. I watched him stalk off. As soon as I got in my car, I put my sister on Bluetooth. "Hi sis. I have a date tonight."

"With Ian?"

"No. Why would you say that? Never mind, don't answer that. It's with a man named Nicholas. He's the EVP for our new client."

"Oh. How nice." She wasn't as excited as I thought she would be, but she gave me suggestions on what I should wear to Pierre's. It was a predictable restaurant for Nicholas. Overpriced and fancy, but at least the food was good.

I left the office early, and to my great delight, without having to see either Mr. Greyson or Alexa. I came home, sank into a bath, shaved my legs, and took my time getting ready. It had been too long since I'd been on a date, so I took extra care and tried to enjoy the experience. I wore my new red bandage dress and some killer heels. I stared at my reflection in my full-length mirror. Not bad for my almost thirty-two-year-old self. The belly dancing was definitely doing its job.

I walked out into the slightly cool air with a spring in my step. I almost put the top down on my car, but I decided against messing up my hair. I felt energized when I reached Pierre's right on time. I didn't know what kind of car Nicholas drove, so I wasn't sure if he was there, but I went right in anyway.

Pierre's screamed high priced the moment I walked in, from the tuxedo-clad host, to the white linens and low lighting, to the string quartet playing. It was lovely, but I would still take the park and peanut butter and jam sandwiches. Oh well. Enjoy the moment, I reminded myself.

It didn't take me long to spot Nicholas. He stood when he saw me walking toward him. His eyes roved over me at least three time before I made it to him. Each go around made his smile get wider. I wasn't sure if I should be flattered or worried. He pulled out my chair. "You're breathtaking," he said as I sat down.

"Thank you. You look great." And he did. He wore a black suit and a gray tie. I'm sure the suit was tailored, as it fit his physique perfectly.

Nicholas didn't take his eyes off me until the waiter brought us our menus and the wine list. He, of course, wanted to order the most expensive bottle they had. I didn't socially drink unless I was well acquainted with who I was going out with. I was about to tell him I would pass, but a familiar voice said, "The lady will have water, with orange slices if you have them."

I didn't know whether I should laugh or cry at his presence, but I could tell my date sure wasn't amused as he looked up at him and glared.

Mr. Greyson didn't let that bother him at all. He smiled at Nicholas and then over at me. "That's what you still drink, isn't it, Kelli?"

"Why yes, Mr. Greyson, how kind of you to remember," I said in mock sincerity, because just outright mocking would be in poor form at the moment.

But he knew, and it made him smile even more.

"Ian, what are you doing here?" Nicholas asked. Stretching his fingers as if he was thinking of curling them up and punching my boss.

"My brother in-law, Sean, is in town for the evening on business." He pointed over to him.

My head whipped toward the bar, curious to see whom Noelle had married. He waved at me. I waved back. He looked like a nice guy.

"And I heard this was one of the best places in town," Mr. Greyson said.

"It is," Nicholas responded dryly.

I took that as my cue. "Well, have a nice evening, Mr. Greyson." I waved goodbye.

"You too, Kelli." Mr. Greyson could hardly keep the laugh out of his voice.

It took everything I had in me not to roll my eyes, especially when he had parting words for my date. "Don't have her out too late, it's a school night after all."

Nicholas didn't respond to that ridiculous statement as Mr. Greyson walked away, finally letting his laugh out.

I turned my attention back to my disgruntled date. "Sorry about that." I smiled in hopes to smooth it over.

He wasn't smiling back. "Do you guys have like a thing?"

"No. He's my boss," I said indignantly.

He smirked. "Because that would be unheard of."

"I think we should change the subject."

Nicholas had no problem with that, but unfortunately, my first impression of him was dead on. He loved to talk about himself. I was treated to the highlight reel of his "fascinating" life. I didn't even need to speak. All I had to do was sit there and occasionally nod or smile. And the only reason I was smiling was because someone besides my date kept staring my way from the bar. Several times I caught both Mr. Greyson and his brother-in-law looking my way and waving or pretending their hands were guns and shooting themselves in the head. That was exactly how I felt.

It got really interesting when the table next to us freed up. Guess who came to occupy it?

It was comical, in a way. At least it made my date take a breath and shut up. He was just starting in on his days as a star basketball player for the University of Tennessee, and I, for one, wasn't interested at all. The new table arrangement also allowed me to be introduced to Noelle's husband, and I had really wanted to meet him.

Mr. Greyson, with no regard, interrupted Nicholas. "Kelli, this is my very lucky brother-in-law, Sean Nixon." My first thought was, that was kind of sweet. Mr. Greyson and Noelle had been close, and by how he introduced Sean, I could tell that was still the case. My second thought was, I bet Noelle didn't love having Nixon for a last name, but I bet she loved Sean. I could sense he was a nice guy. He wore a goofy smile that fit his red hair and freckles perfectly. He looked like the sweet boy next door. I was sure Noelle kept him on his toes.

Sean held out his hand as the introduction was made. "It is a pleasure to meet you. Noelle will be jealous."

"How is Noelle?" I took his hand, eager to know anything about my old friend.

His eyes lit up at the mention of her name. That was a good husband there. Holy envy was creeping in. I wasn't attracted to Sean, but I hoped someday to have a husband who lit up at the mention of my name.

He grinned like he really was the luckiest man. "She's Noelle."

"Please tell her hello for me."

"I'll do one better." He took out his phone. "Ian, stand by Kelli."

Mr. Greyson zipped over to me and held his hand out to help me stand. Naturally my hand found its way to his. His touch made me wish... well... never mind. To make matters worse or better, depending on how you looked at it, he put his arm around my waist. I looked up at him. He grinned like a fool, and foolishly, I liked it. We smiled for one picture before I unloosed myself from Mr. Greyson. It was then I noticed how very unhappy my date was. He was shooting daggers at Mr. Greyson with his eyes. I bit my lip, pretending I was embarrassed, hoping that would ease the tension, but he wasn't buying it. I shrugged it off. I wasn't having that good of a time anyway.

I think Sean and Mr. Greyson could tell and were trying to help me out, either that or they were extremely rude. They kept interrupting Mr. I-scored-fifty-points-in-a-game-once with gems like, "Kelli, tell Sean about the time Noelle climbed out your window during one of our double dates and someone called the cops because they thought she was breaking in." Mr. Greyson was playing dirty. He knew I wouldn't refuse him in front of Sean, which meant I would have to talk about our past. Something I had been refusing to do up to this point. It also wasn't lost on my date.

"You two dated?" Nicholas growled before downing his glass of chardonnay. "I thought you said there wasn't anything going on between you."

"It was a long time ago," I informed Nicholas.

"Seems like yesterday to me," Mr. Greyson said wistfully.

My brows shot up. What was Mr. Greyson playing at?

Nicholas sneered at him.

"Kelli, you didn't tell me your story," Sean jumped in.

Mr. Greyson dared me with his eyes to acknowledge our shared past.

Fine, but I was only doing it because I liked Sean and I missed Noelle. "Once, when *Mr. Greyson* and I were—"

Sean held up his hand. "Excuse me, why are you calling him Mr. Greyson?" He pointed at his brother-in-law.

"That's a good question." Nicholas said, annoyed.

I smirked at Mr. Greyson before addressing Sean. "Didn't he tell you he's all about professional boundaries?"

Mr. Greyson rubbed the back of his neck.

"Ah," Sean sympathized with Mr. Greyson. "I guess given your recent uh...dealings," Sean said clumsily, "that makes sense." I wanted to ask exactly what Sean knew, but I could tell he would be loyal to his family and not divulge anything Mr. Greyson hadn't already shared with me.

"Please continue," Sean requested.

"Oh, um." I almost forgot what I was going to say. "I set Noelle up with a guy I met in my biology class and Ian, I mean Mr. Greyson, and I made dinner for everyone in my apartment. Halfway through dinner the guy throws his barefoot up on the table. We didn't even know he had taken his shoes off," I laughed. "He then proceeds to go into horrific detail about his hammer toe surgery that had gone wrong. Noelle said not a word and got up, we thought to use the bathroom, but twenty minutes later there was a knock on my door. It was Noelle with two police officers."

Sean and Mr. Greyson were laughing hysterically.

"There was no hiding that she had tried to escape her date, but once she told them what her date had done, they let her off. I think the guy transferred out my class."

"Sounds like my Noelle," Sean sounded smitten.

Nicholas was not amused. He took my hand and tried to divert my attention. "Let's focus on the future."

If he thought we had a future he was out of his mind.

Mr. Greyson coughed. "Didn't you say Noelle wanted to talk to Kelli."

"She did." Sean whipped out his phone and dialed his wife. "I have a surprise for you," he told his wife.

Wait. Why was this a surprise to her? I thought she wanted this.

Sean handed me the phone.

"Hello."

"Kelli!" Noelle screamed. "You still look gorgeous. Especially with my brother."

She made me blush. "Thank you. Sean is great."

"I know."

Nicholas began tapping on the table.

"Um, Noelle, can we talk later?" I really was being rude.

"Sure. Sure. Get my number from Ian."

"You can just give it to me."

"Don't be silly." She hung up.

I handed the phone back to Sean. A conspiratorial grin passed between him and his brother-in-law, who never ceased to surprise me as of late. Weird didn't even begin to describe this night.

By the time dinner was over, my date was refusing to take a breath between stories, even if that meant chewing with his mouth open. He refused to be interrupted again by Sean and Mr. Greyson. Not to say they didn't try. Mr. Greyson even tried handing me his chocolate cake to see if I wanted a bite. I swore Nicholas was going to swat it out of his hand if I reached for it.

It was a good thing that Lorelai had already signed our contract. Nicholas was more than out of sorts when it was time to pay the check and depart. He seriously didn't appreciate Mr. Greyson and Sean walking out with us and standing next to Mr. Greyson's car while Nicholas walked me to mine.

When we arrived at my car, Nicholas kissed my cheek. "Maybe next time we could do this alone."

I smiled at him. There wouldn't be a next time. "Thank you for dinner," I responded. "I'm sorry for the intrusion." I wasn't really. Oddly, I kind of enjoyed it.

He took that as an invitation. "How about dessert?"

I had a feeling he wasn't talking about food.

"Good night, Nicholas."

"Maybe next time." He pushed off my car.

I really hated being right sometimes. Nicholas was exactly who I thought he would be. Was I ever going to find Mr. Right?

Mr. Greyson caught my eye and waved. "Drive safe. Good night."

My heart said, *What about that guy?*

No. No. No. He left us and he's with Alexa.

Is he really? my annoying heart asked.

Does it matter? I fired back.

If you want it to, my heart whispered.

Chapter Fourteen

I

T WAS PROBABLY A GOOD thing Mr. Greyson and his plaything were out of the office on Thursday and Friday. I was more confused than ever about my boss.

Mr. Greyson was meeting with some prospects in Memphis and who knew what Ms. Manselle was doing. Maybe she had gone with him. That thought bothered me more than it should. I was also bothered by his behavior at Pierre's. What was he playing at anyway, interrupting my date? Sure, I enjoyed talking to him and Sean more than my date, and I appreciated that they waited for Nicholas to leave before they left. Not that I thought Nicholas would try anything, per se, but it was nice all the same, especially since my first instincts about him were spot on.

How could Mr. Greyson be such a pain in the office, but so Ian-like off the clock?

By the time I got home on Friday I was emotionally and physically drained. The man was wreaking havoc on my life. I longingly looked at my "husband" list on my refrigerator while I contemplated what to make for dinner. Was it really that hard to find a guy who met all my criteria? I told my heart not to even mention you know who, who by the way didn't meet my criteria, having been divorced. Though that was more of a preference than a hard and fast rule. Ugh. It didn't matter.

Saturday morning found me watching my nieces while my traitorous brother-in-law played golf with my boss. I tried not to dwell on the man as the girls and I spent an enjoyable couple of hours at the pool. But as always, as of late, Mr. Greyson showed up in his plaid shorts and well-fitting polo and made sure I was dwelling on him. I swore he looked like he had just done a photo shoot for J.Crew. I looked down at my black swimsuit as I sat on the edge of the pool with my legs dangling in the warm water. I felt vulnerable with so much skin showing. Not like he hadn't seen me in a swimsuit before, but it seemed different now.

His eyes lit up when he saw me. He strutted over to me with golf clubs slung over his shoulder.

I focused on my nieces for safety reasons, theirs and mine.

That didn't deter him. He came right over and sat next to me after he deposited his clubs near one of the lounge chairs. In a surprising move he took his shoes and socks off and dipped his legs in the pool too. "You're looking well today, Kelli."

I playfully nudged him.

He leaned in and whispered, "But not as well as you looked Wednesday night. That red dress, stunning."

Goosebumps erupted all over my body. Where was a breeze when you needed one? He knew those bumps didn't appear because I was cold, and he seemed quite delighted by it.

"Why did you go to Pierre's that night?" I asked.

"I told you. I heard it was the best place in town, and Sean was only here for the night."

"Your Greyson white lies don't work on me anymore."

His left brow quirked. "So, what does work on you? I noticed Nicholas sure didn't seem to do it for you."

"Yes, thanks for ruining my date, by the way."

"I'd like to take the credit, but I think you and I know better."

I turned my attention back toward the girls. He was right, but I wasn't admitting it.

"I know men like Nicholas, too, and I was..."

I looked back over to him, to find him tenderly looking at me. Why did he have to look and act like Ian?

"I wanted to make sure you were treated like you deserve."

I was completely taken aback. I wasn't sure how to respond. "Thank you, but I don't think that's part of your job description."

"Have you actually seen my employment contract?" he teased.

"You're in a mood today."

His finger lightly skimmed my shoulder. "Maybe it has something to do with the Nashville scenery."

Thank goodness the girls swam up to us and splashed us both in the process because my body was about to come unhinged from his soft touch.

"Girls, I want you to meet someone. This is my boss, Mr. Greyson."

"The idiot?" Sam said with no regard or qualms.

Courtney giggled.

My sister and I needed to quit talking around them.

Embarrassed, I bit my lip and turned toward Mr. Greyson who had his eyebrow raised sky high at me, but he didn't address me. He turned to my nieces. "What else has your aunt said about me, ladies?"

"Oh no, no, no..." I cut in.

The girls laughed harder, and I knew I was in trouble. "Well..." they said in unison.

That was it. I jumped in the pool and tried to grab the little trouble-makers, but they swam off to the other side of the pool laughing all the way. I wiped the water off my face and looked up at Mr. Greyson.

"So, this is what you really think of me?" he asked.

There was no sense in denying it. "Believe me, I've thought worse things of you."

It was like I had sucked out all the sunshine in his soul. His entire body deflated. I felt terrible, even though it was true. Did he not understand how much he hurt me so long ago? But still, I should have held my tongue. "Ian...I mean Mr. Greyson, I'm sorry."

"No Kelli, I'm the sorry one." With that he got up, gathered all his things, and left.

I watched him walk away, and part of me ached. When he was no longer in sight, I sank under the water and wondered why I was letting him have such an effect on me.

I didn't see him the rest of the weekend, which was probably a good thing. His actions confused me, and by Monday I was even more confused. I was finally going to see why we were wasting company funds on Ms. Manselle. I was at least happy to know she had actually done some work. Whenever I saw her, she wasn't designing anything—unless you counted her designs on Mr. Greyson.

Matt and I showed up to the conference room, waiting to be dazzled by her new designs. The meeting was supposed to start at nine, but the two love birds were all cooped up in Mr. Greyson's office. I guess they needed a warm-up session. I still didn't get it, and I didn't get him. What did he see in her? Personally or professionally?

They came in fifteen minutes late. Alexa looked frazzled and Mr. Greyson looked out of sorts. Maybe they'd had a lover's spat, but then the presentation started and the kindest word I could think of to describe it was "awful." I could tell Mr. Greyson thought so too, but it didn't keep him from trying to smooth it over. He kept saying things like, "Just visualize this or that." It was pathetic. I mean how could I visualize incomplete and blank slides?

I kept my mouth shut, but Mr. Greyson kept looking at me like he was daring me to say something. I didn't have to, the erratic, incoherent presentation spoke for itself.

Matt's comments tied it up nicely. "I can't work with this. I think it would be better to stick with our current interface." He threw his pad of paper on the table.

I tried my hardest not to smirk, but it was really hard. It was even harder not to go and get my designs. I was even tempted to tell Matt about them and secretly show them to him, but I refrained.

"We'll get this right," Mr. Greyson assured us.

I gave into my urge and smirked at him. Matt shook his head in disgust, and Ms. Manselle pouted.

I will say this, it seemed to light a fire under her. I saw her more at work than at play for the next couple of days.

Thursday rolled around. It happened to be my birthday. I was tempted to give myself the best present ever and not go into work, but Mr. Greyson and I were presenting on Friday to Premier Bank in Nashville. They were a billion-dollar asset financial institution, so we needed all the prep time we could get. At least I was going to be able to have dinner with my family that night before they left for the Magic Kingdom the next day.

I came in at a normal time. I figured I deserved the extra sleep. I was pleasantly surprised to see that Delfia had placed a large bouquet of balloons in my office for me before I arrived. She really was the best. Her hug and homemade blueberry muffins weren't bad either. Just the two of us enjoyed the muffins together in my office. We didn't feel like dumb and dumber were worthy of them, but I felt kind of bad about it later that morning when I got a surprise delivery of flowers.

They weren't just any flowers, either, they were my most favorite of all-time flowers, that only one person would know about. I stared at the beautiful pot full of columbines in disbelief. I didn't even know you could order them like this. There was no note, which made Delfia super curious, but I had no doubt who they were from. Columbines were Colorado's state flower. They grew wild in the mountains. FYI, it's illegal to pick them, but Ian—I mean Mr. Greyson— forgot to mention that to me until after it was too late. I still had those illegal flowers pressed in a journal somewhere. I loved the white and purplish-blue petals. I delicately touched the ones right in front of me.

Why did he have to be nice to me? And why did I have to remember lovely hikes in the mountains, breathtaking views, and kisses with the only man I ever loved? I knew I needed to go and say thank you, but I was hesitant. I considered sending an email, but I had better manners than that, even though he may not agree. I reluctantly got up and opened my door.

Delfia was still trying to guess who the flowers were from. She listed off five more men. I shook my head no at each wrong name. "Is Mr. Greyson in?" I interrupted her.

She looked at me suspiciously. "Yes."

"Is he with anyone?" And by anyone, I meant Ms. Dumber. She shook her head no.

I could feel her stares from behind as I cautiously approached his door and knocked. It didn't take long for him to grant permission for me to open the door. I did so quickly before I lost my nerve. I walked in and shut the door behind me as fast as I could, so no one else would see me or hear me.

He looked surprised to see me, but his eyes lit up. "Ms. Bryant."

"Um...Mr. Greyson."

"Please have a seat," he offered.

"That's okay. I just wanted to say thank you."

He ran his fingers through his hair. "For what?"

I knew he was lying, but I wondered why he would. "I know the columbines are from you. You and I may be the only ones in this state who know what they are."

"Or that it's illegal to pick them in the wild." He grinned.

"Anyway, thank you."

"Happy birthday."

"Thanks for reading my employee file and remembering."

His smile faded away. "I've never forgotten."

"Oh." I always remembered his too. June 16th.

His eyes burned into mine from across the room, and suddenly I wanted to cross the professional boundary line. "Thank you," I said again, flustered, before I ran out of there.

I didn't even react to Delfia's detective work and knowing looks as I walked past her. "Did you know that columbines are Colorado's state flower?" she called with delight in her devious voice.

I ran straight to my bathroom and stared at my flushed reflection in the mirror. What was wrong with me? I decided not to answer, because the answer was ridiculous. Instead, I went back to my desk and tried to concentrate on my presentation for tomorrow before I sent it back to Mr. Greyson. His new laptop was better than mine, and he thought it would be a good idea to use his for tomorrow's presentation.

No matter how hard I tried to concentrate, my eyes kept drifting toward the beautiful flowers, and my mind kept landing on the man who sent them to me. By four, I decided to call it a day. It was my birthday after all. With my balloons and flowers, I made a beeline for the exit. It took me a while to exit the lobby as I had lots of birthday wishes. It was a nice way to leave work, but I wanted to make a quick exit. I wasn't feeling like myself. I was so out of sorts that on the drive home I debated whether I should cancel my birthday dinner with my family or not. Physically, I was well, but I felt weird, if that made sense.

When I arrived home, I carefully placed my flowers front-and-center on my kitchen table. I put the balloons on my coffee table. I didn't want anything to distract from the beauty of those darn flowers. They had become like that silly note he wrote about the coffee filters. I kept staring at them like they would reveal some secret. I finally had to force myself to walk away and get ready for dinner. There was no use in canceling. I knew my excuse of "I felt weird" would never fly with my sister. She would be over here psychoanalyzing me if I gave her such a reason.

As soon as I walked into my sister's home, I was happy I hadn't given into my odd feelings. Court and Sam immediately flew into my arms with birthday greetings and hugs and kisses. They pulled me into the kitchen. It smelled amazing. Amanda and Zane were finishing up dinner, but each took a break to give me a hug. I was definitely feeling the love. For dinner, my sister was making one of my favorites: sweet and sour chicken with homemade fried rice. I felt terrible she was going to all the trouble right before she was leaving on vacation.

She waved off my concern. "I love you, Kelli Jelly."

I sure loved her.

Dinner was beyond amazing, and the cake that followed was just as good or better. Amanda made another favorite of mine, lemon cake with blackberry frosting. She really was Betty Crocker, and I adored her for it. I especially enjoyed the company as I listened to my nieces talk about flying to Disney World the next morning. They were so excited.

"It's not too late for you to come," Zane and Amanda said.

I shook my head and sighed.

Amanda gave me a knowing look.

I put the girls to bed while Zane and Amanda cleaned up. I definitely got the better end of the deal. I had a feeling the girls wouldn't be sleeping well. It was like the night before Christmas for them. They each promised to bring me something Disney related.

"Do you think you could bring back Prince Charming for me?"

They giggled. Too bad I was serious.

I came down to say goodbye to Zane and Amanda. I figured they would want to get to bed, because they had an early flight, but Amanda pulled me into the living room to talk to me for a bit. They both sat on the couch and I took the large ottoman in front of it, trying not to get too cozy.

"So, what's wrong, Kelli? You're not acting like yourself. Did something happen at work today?"

I shrugged my shoulders. "I had a . . . good day."

Amanda tapped me with her foot. "Did Ian bring in another blonde?"

"No," I hesitated, "he sent me flowers today for my birthday."

Both of their faces beamed.

I waved off their excitement. "It was nothing."

Zane reached over and patted my hand. "Kelli, I know we've raised you better than to be this naïve."

I couldn't help but laugh when Zane got all parental on me. He was only like eight years older than me. "I'm not naïve. Ask Amanda, she'll tell you."

She grinned at me but didn't jump to my defense. I kept looking at her expectantly and getting more annoyed by the second as she stared with amusement on her face. I finally blurted out, "Why are you staring at me like a fool?"

"I think we were wrong about the hussy." She tensed waiting for my response.

I rolled my eyes. "I don't agree, but even if it's not what we think, so what?"

"Kelli, you need to open your eyes to the truth," Zane jumped in with his two cents.

"I don't know what you mean."

He took my hands in his like he was talking to his daughters. "Ian loves you," he said point blank.

I laughed in his face and pulled away my hands. "Have you been inhaling laughing gas at work?"

Both he and my sister were looking at me as if I was the high one.

I stopped laughing. "Guys, you know that's not true."

They looked between each other, making me feel more uncomfortable than I already was. "Why do you think that?" My voice cracked.

"Besides it being completely obvious, he said some things while we were golfing that cinched it," Zane answered.

I began to feel weird again. All I could do was stare blankly, with my mouth wide open. Amanda lovingly closed it for me.

"Fine. I'll play your sick little game. Did he say he..." I could barely say the word in relation to him, "loved me?"

"He didn't say the exact words," Zane admitted.

I folded my arms with a fair amount of smugness.

"Kelli, the man loves you."

I jumped up. "No, Zane. The man left me crying and calling his name with no thought at all. Then he went years without contacting me, and when he did show back up, he stole my job and made me call him Mr. Greyson. Does that sound like love to you?"

Both he and my sister each took a hand and gently guided me back to the ottoman. I was on the verge of tears, and I had no idea why, other than I was frustrated with their insinuations and the way my life had been ever since Mr. Greyson showed up.

Zane kept my hand. "Can I tell you a little something about Bryant women?"

Both Amanda and I gave him the look.

He laughed, but braved speaking. "You are the most terrifying creatures on this planet," quickly adding before we really did terrorize him, "but there's nothing greater than being loved by one."

I still wasn't buying it, though Amanda lapped it up. "Aww," she said before she kissed him a little more sloppily than necessary in my presence.

"Ahem," I interrupted. "Okay genius, if that's the case, then why did Mr. Greyson leave me?"

"Kelli, did you ever stop to think that maybe he did what he did because he loved you?"

Chapter Fifteen

YOU DON'T LEAVE THE PEOPLE you love, and that's exactly what I told Zane, and that's the thought I held on to as I drove home. I tossed and turned in bed that night thinking about Zane's conjecturing and how irked I was at all of them. I had begged Zane to tell me what Mr. Greyson said, but he said, "What happens on the golf course between men, stays on the golf course." He added in, "You're a smart girl, Kelli. You'll figure it out."

I woke up tired, and my brain felt muddled. Calling in sick crossed my mind more than once. If only we didn't have that meeting with Premier late that morning. What would've been my excuse anyway? Sick of my boss, perhaps? Or maybe I could blame it on the weird sensation that kept coming over me whenever I thought about Mr. Greyson. In the end, I threw off my covers and started my day by showering and sighing more than was necessary.

I wore my best bone-colored suit that fit me like a glove, and I curled and styled my hair beauty-queen style. I looked in my floor length mirror when I was done and sighed some more. I looked okay, but there was still something different about me. I really didn't feel like myself. I ran my fingers through my hair and sighed again. I threw my hands up in the air. I knew what my problem was—it was that man.

He continued to consume my thoughts as I drove to work. I became increasingly more upset and confused by the mile. I was angry that he would talk to my brother-in-law about me in the first place, and that my brother-in-law, whom I trusted, and whose children I took care of on a regular basis so he and my sister could still pretend to be newlyweds, wouldn't even tell me what he said. If Zane would only tell me, I could clarify for him what Mr. Greyson really meant, because surely he didn't love me. But what upset me more was the thought, *what if he did love me?* I tried so hard not to entertain that thought, because it was completely ludicrous.

I mean really, the man had been married, and let's not forget that he left me and took my job. And let's certainly not forget all of his professional boundaries mumbo jumbo. And then there was Alexa. However, I also couldn't forget that he came to my rescue and brought me a tissue, and he saved me from an awful date. He also remembered my birthday and bought me the most beautiful flower arrangement. Not only that, he was giving me opportunities at work I had never had before.

"AHHHH!" I screamed out in my car on the highway. I couldn't do this. I couldn't let him back into my head, or worse, my heart, the heart he ripped out and casually tossed away like day-old take-out cartons.

By the time I arrived at work, I was frazzled to say the least. I wasn't in a mood to deal with what I had waiting for me when I made it upstairs. I knew immediately something was up by the way Delfia's eyes were bulging out. She didn't even say good morning. All she did was rush me into my office and shut the door. From there she hauled me into my bathroom and shut that door.

I was so stunned I didn't object. "Delfia?"

"Shh," she whispered.

"What's going on?" I whispered back.

"This morning I came in earlier than normal, and little miss thing was here. I was surprised because Mr. Greyson wasn't here yet, and I wasn't even sure she worked."

I nodded my head in agreement with her assessment.

"She was in the conference room talking to someone on the phone, and she obviously didn't know I was here; either that or she's as dumb as we first suspected."

Delfia and I had discussed her at length. We decided she was either really dumb or very smart.

"So, what did she say?"

"She said, 'I may need a little more time, but I'm not sure how much longer I can play the incompetent angle. Also, there's a snag in our plan. Ian appears to have feelings for the regional manager.' Then she went on to belittle you, the little wench."

I rested my hand on Delfia's arm. "Thank you, friend, for being miffed on my behalf, but I don't need or want her good opinion. Plus, I could think of some choice words to describe her."

"If you weren't such a fine lady, I'd ask you to tell me some."

I considered it and then thought better of it. No sense in going down that road.

"Kelli, you need to tell Mr. Greyson," she added to my surprise.

My eyes popped out. "Tell him what?"

"Tell him he needs to fire Alexa."

I shook my head. "I can't do that." Especially under the circumstances.

She looked at me like I should be pitied, and touched my cheek like she was my mother, except my mother was never so gentle and kind. "Kelli, it's about time for you and Mr. Greyson to come out of the closet," she snickered.

I batted her hand away. I was beginning to think everyone had gone crazy. The notion that Mr. Greyson had feelings for me was, not to use an "Alexa" word, but silly. Right?

"Come on now," she said. "Neither of you are fooling anyone."

I opened the bathroom door and marched out. I didn't need this today. It only added to my befuddlement, and now I was beyond furious. I knew that Ms. Manselle was bad news, I just couldn't believe Mr. Greyson was taken in by the bimbo. Who was Alexa conspiring with, and what plan was she talking about?

I sat down at my desk and rubbed my head.

Delfia grinned at me as she walked out.

My head began to pound, so I took some Tylenol as my laptop came up. Of course, well enough couldn't be left alone.

Mr. Greyson popped in. "Your presentation looks good. I only tweaked it a little." He ran his fingers nervously through his hair. It wasn't like him to act in such a way. "Would you...like to drive together?"

I bit my lip and mulled it over. Maybe I should. What Delfia told me was getting to me. Alexa really did need to be fired, and the ride over would allow me to talk to him. "Sure," was all I said, but it was enough to make him grin from ear to ear.

"I think we should leave at 9:45," he suggested.

"Sure," I responded blandly.

The next couple of hours were practically pointless. The only thing productive I accomplished was saying goodbye to my family as they waited for their plane to leave Nashville International. My nieces were so excited, I wondered how they would do on the plane. I reminded them, though, that they promised to bring me back something pretty, like Prince Charming. They giggled and promised they wouldn't forget. I wanted to talk to Amanda and Zane about what Delfia had told me, but I was afraid I would be overheard, and I didn't need anyone else telling me I should be with Mr. Greyson this morning. Instead, I said my goodbyes and told them I loved them.

I already missed them.

At 9:30, I freshened up and tried to do some relaxation techniques before Mr. Greyson came to retrieve me. I was more nervous about driving with him than presenting before a billion-dollar institution—an institution that could put my software on the map if we played our cards right.

9:45 came and went. It was very unlike Mr. Greyson to be late, he was often early, so at 9:50 I thought maybe there was a miscommunication and he was waiting on me. I only needed to grab my purse since he was driving, and we were using his laptop this go around. I walked out of my office to find no Delfia. I looked over to see that Mr. Greyson's door was closed, and I figured she was in there receiving orders. I smiled to myself thinking about how much she loved that. In my happy thoughts, I didn't think, I just walked over and opened Mr. Greyson's door to tell him we were going to be late and he could bark orders later, but opening that door unannounced was a horrible reminder of why knocking was so very, very important.

I stood there stunned at the scene before me. Ms. Manselle had nothing to worry about from the looks of it. I think her plan was falling right into place. Their lips were locked as she sat on his desk, holding onto his red tie.

"We're late!" I shouted louder than I meant to.

Mr. Greyson pushed Ms. Manselle away, almost knocking her off his desk. "Kelli," he said.

I slammed the door and ran toward the stairs. I would drive myself if I could manage it. The nauseous, rolling feeling was back, and I felt a little lightheaded. How dare he act so pompous and self-righteous and then come in here and make out with his floozy on company time. He was the biggest idiot, and she was playing him like a fool.

I barely remember making it outside to my car. As I rifled through my purse, I realized I should have remembered something else, my car keys. How could this be happening? We were going to be late for the most important meeting of my career, and it was entirely his fault. I marched myself back toward the office, all while trying not to cry.

In my haste, I ran into him, and he grabbed my arm.

"Ms. Bryant, where are you going?"

I yanked my arm away. "I'm going to get my keys." I stormed off, only to be pulled back. I stared directly into his wide eyes. "Don't touch me."

He dropped his hand. "Please, we're going to be late."

"And whose fault is that?" I yelled unprofessionally.

"Please," he pleaded with his tone and eyes.

"Ugh!" I turned and walked toward his car.

He ran after me, and he was smart enough not to open my door; instead he hit the unlock button on his key fob. I got in and immediately turned to look out my window. I hated him.

We drove in silence for several minutes.

"Can we please talk about what happened?" he asked.

I turned toward him, and the sight of him made me snap. "Yes, let's talk."

He glanced at me warily.

"How does this work for you? I quit!"

"Why?" he spluttered while trying to stay focused on the road.

"Are you kidding me? You've done nothing but belittle me, and then you bring your girlfriend on board so you can have rendezvous with her at your convenience in your office."

"How many times do I have to tell you that woman is not my girl-friend?" he yelled back.

I had this desire to smack him. "Whatever, Mr. Greyson, but by the way, she's playing you like the fool you are. You deserve each other."

"For the last time, I don't want her!"

"Wow! I better get my vision checked then, because from my point of view, it looked like you already had her."

He glanced over. "What you witnessed in my office was a misunder-standing."

A maniacal laugh escaped me. "What? You tripped and your lips fell on hers I suppose?"

"Why does this bother you so much?"

"It's completely unprofessional!" Wasn't that obvious to him?

"I don't think that's what's bothering you." His voice was calm, cool, and collected. "I'm sure that wasn't the first kiss you've ever witnessed in that office."

So maybe it wasn't. I had seen Holly and Boss kiss lots of times in there, but that's beside the point. They were married, and you know, he's the owner and not hypocritical, and oh man, did that sound lame in my head. "Please quit talking to me," I responded.

He had the gall to laugh at me as I turned back toward the window and folded my arms in a huff.

"Can't you admit what this is really about?"

I ignored him. I had no idea what he meant. *Or did I?*

Like always, though, he couldn't leave it alone as he sped toward our destination. "By the way, congratulations."

I turned toward him. "What does that mean?"

"You're the new director."

I didn't even know how to respond to his sick joke.

"I promised Gary if you ever decided to resign during my tenure, I would leave Chandler."

I sat stunned for a moment more. "Why would you do that?"

He took one hand off the wheel and threw it up in the air. "Why do you think? Maybe you should get your vision checked."

"Well maybe…" I started to say, but suddenly I felt myself being pushed back by Mr. Greyson, and the last sound I heard was him screaming my name and the sound of tires screeching.

Chapter Sixteen

"KELLI... KELLI... Please Kelli... Please God."

I couldn't tell if I was dreaming or awake, but all I knew was I could hear someone calling my name and pleading for me to be okay. I was having a hard time opening my eyes and responding. I wanted to, but I couldn't. The voice sounded so upset that I desperately wanted to make whoever it was feel better. If only I could open my eyes and make my mouth work.

I'm not sure how long I tried, but finally the smell of jet fuel overcame me, and I was able to slowly open my eyes. What I found, when I did, was Mr. Greyson calling my name and smiling at me in relief.

"Don't you mean, Ms. Bryant?"

He rested his hand on my cheek. "Kelli," he whispered.

I tried to move my head, but he used both his hands to gently hold it still. "Please, Kelli, don't move your head. I don't know how badly you've been injured."

It was then I realized I hurt all over. I felt something wet and sticky on my face. The airbags all around me were deployed. That explained the jet fuel smell. I tried to reach up and touch my face, but moving my right arm caused pain like I had never felt before. I cried out.

"Please don't move at all," he pleaded again. He grabbed a handkerchief from his suit coat pocket and used it to apply pressure to the right side of my head.

"What happened?" I managed to ask.

He applied pressure with one hand, while sweetly stroking my face with the other. He looked as if he were on the verge of tears. "A truck ran a red light, and I wasn't paying attention. I'm so sorry."

I was able to move my left arm, so I reached up and patted him. "It's not your fault."

"This whole thing is my fault."

"Mr. Greyson, are you okay?" I thought I should make sure, even though I couldn't see any cuts or abrasions on him.

He kissed my forehead. "Please don't worry about me. Just hold still. The paramedics are on their way."

"I think that crosses the professional boundary line, Mr. Greyson," I couldn't help but say it.

He chuckled. "To hell with the line, Kelli."

I tried to laugh, too, but found it difficult. "I don't feel very good."

I could see the worry in his eyes. "It's going to be okay."

Then, as if on cue, I heard the sirens, and suddenly there was a flurry of activity going on around us. I heard emergency personnel communicating with Mr. Greyson, but he wouldn't let go of me. I was thankful for that. His presence was more calming than I would have thought.

From what I could tell, without moving my head, the truck that hit us needed to be moved and my door had to be pried opened. Once the paramedics got to me, they convinced Mr. Greyson to let me go. I missed his touch immediately, but that quickly gave way to panic as I found myself being placed in a neck brace and I heard talk of my face needing stitches. They also said something about a possible broken arm and a concussion. Once they finished their initial assessment, they asked me a series of questions: "What's your name? Do you know what happened? Do you know what day it is?" I guess they were checking to make sure I hadn't mentally checked out. I was able to answer each question satisfactorily, I think.

The paramedics carefully removed me from the vehicle and placed me on a stretcher. I winced several times due to the pain. Once on the stretcher, Mr. Greyson came into my line of view. "Do you want me to call Amanda?"

"No," I cried. "I don't want her to worry." I knew if she found out, she would come straight home, and I didn't want to ruin the vacation they had all been looking forward to.

Mr. Greyson picked up my left hand. "It's okay," he said trying to soothe my emotional state.

I had never been in an accident like this before, and I admit, I was a little freaked out.

"Would you like to ride with your wife to the hospital?" One of the paramedics asked Mr. Greyson.

"Of course," Mr. Greyson responded before I even had a chance to correct the paramedic's false conclusion.

If I could have scowled properly, I would have. "Mr.—"

Mr. Greyson leaned down and silenced me by crossing way over the professional boundaries, and the worst or maybe the best part was I couldn't move to stop him. His lips gently pressed against my own, making me forget for a moment I was in any pain. All I felt was our surreal connection. It hadn't gone anywhere after all this time. His lips glided off mine before he pulled back to meet my eyes. "I think you meant, Ian."

"Ian," I repeated back without thinking.

I was wheeled away with Mr. Greyson, or Ian, or whoever the heck he was, holding onto my hand and following me. The jarring from loading me into the ambulance unfortunately made me moan in pain.

"Can't you give her anything?" Ian asked.

"I'm sorry, Mr. Bryant, we can't until we know the extent of her injuries," replied the paramedic.

I had to tell the truth. "His name isn't Mr. Bryant, we aren't even—"

"My last name is Greyson," Ian interrupted. "I've been trying to convince her to take my last name, but you know how women are today."

The paramedic chuckled. What was this? Comedy hour? I was in pain and my boss was a liar. He was also doing and saying things that made my already-pounding head hurt more, and even worse, my heart ached. It ached for things I wish I could've had, things I was now pretending to have.

Ian stroked my cheek before I could rebut his asinine comment. "But maybe someday she'll take my name."

I closed my eyes. I felt nauseous, but I wasn't sure if it was from the accident, the ambulance ride, or my pretend husband. But then I remembered something. My eyes flew open. "What about our meeting with Premier?"

Ian smoothed my forehead. "Relax. I'll call Delfia when we get to the hospital." He paused. "That is, if you want me to, *Director*."

I had forgotten that. Was he really willing to give up his job for me? Then I thought, did I really want him to? He was opening doors for me that had once been closed. My baby was set to fly because of him. And despite his, let's say sometimes abrasive on the clock attitude, he was a good leader. He was brilliant and we made a good team. "What I said in the car, I didn't mean it."

He kissed me again. "I'll call Delfia then."

I closed my eyes again, tried to breathe, and not to think about the pain I was in, physically and emotionally.

It didn't take us long to get to the hospital where I was rushed into the emergency room. I heard them repeat to the doctor and nurse my vitals, which were thankfully normal, and what my injuries and symptoms were. The doctor, who I believe said his name was Dr. Ellis, asked my "husband" to wait outside while they examined me. When Ian objected, they said he could come back in a moment. I didn't say anything. I still couldn't believe he was continuing with this charade.

Dr. Ellis examined me from head to toe, and when he got to my arm, I yelped. The sharpness that went from the shoulder to my fingertips was like nothing I had ever experienced before.

"I think it's a safe bet to say your shoulder is dislocated. I'm going to have to manipulate it back into place, and your forehead is going to need some stitches," Dr. Ellis said like it was no big deal. It was a big deal to me.

I desperately wanted to see the cut on my forehead and the word manipulate never sounded good. At least he didn't think my arm was broken, but he was ordering x-rays just in case. But he was concerned about a concussion, so they were going to monitor me for a while, perhaps overnight. *Oh joy.* I was even more overjoyed when the nurse informed me I needed to be changed into their lovely attire. I had a choice between a blue and a pink hospital gown.

"I choose door number three."

She laughed but wouldn't let me stay in my blood-stained pant suit. She unceremoniously started undressing me since my right arm was immobile and they refused to take the neck brace off until after the x-rays. It was a good thing they had asked my pseudo significant other to wait outside. He would have gotten quite the show. Once they were done exposing me and poking me, they let him in.

Ian rushed to my side and took my hand, then began assaulting the doctor with his questions regarding my condition.

"Bad news, I'm going to make it," I teased.

He kissed my hand. What was up with him?

The nurse handed Ian a clipboard as she left the room. "You and your wife will need to fill out her medical history and insurance information. As soon as that's complete, I'll take her down to x-ray."

"I'll take that." I tried to reach for the clipboard with my left hand, the only hand I had available to me.

He pulled it away from me. "Aren't you right-handed?"

"So?"

"Please let me help you."

"Why are you being so nice to me?"

He dropped the pen the nurse had given him. "What does that mean? I'm always nice to you." He sounded hurt that I thought otherwise.

"Not always," I choked.

He scooted closer and rested the clipboard on my bed. "Kelli, I know we need to talk. I've wanted to talk to you about our past. But I don't think now is a good time." He was right.

Part of me ached to know the why of it all, but admittedly, part of me was scared to know the truth. "I guess you can fill out my medical history," I conceded.

"Thank you." He picked up the pen and clipboard. Not surprisingly he knew so much about me he could fill in several blanks without asking me. But then he got to the fun stuff.

"Are you pregnant?"

"Uh. No."

"Start date of your last period?"

If you're not pregnant is it really necessary to know that? "Are you serious?"

Ian nodded.

I had to think about it for a second. "April 5th, I think."

Ian seemed to be enjoying this more than he should, by the smirk on his face.

"Do you take birth control? If yes, what type?" Ian was more than interested to know the answer to this question based on the way he was tapping the pen against the form, trying to be nonchalant about it. Did that mean what I thought it meant? This was all so confusing to me. Was my brother-in-law right about Ian's feelings for me?

I wasn't sure how I should feel about it all. "You know what?" the frustration and confusion of the situation and the pain I was in bubbled over. "Just write thirty-two-year-old virgin across the dang page and be done with it." My hand flew to my mouth. Why did I blurt that? Not even my sister knew.

Ian fumbled the clipboard. His eyes blinked about a thousand times. When he got control over his shock, he set aside the paperwork and took my hand.

His touch made me cry. Tears silently poured down my face and dripped onto the uncomfortable neck brace that was making it hard to get a good read on Ian's facial expression.

His free hand rested on my left cheek. His thumb swept across my cheek, wiping the tears as they fell. I wanted to ask him how the right side of my face looked. I had a feeling it wasn't looking so hot. Ian stood enough to hover over me. His rich chocolate eyes penetrated my own. In his I read several conversations we had many years ago. My experience, or lack thereof, in the sex department was a frequent topic when we were dating.

"I told you it wasn't unrealistic for me to wait." Though I never expected I'd be waiting this long.

His hand moved up and tenderly brushed my bangs to the side. "I never said it was unrealistic for you. I said it was unrealistic for us. I still stand by that."

"You must think I'm some Pollyanna."

"No. I was thinking how incredibly beautiful and amazing you are."

I closed my eyes, wanting to believe he meant what he said. "I didn't mean for my life to turn out this way. I've just been waiting for someone I loved, who was committed to me and loved me as much as I loved him." For some reason those three ingredients never came together for me. Why I was being so honest with him I don't know. It was as if I had my best friend back. I realized in that moment how much I had truly missed Ian. How much I had wanted him to be the person to make the perfect recipe with.

He kissed my head. "I wanted that for you too."

Chapter Seventeen

WHAT A DAY IT HAD been. I kept staring at Ian while they stitched my head, not sure what all this meant. It was a lot easier to look at him now that the neck brace was off. In other good news, my arm wasn't broken. Unfortunately, my shoulder really was dislocated. The manipulation thing didn't sound all that pleasant, even if they were going to do it under localized anesthesia. I prayed it worked or they were going to have to put me under. Maybe some general anesthesia wouldn't be all that bad. An hour with no thoughts at all. Thoughts like, what am I going to do about the way my boss was staring at me like Ian used to. The stare that said, I'm crazy about you. I might go crazy after all this.

"Do I look like the bride of Frankenstein?" I asked Ian once the doctor was done stitching me up. I still hadn't seen myself.

He kissed my hand. "Never."

The doctor left, giving us another moment alone before the next procedure. It was a good time to ask, "Why did you tell them you were my husband?"

"I was afraid they wouldn't let me come with you if we weren't related."

"I think you've watched too many TV shows, and even if that were true, you could have gone with brother or something."

He moistened his lips. "I've never had a brotherly thought about you."

My cheeks warmed. "What's going on between us?"

"Kel." He brought my hand up between his. "I—"

Dr. Ellis and a nurse named Janelle walked in, interrupting us.

Ian lowered my hand. My heart was racing and there was no hiding it. The machine monitoring my pulse broadcasted it.

Janelle went into nurse mode. "Don't you worry, you're not going to feel a thing."

Oh, she had no idea. I was feeling things. Like all the things.

Ian's lips twitched. He knew he was the cause of my erratic heartbeat. I hoped he wasn't getting too cocky about it. I wasn't sure about any of this, especially him. I wasn't even sure I knew who he was. Was he Ian or Mr. Greyson?

Janelle started administering pain meds through my IV. I wanted to kiss her. My entire body ached. Dr. Ellis asked Ian to wait outside while they manipulated my shoulder. Before he left, he kissed me softly on the lips. My heart monitor told the story of how much it affected me.

"Mr. Greyson, I think we need to talk about your behavior," I whispered. The pain meds were making me feel sleepy.

"Later," was all he said before he left me feeling overwhelmingly confused and wonderful. I had missed his kisses like Charlie missed his squeaker toy.

"That's so cute that you call him Mr. Greyson," Janelle said.

Yes, it's adorable, I thought.

And with that thought, the doctor began manipulating my shoulder back into its socket. All I had to say was, pain relievers were a gift from God, as were doctors. As soon as my shoulder was in its rightful place, I felt instantaneous relief. It still felt sore, but the throbbing pain was gone.

I thanked Dr. Ellis, and he gave me a list of instructions to follow, along with the best news of the day: I could go home that evening. Hallelujah. I had no desire to stay overnight, but there was a caveat. Someone needed to stay with me and monitor me, just in case. That was going to be tricky with my sister and Holly both being out of town. I wondered if

Delfia would want to. We weren't friends out of the office, but there was no reason we couldn't be.

It was just about this time that Janelle let Ian back in and, unfortunately, he caught the gist of the conversation. "Don't worry, I'll keep a careful eye on my wife tonight."

I wanted to challenge him right then and there, but if I had, I would have looked like a liar. And okay I was a liar. I was letting these people think I was married to my ex-boyfriend who was currently my boss.

As soon as the nurse and doctor left us alone, I turned to Mr. Greyson or whoever he was. "You can't monitor me over night."

"Why not?" He was surprised that I would disagree.

"Mr. Greyson, you're my—"

He sat on the edge of my bed and placed his finger to my mouth "Please call me Ian."

"Even at the office?"

He thought it over for a moment. As he mulled, I wondered why this was such a hard concession for him. What had happened to make him this cautious? I mean, he had always been cautious, but I had a feeling there was more to the story.

He ran the back of his hand down my cheek. "Even at the office," he conceded.

I smiled at his concession, but he still wasn't staying with me. "Okay then, *Ian*, I don't think it's appropriate if my boss spends the night with me."

"Fine, I'll quit right now."

"Who says I would let you stay even if you weren't my boss?"

He pressed his lips together. "You know, it wouldn't be the first time we spent the night under the same roof."

I could feel the heat rise in my cheeks. He spoke the truth. We had spent five days together at his parent's place. I had slept in his old room, and he slept on the pull-out couch that had a sprung spring. Those were some of the best days of my life.

I bit my lip.

"I'll stay on your couch or even the floor," he said it like that settled the matter.

I shook my head, well as much as I could. My head was still pounding. "What's going on with you?"

He brushed my hair back. "Seeing you hurt and unable to move today reminded me how short life is, and I've already wasted so much time."

I was about to ask for clarification on that statement. But his phone rang. It was his insurance company, and he was arranging a rental car with them. I had forgotten we were both without transportation.

He shoved his phone back in his pocket. "I need to go, but I'll be back to take you home."

It was then that I remembered my keys were at the office. "Could you stop by the office and get my keys and laptop?" I wasn't too worried about my car. Our office was in a good part of town, so it could wait until tomorrow.

"Of course. I need to take care of something there anyway."

"And...can you ask Delfia if she can stay with me tonight?"

"Sure." He grinned. Why did I think he wouldn't be asking her?

He kissed my forehead before leaving, which left me feeling all sorts of weird, and it wasn't from the drugs that were pumping through my veins.

As soon as he left, I called Janelle back in so she could help me to the restroom. It was time to take a look at the damage that had been done to me. I knew there was some, I could feel it. She helped me walk over while wheeling the IV.

Once I was left alone, I faced the mirror and it wasn't pretty. The entire right side of my face was already beginning to bruise, and my right eye was slightly swollen. The stitch line on my forehead was going to leave a nice scar. I was suddenly grateful I had decided last year to get bangs. It looked like I would always be keeping them. I chanced to look down at my lovely hospital-issued attire and found more bruising down my right side. I was surprised Ian hadn't mentioned how horrible I looked, but it did explain the look of concern in those chocolate eyes of his.

I couldn't stand too long. I wasn't sure if it was the trauma or medication, but I really didn't feel all that hot, and Ian wasn't helping with him being all Ian. If I thought I was confused before, there was no comparison to the way I felt now. I was beginning to think Zane and Amanda were right, even though it made no sense at all. I mean, we'd spent thirteen years apart. And he told me coming here was all about business, but he sure wasn't acting professional.

I'll admit, there was a part of me that welcomed it, but how did I reconcile the years of separation and pain? And what about trust?

Janelle settled me in my bed once I was finished in the bathroom. She took my vitals, all while making small talk. "How long have you been married?"

Grrr, Ian. He was turning me into a liar. "Not long at all." Was that kind of the truth?

"Oh, newlyweds," she squealed.

I had a feeling she would like to be one. The cute perky nurse had that new-love aura around her.

"Do you have anyone special in your life?" I asked while she took my pulse.

My assessment of her was dead on. She began to gush about Carson. "We've been dating for three months, and I know that isn't very long, but I know he's the one. I mean, is that even possible? How did you know your husband was the one?"

I thought about her question, and at least I didn't have to lie. "It's like drowning in pure intelligence," I said. "You have this peaceful, all-encompassing feeling that says you've come home."

She sighed like a Disney Princess. She didn't have to say anything, I knew she understood exactly what I had said, and even more, I knew she felt it. I only hoped her story ended better than mine, and that her Carson felt the same way she did.

She let me be and turned down the lights. "Try and get some rest, we'll monitor you for the next little while, and if everything looks good, you can go home early this evening."

I closed my eyes and let the medication take me over. I fell into a fitful sleep. The medication seemed to be fighting my mind for control, it was saying sleep and my mind was saying let's overanalyze everything Ian has said or done in the past two months. Heck, even the past fourteen years. Eventually the two did seem to make a compromise. I got to sleep, but my dreams were laced with Ian. I was almost grateful when the pain meds wore off and I woke up, even if I did hurt all over.

I found, though, that I wasn't alone, and my dreams had suddenly become reality. There Ian was, on the edge of my bed, holding my hand. He had changed out of his suit that had some of my blood on it. He was now casual, in jeans and a polo shirt, looking more like the Ian I used to know.

He touched my brow as soon as my eyes opened. "How are you feeling?"

"Like I've been hit by a truck."

His head hung.

"Hey, it wasn't your fault."

He didn't respond verbally, but I knew by the look on his face he blamed himself, and nothing I could say would change his mind.

"So are Delfia and I having a slumber party tonight?"

A devilish grin appeared on his face. "She has a date, so it looks like it's just you and me."

"Hmm."

"Come on, Kelli. We're both adults."

That was the part that worried me. "Did you tell her I was injured and how important this was to me?" I mean, surely her date with Matt could wait a night.

"I didn't think that was wise."

"Why not?"

"Did you really want me to disclose to Ms. King that I was the alternative?"

"Well, no, but I don't think we should be having a sleepover." Taking my chances of slipping into a coma sounded like a better and safer idea.

"I cleared it with your sister, if that makes you feel better."

I sat up as straight as my body would allow me to at the moment. I was finding movement of any kind to be painful, and my right side was a little numb from the local anesthesia they had given me before they manipulated my shoulder. "When and why did you talk to Amanda?" I didn't want to tell her until she got back.

He touched my shoulder gently as if to tell me to relax. "I knew she would want to know, and I had to get the code to your apartment."

"What?"

He reached down, grabbed a bag, and placed it gently on my abdomen. "I thought you would want some more comfortable, non-blood splattered clothing to change into."

His thoughtfulness surprised me. "Thank you, but..." I didn't know what to say. The guy was throwing me for a loop.

"But, what?" he grinned.

"You shouldn't have called my sister. I don't want her to worry."

"She's happy I called her, and I promised her I would take good care of you, so there was no need for her to worry."

"And she believed you?" I spluttered.

"You know, some people actually think I'm a pretty good guy."

I exhaled loudly.

He leaned closer and lightly touched the bruised side of my face. "I don't blame you for the misgivings you have about me. They are well deserved, but I know somewhere in that willful mind of yours, you know it's true."

I so badly wanted to believe him, especially when he looked at me so tenderly, but I had spent years trying to get over him, only to have him hang over every relationship I'd tried to have. Instead of words to respond, my body decided tears were a good way to go. It wasn't the best option in my mind, but I couldn't hold it liable; after all, I was tired and battered, physically and emotionally. A body can only take so much. To make matters worse, Ian carefully drew me into him and held me. Against my better judgment, I sank into him and bathed his shoulder with my tears.

That overwhelming feeling of peace and rightness suddenly washed over me. But how could that be? I had loved him, and because of that, he left me. I extricated myself, settled back against the bed, and closed my eyes. He pressed a kiss to my forehead.

I heard my nurse come in. "I've come to spring you," she announced.

It was the best news I'd had all day.

She came around to the side Ian occupied. "I'm going to need you to move. I need to check your wife's vitals one more time, but don't worry, I'll have her back to you in no time." She winked at me.

It was all I could do to not roll my eyes.

It didn't take her long to remove all the medical paraphernalia attached to me. Once she was done, she went over a list of things I should and shouldn't be doing for the next week. Heavy lifting and driving were off the table. She also gave me a list of exercises to do with my arm and shoulder. She turned to Ian and gave him warning signs of concussions to look for. "Also, your wife may be unsteady for a day or two, so it would be a good idea to help her with everyday tasks like bathing and dressing."

"Don't worry, I will be happy to help her with *anything* she needs." Ian patted my hand.

My brows raised so high, the cut on my forehead began pulsing.

She handed Ian a couple of prescriptions for pain relief. "Just let me know as soon as your wife is dressed, and I'll bring in a wheelchair to take her down to your car." How many times was she going to call me his wife?

As soon as she left, I sat up slowly and grabbed the bag of clothes Ian had brought me with my left hand.

He helped me stand. "Would you like some help dressing?"

"I think I can manage."

"Doctor's orders," he whispered in my ear.

I nudged him away with my hip. "I'll be right back. Keep your eyes to yourself." I wasn't sure how much of my backside was showing. Hospital gowns were the worst.

"You have my word. I'll be here if you need me. I put a button up shirt in there, so you don't have to reach above your head."

He always thought of everything. I crept my way to the bathroom. I was definitely getting those prescriptions filled. Every step felt like I was dragging a ton of bricks, and the bricks shot needles every time they were moved. Once in the bathroom, I realized why Janelle said I would need help dressing. It was all I could do to get my jeans on, but I had to. There was no way I was having Ian help me and calling Janelle in here would blow the whole we're married thing. I silently cursed Ian as I slowly pulled up my pants with only my left hand. My poor right side still wasn't functioning. The anesthesia hadn't worn off yet. It took everything I had not to cry. It was then I realized I couldn't button them with only one hand. I had the same issue with my shirt.

I came out of the bathroom holding my shirt together with one hand to find a smug-looking Ian right by the door waiting for me.

"Do you need help, honey?"

"Don't even think about looking down my shirt or pants," I warned.

He grabbed my shirt, pulled me to him, and began buttoning my shirt while his dancing eyes stared directly into my own. Not once did he look down.

"Don't enjoy this too much," I growled.

He pulled me a little closer to him. "Maybe you don't know how this works for guys, but we typically enjoy *unbuttoning*."

"Did you really just say that to me, Mr. Greyson?"

"No more Mr. Greyson, Kelli," he pled.

He had two buttons left when he stopped. "Is that sufficient?"

I nodded, and without a word, he buttoned my jeans for me. "Thank you," I whispered.

"My pleasure." He led me to the bed and helped me sit down. There he bent down and put on my shoes for me like I was four years old. He stood. "I'll let your nurse know you're ready to go, and I'll pull the car around."

"Thanks."

He leaned down and kissed the top of my head. "I'll see you in a minute."

Yeah. This was going to be an interesting night.

Janelle was there within a couple of minutes. She wheeled me out into the warm evening air. I loved that it was staying lighter later. It was around six, but there was still plenty of sun. Ian waited by the passenger side with the door already opened. He had some black sporty-looking car. I couldn't tell off hand what the make was, but it looked expensive.

Janelle helped me up, and Ian took it from there, helping me into his car. He even buckled me in. I was beginning to feel like a toddler.

"You ready to go?" he asked.

Not even a little.

Chapter Eighteen

I SAT ON MY COUCH WATCHING Ian be Ian. He did all the Ian things, like ordering my favorites from Alicia's and having them delivered. I didn't even know that was an option, but Ian had worked it out with Jose. Then he made sure I was as comfortable as I could be on the couch, propping pillows around me. He also filled my prescriptions for me.

Ian brought me my dinner and some pain meds. The doctor said I could take a higher dose up front and I planned to. This way I would fall asleep fast and my sleepover with Ian would be over before I knew it.

Dinner was mostly a silent affair, but the looks and body language were loud. Ian shifted several times on the opposite side of the couch from me. We kept glancing at each other with vacant expressions. Sometimes his was more like puzzled. He probably thought I was a freak of nature, someone they could a make a documentary about. It could be called, *Virgin Tales.*

There was so much that needed to be said, but I didn't know where to begin and my head was a little fuzzy. I also had a feeling Ian wasn't ready to deal with it either. I'm sure he had a plan and a timetable, but somehow the accident changed all that.

By the time I was done picking at my smothered burritos, I was feeling more than loopy. Unfortunately, I had no desire to sleep in jeans and my arm and hand were still under the influence of anesthesia. Ian was going to have to help me undress.

"I'm tired. I need to change into some more comfortable clothes." I cringed.

To his credit he only half smiled. "Would you like my help?"

I bit my lip. "I don't think I have a choice."

He slid across the couch and took my plate before setting it on my coffee table. "You'll always have a choice with me."

He had said the same thing to me before. Never once when we were dating had he tried to take advantage of me. I probably pushed the line more than him, but he always made sure we never crossed it. "What choices are you offering me?" I rubbed my head with my working hand. The medication was really kicking in.

He stood and pulled me up. "You're tired and we've both had a long day. Let's talk later."

That was probably a good idea. It was probably good, too, that I wasn't fully cognizant when he started unbuttoning my shirt. His eyes never drifted down even though I was doing my best to keep it from falling wide open. Being so close to him, though, had me wanting to get lost in his eyes and fall into his arms. Maybe it was the drugs, but this urge came over me and my lips fell on his.

At first, he kissed me back, but just as he was about to part my lips he stopped abruptly. "Please don't tempt me right now," he whispered against my lips.

I backed away shaking my head. "I'm sorry. I don't know what came over me."

He ran a finger down my cheek. "Don't apologize, you're in a vulnerable state now and I don't want you to do anything you'll regret."

I was already regretting allowing him to sleepover. I mean, what were the odds of me having any concussion symptoms? And one-handed people functioned all the time. I held onto my shirt and walked away toward the hall leading to the bedrooms.

Ian gently grabbed my arm on the way. "Hey. Please don't be embarrassed." He knew me too well. "I was trying not to enjoy myself too much. You're making that difficult," he added.

The conversation we had in the hospital about men enjoying unbuttoning rang in my head. "I should go change."

"I'll get the couch ready for you."

I had decided it was best for me to sleep on the couch while he was here. He had volunteered to sleep on the floor in my room, but the thought of him sleeping in my room was going to throw me over the edge. I had imagined us sharing a room and a bed too many times, you know until death do us part, or forever. If I couldn't keep my lips off him, who knew what would happen. Probably nothing, because Ian wouldn't allow me to do anything I would regret.

I walked into my room, shut the door, and tried to breathe normally. He was getting to me. It was then I decided I was wearing sweats; they had elastic bands. I also managed to get on a t-shirt. It hurt like heck, but there was no way I was asking Ian to help me. I could imagine Amanda and Zane laughing now. It didn't take long before I was treated to the real thing. While brushing my teeth and lamenting over how awful I looked—bruises weren't my color—my phone rang.

"How are you? Tell me everything that happened. Is Ian there with you?" Amanda spouted out so quickly I barely comprehended what she was saying. It didn't help that I was feeling higher than a kite.

"I'm fine, and yes, Ian is here."

Amanda squealed like a preteen. "I can't believe you're sleeping with him."

"We're not sleeping together. He's sleeping on my loveseat and I'm sleeping on the couch."

"I'm pretty sure two can fit on your couch."

"Amanda, he's my boss and you should see how I look. Besides, I can barely walk, I hurt so bad."

"Oh, honey, I'm so sorry. I wish I was there to take care of you. Are you sure you're okay?"

"Yes. Ian has been taking great care of me."

"You know he cares for you, right?"

I sat down on my bed. I was feeling woozy.

"Kelli?"

"I'm here. I'm really confused right now."

"Try not to over think it. You're good at that."

"It's kept me from getting involved with some real idiots."

"It's also kept you from some great guys too."

"You think Ian is a good guy?"

"I think Ian has made some choices he regrets, like we all do, but I like a man who is willing to do whatever it takes to right them."

"Is that what you think he's doing?"

"The question is, do you?"

I painstakingly laid down on my bed. "I don't know. He thinks I'm too vulnerable to talk right now."

"I'm liking him even more."

Yeah, I kind of was too. "I better go."

"Hey, don't do anything I wouldn't do tonight." She evilly laughed.

"Good night, Amanda."

I threw my phone on my bed and walked out to find blankets and pillows on the couch. Ian rushed to my side to help me to the couch and settle in. He sat on the edge, close to me, and touched my face softly. "I'm so sorry," he kept repeating.

I had a feeling he wasn't only talking about the accident. I reached up and grabbed his hand and held it. "We really need to talk."

He leaned down and pressed his lips to mine. "Not tonight," he whispered against my lips that already missed his.

I was so torn, part of me wanted to pull him back and kiss him thoroughly. The other part wanted to shake him and make him tell me why, after all these years.

"But…" I barely managed to say. My eyes were already becoming heavy.

"Just sleep," I heard him say before I did as he said.

I don't know how long I slept, but I woke up in the pitch dark of night feeling disoriented and hurting. I tried to sit up, only to find that difficult. I cried out in pain.

"Are you okay, Kelli?"

That voice jarred my memory, as did his touch. He was by my side lightning fast, helping me to sit up. As my eyes adjusted to the dark, I could see him. The "him" that had left me and hurt me. A wave of memories and pain washed over me. "I loved you and you left me. Why?"

Even in the dark I could see his eyes widen. "Kelli, I don't think we should talk about that right now."

"Stop saying that," I cried. But before he could answer, I snapped, and a flood of uncontrollable words fell right out of me. "It's because I don't have big boobs and blonde hair like Alexa and your ex-wife."

His jaw dropped.

"That's right, my sister and I googled you and your big-breasted wife."

He chuckled. "Kelli, you don't know what you're saying right now."

"I do know what I'm saying, I just can't help what I'm saying. I deserve to know after all these years."

He took my hand and I tried to pull away, but he wouldn't let me. "Please Kelli, let's have this conversation when you aren't under the influence of painkillers."

"Maybe you should go." I sniffled.

"Fine," he sighed, "we'll have it your way." He let go of my hand and ran a finger softly down my cheek. "Kelli, first of all, this has nothing to do with the size of your breasts or the color of your hair. You are the most beautiful woman of my acquaintance, but you were so young and innocent. It was against my better judgment to get involved with you in the first place."

"So, you never wanted me?" My emotional state came right through. On some level, I knew I would regret it, but the drugs in my system were having a heyday.

He shook his head. "I didn't say that." He moved in closer. "I never wanted another woman more than you, but I wasn't ready for you and you lacked experience with men and relationships."

"What is that supposed to mean?"

He stood and began pacing the floor, just like he had the night it all fell apart. He didn't speak for a couple of minutes, and when he did, he still kept pacing. "It means I wasn't ready to get married, especially to a girl who hadn't even experienced life."

"I didn't ask you to marry me. I knew you didn't want to at the time."

He stopped pacing and faced me. "The problem was," he paused, "I wanted to marry you."

What? I shook my head in confusion, well as much as I could. My head was pounding. "I don't understand."

He knelt next to me beside the couch, so that he could look directly into my eyes. "I loved you and I wanted nothing more than to be with you, but I had nothing to offer, and you were so young."

"Then why didn't you just tell me that instead of walking away like I didn't matter to you at all? Wait…did you say you loved me?"

He leaned in and kissed my forehead, lingering for a moment before he answered. "Yes…I loved you, but I couldn't tell you because I knew you and how you would respond. And I knew it wouldn't take too long before I would have been begging you to marry me."

"And that was too horrible a thought for you?"

"Kelli, you were nineteen and I was barely out of grad school," his voice pleaded for understanding.

But I wasn't sure I could understand that. "So, because I was young, you decided to toss everything we had together aside, all while knowing how I felt about you? Do you even know how much you hurt me? Did you even care? Did you really love me?"

He didn't answer, he just kept gazing into my eyes.

"I would have waited," I said through tears. When he didn't respond I laid back down. "I don't feel good."

He got up and walked toward my kitchen. Soon he was back with water and more painkillers. I gratefully took both and closed my eyes.

He stayed by my side. I could feel his body heat and the sound of his deep steady breaths. Seconds later he caressed my cheek. "I loved you more than you know, and I'm sorry I hurt you. I thought I was doing what was best at the time."

I didn't know what to say. Tears streamed down my cheeks while I waited for the medicine to kick in. It took a long time, or what seemed like a long time, to fall asleep again as I pondered everything over in my head. I was having a hard time reconciling him walking away because he loved me. And what about Marissa, his ex-wife, or Alexa? It all made my head hurt, and when I did fall asleep, it was fitful, even with the medication.

I was awakened to the smell of something wonderful, but as soon as I sat up, I remembered who was here and all that was said in the middle of the night, right down to the big boobs. I wanted to crawl back under the covers and die. This was the reason why my dad warned me never to do drugs.

I wondered if Ian would notice if I crept to my room, locked the door, and stayed there until he left. I contemplated dropping to the floor and army crawling my way over there, but I knew in my condition that was a no-go. Knowing my luck, he would probably notice, and I would look like a bigger idiot crawling on the floor. It occurred to me I could keep pretending to sleep, but my bladder wasn't too fond of that idea.

I decided I needed to be a big girl, so I stood slowly and painfully. None of which went unnoticed. There was a clear view from the kitchen to the living room, and before I knew it, he was by my side.

"How are you this morning?"

I couldn't help but look at him and think, *so this is what it would be like to be married to him.* He was still in pajama bottoms and a t-shirt. His hair was ruffled and he had the perfect amount of scruff on his face. But then I remembered how embarrassed I was about my breakdown in the middle of the night. I pointed down the hall. "I'm going to my room."

"Breakfast is almost ready," he called out.

I closed my door and let out a deep breath. I decided then and there I was only taking Tylenol or Advil. I headed straight for my bathroom and looked in the mirror. To say I looked horrible was putting it nicely. The right side of my face looked like a paint palette. No amount of make-up would help the monstrosity that was my face. Only time and ice would help, but I did the best with what I had. I brushed my teeth and my hair. I managed to get my hair up in a bun. Thankfully my hand was working a little better. I washed my face, and for fun I threw on some lip gloss and mascara. I figured it couldn't hurt. Reluctantly and slowly, I walked back out to tell Ian his services were no longer required. I also thought about quitting again, which I guess in essence made me the boss. How could we work together now? I felt so stupid about last night. And there were feelings, lots and lots of feelings.

Ian was in the kitchen when I came out. His face brightened upon seeing me. "Sit on the couch and I'll bring breakfast to you."

Why did he have to be so kind this morning? I stood there and stared at him.

"What's wrong?" he asked.

"Maybe you should go."

He set down the plate he had in his hand and walked over to me. Before I knew it, I was wrapped up in his arms. That wasn't helping the situation.

"I think we need to talk." He kissed my cheek.

"Yeah, about last night, maybe we should forget about it."

He laughed and led me over to the couch where I obediently sat while he went to retrieve our food. He brought me a plate filled with homemade coffee cake and fresh fruit. It smelled fabulous, and I knew it would taste just as good. Ian was an excellent cook.

I wasted no time tasting his offerings, and I wasn't disappointed. "It's delicious, thank you."

"You're welcome," he said from where he sat next to me. We both ate in silence for a few minutes before he set his plate down on my coffee table. I wasn't putting mine down until it was all gone. I had missed his cooking, and I was starving.

Charlie decided to jump in the middle of us. He typically didn't like company, but I guess as Ian had been there all night, he was tired of waiting to be adored. Ian did the honors and scratched his head while I continued stuffing my face.

With Charlie purring and my mouth full, Ian took his opportunity. "I'm not going to beat around the bush anymore. I'm hoping for a second chance here."

I lowered the piece of pineapple I was about to eat. "So, you lied to me?"

He shook his head in confusion. "I've never lied to you."

"Ha! You told me the first day you were here that you working for Chandler had nothing to do with me."

"It didn't and it doesn't. I was hoping to woo you outside the office, but you've made that nearly impossible. Hell, you would barely even acknowledge that you knew me previously. You're the most stubborn woman I know."

I had to smile at the irritation I had apparently been causing him and the title he had given me. I took it as a compliment, but he was still a liar. "So, you're telling me you, by happenstance, came to work for Chandler and it had nothing at all to do with me?"

"Heading up Chandler made it convenient, but I could have and would have come to Nashville regardless."

I nudged him with my elbow. "I don't find your Greyson white lies charming anymore."

He took my plate out of my hands and set it next to his before resting his hand on my unbruised cheek. "Kelli, can you please forget about Chandler and tell me how you feel?"

"Not until you admit you lied to me."

He groaned. "I didn't lie to you. When I met Gary last year, I had no idea that you worked for Chandler, but when I found out, I felt like maybe it was Kismet or something. Like the universe was giving me a second chance. And I meant what I said, your software idea is unique and challenging. I didn't want to mix business with pleasure, I still don't, but I want us to be together."

I sighed. "Ian, you're my boss and I've spent thirteen years wondering why you left me."

His thumb glided across my cheek. "I'll resign right now and then spend the rest of my life trying to undo the past."

"Ian, it's not that simple."

"I know that. I've spent the last thirteen years trying to forgive myself for letting go of the best thing that ever happened to me."

"You think I'm the best thing?"

He tucked some of my loose hair behind my ear. "I know you are."

"Ian," I breathed out and breathed him in. He was close enough to taste.

"Kelli," he closed the gap, "tell me what you want."

Oh, him. Wait. This was moving too fast. There was so much to talk about.

His lips skimmed mine.

Who needed to talk?

He pulled my legs across his lap. His lips pressed against mine, but this time he didn't stop there. His tongue slid across my lips, parting my own. My sister was right. It was all in the kiss, and no one kissed like Ian. His hands did all the right things, running through my hair and gliding down my back, drawing me closer to him. When his mouth wasn't entangled with mine, he was pressing gentle kisses down my neck and even on my bruised cheek, as if he could kiss the hurt away. It was helping. I felt nothing but him.

"I missed you," I admitted between kisses.

"I missed you more," he nuzzled my ear, sending shivers down my entire body.

"I think we've crossed the professional boundary line."

"No, Kelli, this is all personal."

Chapter Nineteen

WOKE UP EARLY IN THE afternoon laying in his arms after a long nap. The accident and residual pain medication were kicking my butt. Ian was peering into my eyes the second mine opened.

"I could get used to this." He kissed my nose.

"Me too." The contour of my body seemed to fit perfectly with his, like two puzzle pieces. Like he was my missing half. "But we need to talk about how we'll make this work, and about your past."

His jaw clenched.

"You don't want to tell me about your ex-wife? Or Alexa?" I spewed her name.

"I fired her," he snarled.

"What? When? Why didn't you tell me?"

"Relax. I fired her when I went back to the office to get your keys and laptop. I didn't mention it because I had more important things to worry about. Namely you."

"Why did you hire her in the first place? You seem smarter than that," I teased, sort of.

He let out a heavy breath. "She introduced me to my ex-father-in-law and Marissa," he growled, "they own a VC firm and their initial investment helped me launch IAG. On top of that, Alexa did a lot of design work for me at the beginning for free. She's hit a rough patch lately, so I wanted to help her, like she helped me."

"I'm pretty sure she only wanted to help herself to you."

"Her advances were never welcome. That kiss you saw yesterday, was all her, I swear. I never had feelings for her other than as a colleague."

"What about your feelings for your wife?"

"Ex," he was quick to add.

"Okay, your ex-wife."

He stared out into the room, thinking about what to say before pulling me closer to him. "Marissa was a mistake. We mistook our business relationship for something it wasn't, and it turned personal. I'm still paying for it. She's the reason I had to return to Colorado. She's suing me over the sale of my company."

"Oh."

"I'm not worried about it. The lawsuit has no merit. This is to spite me."

"What reason does she have?"

"She's mismanaged her father's firm and she's looking to blame someone. It's a power play." He stroked my hair. "Let's not talk about it anymore. You need to rest."

I snuggled into his chest. "Ian, maybe we shouldn't mix business with pleasure. What if we're mistaking this for something it's not?"

He leaned away from me, his brow crinkled. "Kelli, I know you don't agree with my professional approach, but I'm not going to make the same mistakes I made at IAG. Too much is on the line this time. If I have to, I'll quit, but I think you and I together can take Chandler to the next level. But more importantly, I can't imagine my life without you."

"So, you're admitting you came to Chandler because of me." I flashed him a crooked smile.

He nuzzled my neck. "You are so infuriating sometimes."

"The feeling is mutual, but you didn't answer the question."

"Yes, okay, you were *part* of the reason I came to Chandler, but you are *the* reason I came to Nashville. You are my reason for everything."

Oh. Wow. "That might be the sweetest thing you've ever said to me."

"It's true."

I rested my head back on his chest. "I still need time to think."

"Take all the time you need. I'm not going anywhere."

"Promise?"

"You have my word."

I drifted back to sleep with that lovely thought.

That night after dinner we curled up on my couch and watched a movie, you know, between making out. I figured while I was thinking about giving him a second chance I might as well test out the merchandise. Did he ever make me want to buy in. The man had a gift. My toes were going to be permanently curled.

While taking a breath between kisses, Ian reached into his pocket, pulled out a piece of paper, and placed it on my lap. "We need to talk about this list."

I picked up the paper and laughed when I realized what it was. It was the husband list I had stuck to the refrigerator.

Top Ten Husband Qualities

1. Gainfully employed.
2. Good kisser.
3. Must want children.
4. A non-yes man.
5. Handsome and well groomed.
6. Must adore me.
7. Challenges me to be better.
8. Preferably never married.
9. Minimal baggage. See number 8.
10. Above all, faithful to me.

He took the list back and went down each number, one by one. "Number one, no problem." He kissed me and smiled. "I've got two covered."

"Uh, don't you think I should be the judge of that?"

He tapped my nose. "Believe me, I can tell you agree with me."

I couldn't deny it. It was so true.

"Number three, yes."

I don't know why, but the thought that Ian wanted children, and perhaps with me, made me blush.

"Number four for sure, as well as five."

I rolled my eyes at his arrogance.

"Number six. I absolutely adore you," he whispered in my ear.

"Numbers seven and ten are not problems, but we need to talk about numbers eight and nine."

I'll admit his past made me wary, and it was a sticking point in my mind.

I know he didn't want to talk about his ex-wife, but I had to ask. "Do you still love her?"

He sighed. "The question you should ask is if I ever did."

"That's kind of worse in my mind. Why would you marry someone you didn't love?"

He took my hand and his thumb swept across it several times. "I told you I made mistakes, and I've done things I'm not proud of. Remember when I said that I tried to forget about you and that's where I went wrong?"

"I remember you saying there was a woman."

He held my hand up and kissed my palm. "In my pursuit to get over *you*, I made some very poor choices, Marissa being one of them. But in my defense, she didn't really love me either."

"I don't know if I can be with someone who takes marriage so lightly. And how long will this legal battle with her go on?"

His brows creased. "Kelli, I don't take marriage lightly, and I didn't take it lightly. Love and marriage don't always go hand-in-hand. Yes, that's the best way and the way I would prefer it, but I was faithful to the vows I made, and I only divorced her because she was unfaithful. Don't get me wrong, I regret marrying her, but don't think for a second I did it lightly. And to answer your question, the litigation should be done within the month, with any luck."

I wasn't sure what to say.

He didn't seem bothered by my silence. He brushed my hair back. "Do you think you could possibly get over the fact that I'm divorced?"

I tapped my finger against my mouth. "Hmm. Dating my divorced boss who broke my heart when he left me? It sounds so tempting."

He carefully pulled me onto his lap, doing his best not to jostle me. He held me close. My head rested on his shoulder. "How about dating a man who has learned from his mistakes and is crazy about you?" He paused for a moment. "How about a man who is still in love with you?"

My head popped up. For a second I thought it was the drugs talking. "You love me?" I stuttered.

"I love you, Kelli."

Chapter Twenty

SUNDAY STARTED WITH A PHONE call from Ian. He had left my apartment around midnight. As much as I enjoyed sleeping in his arms, I needed to be in my bed and have some time alone to think. He had thrown a lot at me. I couldn't believe he was still in love with me. I wasn't sure if I was still in love with him, but I had a feeling if we kept on this road it wouldn't take long.

"I have a surprise for you," he informed me.

I wasn't sure I could take any more surprises from him. "Um, is it a good one?"

"Very good."

I sat up from my nesting spot on my bed and ran my fingers through my hair. "I'm intrigued."

"I have to go pick it up. I'll bring it by around one. I just want to make sure you didn't need anything before then."

"You're not going to tell me?"

"No."

"You don't need to do anything else for me. You bought enough food yesterday to feed an army, and my apartment has never been so clean."

"This is so much better."

"If you say so."

"I do. Call me if you need anything before then."

"I will."

"See you soon."

I admit I was looking forward to it. He was kind of addicting, even if he was turning my life upside down. But in a weird way, it brought a peace I hadn't felt in a long time.

After I tried to make myself look at least semi-human, meaning I put on some yoga pants and applied some mascara and lip gloss, Delfia called. I could tell immediately she had some juicy news to share. She tried to show decorum by checking on me first. "How are you doing? We were all worried at the office."

"I'm sore and bruised, but all right."

As soon as she knew I was on the mend, she jumped right in. "I've been dying to tell you this all weekend," she started out. "I wish you could have been there, or I wish I would have thought to record it, because it was fabulous."

"What?" I was anxious to know.

"Friday, when Mr. Greyson came back to the office after the accident, he walked in with this look of pure disdain on his face. Without even a hello he asked where Ms. Manselle was. I was honestly a little terrified of him, so I just pointed to the bathroom. He walked right over and waited for her to come out."

I had never heard her so giddy, and that was saying a lot.

"As soon as that little wench came out, he let her have it. It was amazing."

"What did he say?" He hadn't given me any details.

"He told her she was classless and that she would never work for him again. Then he told her to pack up her belongings, and she should consider her advance as final payment because he would never use her designs. But the best part was when she asked if this was about you and he told her that if she ever spoke your name in any way that was degrading or defamatory, he would personally make sure she never worked again."

"Really?"

"Kelli, seriously, it was the best."

"I'm sorry I missed it, especially since I was lying in a hospital bed."

"Speaking of that, when will you be back in the office?"

"I'll probably work from home this coming week. I feel pretty wretched, and I look worse."

"I'm sure you look gorgeous as always, but I do hope you feel better soon."

"Thank you."

From there, we said our goodbyes. I hung up with her, feeling even more peaceful than before. I was so happy I didn't have to go back to that bimbo in the office.

While I had my phone in my hand, I decided to call Amanda. I really needed her advice about Ian. She was going to flip when I told her that Ian was still in love with me. That was after she rubbed in how right she was.

She picked up on the first ring. "Are you okay?"

"I'm alive. How's Disney World?"

"You know, it's lost a lot of the appeal it used to have when we were kids, but the girls are having a great time, so it makes it all worth it."

I smiled to myself. Amanda was such a good mom.

"So, tell me how you are. I mean, of course, Ian has been keeping us updated, but I've been worried about you."

Why didn't it surprise me that Ian had been giving them updates? "Really sis, I'm fine, but I wanted to talk to you about Ian. Do you have a moment?"

"Uh, yeah. Spill your guts. I've been waiting to get the scoop. Zane wants to know too."

Of course, he did. I'm surprised he hadn't called Ian himself since they were buddies now.

"So . . . Ian wants to get back together and he may have said he still loves me."

"I knew it! Zane," Amanda yelled, "we were right. He's totally in love with her." I could hear Zane laughing in the background.

"Now that you got that out of your system, tell me what to do."

She thought for a moment. "Oh honey, only you can answer that. But I think you know what to do, you're just afraid. And rightly so. But I will say this, ever since he's come back, I see that spark in your eye that's been missing for a long time. And for what it's worth, Zane really likes him."

"Well, that cinches it."

She laughed. "I'm glad your sass is still alive and well."

"I love you."

"I know. I love you too. Listen to your heart. It hasn't steered you wrong yet."

I leaned back on the pillows on my bed and let out a slow breath as I contemplated what to do. I thought about making a pros and cons list, but Ian would probably find it and talk me out of all the cons.

I spent the rest of the morning watching reruns of *Friends* and snuggling Charlie. I also had to do the exercises my doctor gave me for my arm. I might have cried out in pain a time or two, but at least I could use it. It made bathing and doing my hair and make-up so much easier, although I'm not sure why I bothered with make-up; half of my face still looked like Sam and Court's old finger paintings.

Ian didn't seem to mind the bruises. He had been kissing them all weekend, as if he could make it better. I wish. I knew he blamed himself for the accident, though it was clearly the truck driver's fault for running the red light. But Ian kept saying he was distracted. I reminded him that we were both arguing at the time, so it was my fault too. He wouldn't allow me to take any of the blame. I had a feeling he blamed Alexa and it's why he was so harsh with her. I'll admit I was okay with that, especially because she was playing him, not to mention she was a terrible designer. It made me wonder if I should show him my designs now.

Just watching TV and the few exercises I had to do left me feeling exhausted. The doctor said it would take my body a while to heal, but it made me feel pathetic. I also wondered if it was pathetic how much I couldn't wait for Ian to return. Maybe the better question would be, was it pathetic that I was even willing to consider letting him back into my heart? The heart he tore apart, that never fully mended. And what about the fact that he was my boss? It's not that I had never had a relationship with someone I worked with, but dating the boss's son was a tad different than dating the boss. Ian insisted it wouldn't be an issue as long as we kept our professional and personal relationships separate. To me, that was easier said than done, especially since I wasn't good at compartmentalizing like he was.

I only got a few episodes in before there was a knock on my door. I extricated myself from Charlie and got up to answer the door with a little flutter in my heart. With anticipation, I opened the door, expecting to see Ian, which I did, but his surprise was more than surprising. She didn't hesitate for a second, she threw her arms around me. "Kelli!"

I was so happy to see her, but my body didn't appreciate her iron tight grip. "Noelle," I moaned in pain.

Ian was quick to rescue me. "Noelle, her whole right side is bruised." She backed off. "I'm so sorry."

I leaned on Ian. "It's okay. What are you doing here?" I couldn't believe she was actually here.

She playfully pushed Ian's shoulder. "My dear big brother here was so worried about you he asked me to come for the week to take care of you while he's at the office."

I gazed up at him. His cheeks had pinkened. I think he was embarrassed, but I didn't know why. I stood on my tiptoes and kissed his cheek. "You are so thoughtful. Thank you," I got choked up.

He smoothed my brow. "I know you can take care of yourself, but I thought you might like the company and someone who could drive you around when I'm not available."

Noelle was Noelle. "Whatever, Ian. He was a wreck when I talked to him. I've never heard him so worried."

Ian wrapped his arm around me. "I think we should let Kelli sit down." He led me in out of the warm spring day. It was a shame I couldn't be out enjoying it. Not to say I didn't enjoy being in Ian's arms. I stopped him before we made it to the couch and kissed his lips. "You know you aren't playing fair."

"I'm playing for keeps."

Dang. That sent a thrill down my body.

"Aww, look how cute you two still are," Noelle interrupted.

I kept staring at her. I couldn't believe she was here. I hadn't seen her in almost thirteen years, and there she was, looking different, but I still recognized the mischievous glint she always had in her eyes. She had let her pixie cut grow out, and it wasn't dyed crazy colors anymore. Instead, it was her natural dark hair that was similar in color to Ian's. She looked more settled. I assumed motherhood had added that layer. It was weird that she was married and had a baby before me. She was the one who had always said she was above such nonsense, but I guess meeting Sean had changed all that. I was happy for her.

Ian and I settled on the couch together and Noelle sat on the floor in front of us. She'd always preferred the floor.

"You look great, Noelle."

She waved my compliment away. "You're the one to talk. Look at you. Even banged up from an accident you look like a million bucks."

"I don't feel that way."

"How are you?" She patted my knee.

I glanced at Ian. "Your brother has done a great job of nursing me back to health."

"You don't know how happy it makes me to see you two together."

I was beginning to feel the same way.

We spent the most pleasant day together talking and catching up like old friends do. We even reminisced about the past, and I found it didn't hurt as much as it used to. The Thanksgiving we all spent together many years ago was brought up, and we all decided it was one of the best. I watched Ian carefully during our conversations, he looked hopeful. He also never let go of me unless he was making dinner, or we were eating.

He was either holding my hand or he had his arm around me. I found myself very comfortable with him.

The day and evening passed too quickly. I was sad to see them leave late that night, but I knew Noelle needed to get settled, and Ian was returning to work the next day. Before they left, Ian took me up in his arms after asking his sister to wait outside for him. He kissed me gently on my lips before leaving a trail of kisses on the way to my ear. "I don't want you to think about work this week, just relax and get well," he whispered.

"But I have so much work to catch up on."

"Boss's orders."

"Are you bossing me around?" I teased.

He pressed his lips hard against mine, enough for me to taste the red wine we'd had with dinner. If his sister wasn't waiting for him, I would have drank him in deeply.

"Believe me," he groaned against my lips, "you are in charge of me. Good night."

Whoa. I watched him walk out. He left me feeling all sorts of weird, but this time I recognized it—it was the way he had always made me feel. It wasn't really weird, it was wonderful. I think it had just been so long since I had felt that way it seemed foreign to me.

I lay in bed that night thinking about what kind of man flies his sister in to keep me company all week when my own sister wasn't available. Not to mention all the cooking and cleaning he had done. I guess he was the same kind of man who helped me not only pass calculus, but pass it with flying colors; or the same man who always took time out of his busy school and work schedule to see me every day, even if it was only to kiss me and tell me he was crazy about me. And he was the same man who was doing everything he could to make sure my baby took off. So, what was thirteen years apart?

Chapter Twenty-One

NOELLE WAS AT MY DISPOSAL until Friday. I still couldn't believe she was here. I felt a little guilty about it as she had to leave her son, Jax, and her husband behind.

"It's good for Sean, and I deserve a week off," she said, but she was quick to show me hundreds of pictures of her little guy on her phone while we hung out on my couch. He was adorable, with wispy brown hair and big blue eyes that had a hint of mischief in them. I bet he was going to give his parents a run for their money.

The first day we spent talking without the listening ears of her brother around. It made talking about him so much easier. It felt like we were back in college, stuffing our faces with junk food and gossiping.

Noelle had to throw in her two cents about her thoughts concerning Ian and me getting back together. "You are probably a fool to date Ian again," she teased.

I tilted my head. "Do you think so?"

"No. Besides Sean and my dad, Ian is the best guy I know. He's uptight as all get out, but you already know that about him. It's kind of endearing now."

I giggled. It kind of was.

"You know he was really upset and depressed for a long time after you broke up?"

"He was?"

She nodded.

"Then why do you think he didn't contact me, or better yet, why did he wait so many years?"

"Those are good questions, but you know Ian. He doesn't talk much about his feelings. From what he did say, I think he was afraid that after what he did, you would never take him back. Then he became so focused on making IAG work that it became his life. But last year when he called to tell me he had found out where you worked and that you had moved back to Nashville, it was the first time in years he sounded happy. I encouraged him to come out here, but I didn't need to. I think that was his plan from the second he found out."

I bit my lip. "Really?"

"Oh, yeah. He was himself for the first time in a long time." She grabbed a handful of white cheddar popcorn. "Enough about my brother. Tell me about you, Miss Hotshot Executive."

I gave her a thirteen-year recap. We caught up on her life as a wife, mother, and editor. She edited textbooks at home part-time.

But what I really wanted to know was, "What made you change your mind about marriage?"

She smiled wide and her eyes brightened. "Have you ever had one of those moments when, in an instant, your whole life changes?"

I couldn't help but think about walking into a library almost fourteen years ago.

"Well for me, that moment came in Starbucks almost five years ago. Some guy who wasn't paying attention spilled hot coffee all over the front of my shirt. He didn't even pause to say he was sorry. But then this guy who was standing behind me in line grabbed a hold of him and made him apologize to me and give me money for dry cleaning as well as for coffee. No one had ever been that chivalrous to me. I had never been one to care about chivalry until that moment. Maybe the pink and purple hair was a turn off." She laughed, making me laugh too. "But that didn't matter to Sean. He saw past the hair and into my soul."

I wasn't sure I had ever heard her speak in such tones. I really was happy for her, but the reverent tones didn't last long as we moved to the topic of her ex-sister-in-law, whom she despised. The way she talked about her made me almost feel sorry for Ian, almost. She sounded like a real prima donna who cared more about appearances and keeping up with the Joneses. I guess she even refused to have any holidays at the Greyson's ranch. They all had to be at her dad's mansion in Cherry Creek. She had no idea what she was missing out on—holidays with the Greysons were the best.

That night Ian joined us and cooked for us again. He was going to spoil me. We stayed up late playing Canasta. It was a card game the siblings had taught me over that magnificent Thanksgiving break. You'd never met two, okay three, more competitive people in your life. I'm not sure if we argued or played more, but it didn't matter because either way I was having the time of my life.

The rest of the week Noelle made me get out and show her Nashville, even though I looked horrible and felt the same. Though I had to say, it was better than lying on the couch all week. The bruising was beginning to turn awful yellow and green colors, but she said if anybody made remarks, she would handle it. Ian kept telling me bruises or no bruises, I was still the most beautiful woman in his eyes, so I swallowed my pride and showed my friend why I loved my hometown so much. We did music row, Opryland, a river cruise, the Parthenon and Cheekwood. It was the best staycation ever.

The nights were even better, as we spent them with Ian. Noelle's last night was spent at Ian's place. I was finally getting to see what a thousand extra dollars a month bought you, and it was pretty nice. His apartment looked more like an urban loft. He had it handsomely decorated in tones of gray and tan. He reminded me I was welcome there anytime, and by the time he and I took Noelle to the airport Friday night, I was pretty much committed to the whole let's-give-this-a-second-chance thing. I hadn't felt this weird or wonderful in years.

Saturday only added to my wonderful weirdness when I got to see my family back from their Magic Kingdom vacation. Ian drove me over, and while he and Zane bonded over the rounds of golf Zane played while in Florida, I helped my sister with laundry and unpacking, all while listening to Court and Sam give me a blow-by-blow account of each and every ride, each and every day.

They hadn't forgotten their promise to buy me something pretty at Disney World. Sam and Court each handed me a Disney bag. I opened the first bag and pulled out a Minnie mug that was personalized with my name on it. I loved it. I opened the next bag to the sounds of snickers and giggles. It made me curious. I pulled out a Mickey mug, and all the giggles made sense. It was also personalized, but with Ian's name on it. I pulled those troublemakers to me and squeezed them hard. "Thank you." I gave my sister the evil eye. I knew she was behind it all.

She grinned unabashedly. Then had the audacity to ask, "Hey…do you think you could watch the girls tonight? Zane and I could really use some alone time."

I almost said no because I really wanted some alone time with Ian, but I could never refuse her. Ian made it an easy choice as he agreed to join in on the fun.

First, we went back to his place and he made us homemade pizza. He amazed my nieces when he tossed the pizza dough high in the air and then caught it with one hand. He let them help add the toppings. I had never seen him with kids before, and I liked it very much. While the pizza baked, we tried to teach them how to play Canasta, which was more difficult than I thought, but still enjoyable. After dinner, we took them to the movies where we could at least raise the arms of the chairs and sit close to one another.

I don't think Ian watched the movie at all. He kept whispering in my ear what he wished we were doing instead. It made me realize why my sister solicited my services so often. I loved my nieces more than anyone, but at the moment, I found myself wishing I was in Ian's arms without their prying eyes. They were very interested in this man I was introducing into our lives.

Sam asked, "Why do you like him now? I thought you said he was an idiot." Yep, that was Sam. And it was a good question.

After the movie, it was straight home for the cuties, where we declined an invitation from Amanda and Zane to stay for dessert. They gave us knowing looks, and we took that as our cue to flee. We ran to the store for ice cream and plastic spoons, then made a beeline for the park where we laid out a blanket and enjoyed our ice cream and our favorite park activity.

Under the starlit canvassed sky, I lay my head in his lap while he stroked my hair. I felt like all was right in the world. I sighed, "Thank you."

He gazed down at me. "For what?"

"For this whole week. You've taken such good care of me."

"I missed you, Kelli."

I grinned. "I missed your cooking."

He pulled me up gently, so we were face-to-face.

I looked into those chocolate eyes of his that were framed by eyelashes that would make any woman green with envy. I outlined his face with my finger. "Did I forget to mention how much I've missed you?"

He kissed my forehead, before resting his chin on my head. "Does this mean we can give this another go?"

"Are you asking me to go steady, Ian?"

He chuckled. "For now."

I pulled away and raised my brow. "Only for now?"

"That's not what I said."

I bit my lip. "Oh."

He captured my lips and kissed me like that's all he wanted to do forever.

Chapter Twenty-Two

I T WAS A GOOD THING we had such a wonderful week and weekend together, if not we may have broken up before we ever really started again. Ian wasn't kidding when he said he wanted to maintain professional boundaries while in the office. I agreed with him, but I guess I thought he would have lightened up some, or at least softened on how he approached me.

Monday morning started off all well and good. I came in to find Delfia anxiously waiting for me in my office that was now filled with flowers and get-well cards. I noticed, too that some furniture rearrangement had been done in my absence. The credenza was now back to its original place.

Delfia was to me in no time, hugging me. When she pulled away her eyes were all alight like she knew something. I'm sure she had her suspicions about me and our boss. "By the way, Mr. Greyson would like to speak to you."

"Thank you." I tried not to give anything away. I'm not sure how well I did because her toothy grin was pretty wide.

I set up my laptop and read some of the cards before I made my way to the adjoining door. As I approached it, I wondered if I should knock, or if he would mind now if I just walked in. I decided I would test the waters. I opened the door without knocking. I peeked in and found him sitting at his desk, looking like Mr. Greyson.

"You wanted to see me," I said as a way of announcing myself.

He looked up and smiled, so I guess it was okay that I didn't knock, but then... "Yes, Ms. Bryant."

I shut the door and frowned. "Ms. Bryant? I thought we decided to cut that nonsense out?"

"I said you could call me Ian," he didn't miss a beat.

"Well, if you need my permission, you have it, please call me Kelli."

"I can't." He set down the pen he had been holding.

I didn't even know how to respond to that ridiculousness, so I stood there dumbfounded.

He waved to the chairs in front of his desk. "Would you please sit down?"

I did as he asked, but I wasn't happy about it. When I took one of the seats in front of his desk, I looked at him as if to say *this better be good, really good.*

"Ms. Bryant," he said with a smile. "I have a good reason for not wanting to call you by your first name."

"Care to share with the class, *Mr. Greyson?*"

My snarkiness didn't faze him. "Besides it making it easier to separate our professional and personal relationships, I can't call you Kelli in the office because there is no hiding how I feel about you when I say your name. I'm trying to prevent any undo backlash that may come your way if people in the office honestly knew how I felt about you."

So, it was good, really good, but I still didn't like it. "You know, I've dealt with that before. There were a few people who were very unhappy about me receiving my current position. They chalked it up to nepotism and the fact that Gary and Holly had wanted me to marry their son."

"And you think I want you to have to deal with that again?"

"No, but you don't have to protect me. I'm a big girl now, and I just happen to be their boss too."

He sighed in frustration. "Please, can you just trust me? I'm trying to prevent any unnecessary complications."

I narrowed my eyes.

"That's not to say you're a complication," he quickly added, "but regardless, I have Chandler's reputation to protect as well."

I could understand that, so I dropped it for now. "So, what did you want to see me about? I'm assuming it wasn't to discuss name preferences."

His eyes begged for me to understand before he clicked a few things on his laptop and turned it around to face me.

I was surprised by what the screen held. There were my designs, front and center. My eyes drifted from the screen back to him. "Where did you get those?"

"When you asked me to retrieve your laptop after the accident, I noticed the folder on your desktop."

"So, you thought it was a good idea to open it without my permission?"

"Do I need to remind you about the disclosures you've signed pertaining to anything on company computers?"

I shot daggers at him with my eyes. "Need I remind you—"

He headed me off at the pass, "Ms. Bryant, your designs are perfect."

"Yeah . . . well . . . thanks." His flip-flopping was giving me a headache.

"Why didn't you show these to me in the first place?" He admired them.

I sat up a little taller. "I was planning on it, but then you brought back that 'contracted designer.'" I used air quotes as I loosely said the term. She couldn't design herself out of a box.

He cleared his throat. "Yes, well, I still would have liked to see them."

"Especially since we've got nothing better right now," I teased.

He didn't take the bait. "I would like to set up a demo with Matt for this afternoon to show him this so he can get to work on adding it. Are you available at three?"

I nodded. "Is that all?"

"Just one more thing. You are a talented graphic designer, but I need your attention focused elsewhere."

I glared at him. "Fine, Mr. Greyson." I got up and stalked off, slamming the dang adjoining door as I went. He was the most infuriating man I had ever known. This was why all the experts advised people not to date their coworkers.

I sat down at my desk fuming. My phone rang almost immediately. I saw the number on the display screen and considered not answering it, but then I figured he would probably come marching on over here if I didn't, and I wasn't in any mood to see him even though he was looking quite fine today in his blue suit. "Hello."

"Kelli."

"Didn't we just have this conversation? Don't you mean, Ms. Bryant?"

I could hear the smile in his voice when he replied, "I should clarify, this is Ian, and I was calling to make a lunch date with the woman I love, who, by the way, looks stunning today."

"You know this is ridiculous, right?"

"Ridiculous? I thought women liked their boyfriends to call them during the day."

"Typically, we do, but not after said boyfriend just criticized her."

"I'm sure you took it the wrong way because I know for a fact that your boss thinks you're amazing and talented."

I sank into my chair and sighed. "Ian, how are we going to make this work?"

"Kelli, we're not the first couple to work together. We both need to be determined to make it work, and please know there is nothing more important to me than making us work. So, will you go to lunch with me?"

How could I refuse after such a sweet speech?

We met at his rental car at high noon. His Infiniti had been totaled and he hadn't purchased a new car yet. In fact, he asked me if I wanted to go car shopping with him that night, something else I agreed to do.

Lunch was fabulous. He took me to the park and we ate peanut butter and jam sandwiches, but the best part was just lying in his lap while he stroked my hair. We talked about all the somethings and even the nothings of life while we enjoyed the warm sunny weather. It made me not want to return to the office where I became Ms. Bryant again.

"Please try and understand. I don't want to repeat past mistakes, especially when so much hangs in the balance," he begged on the way back to the office.

It was a sweet sentiment, and on many levels, I got it. It was just hard for me.

"So, hypothetically speaking, what's going to happen if, you know...our title changes to a more forever type scenario? Will you call me Mrs. Greyson in the office?"

He picked up my hand and kissed it. "I like the sound of that, but no, I wouldn't call my wife that."

"So, what would you call me?"

"Are you saying you want to get married?" he asked instead of answering.

It was very warm all of a sudden. I had imagined marrying him more times than I could count, but I wasn't ready to take the plunge with him...yet. I wanted to work on getting to know him again, to see if we were still the right match. My guess was we still were, but thirteen years is a long time to be apart, and I needed time to learn how to trust him again. I shrugged my shoulders. "Maybe someday."

He kissed my hand and smiled. "Well, then, someday I'll tell you."

"Has anyone ever told you how infuriating you are?"

He laughed. "You're not the first."

"Well, you know the first step to recovery is admitting you have a problem," I quipped.

His smirk said he probably wasn't going to change. I figured that was the case.

I did get some vindication that afternoon as we met with Matt and he was blown away by my designs. What did he say? "Kelli is the only designer we need for this project." I tried not to smile too big. But sometimes it was so difficult to be professional.

Chapter Twenty-Three

A S THE WEEKS WENT BY, we eased into an uneasy pattern, at least for me. We kept it professional at the office and passionate on the off hours and weekends. With each passing day I wanted more and more to be just Kelli. But I soon got an up close and personal view on why Ian was so adamant about keeping the two separated.

A few weeks after the accident, Ian and I were having lunch together. I reveled in that hour every workday where I was Kelli and he was Ian, but that particular day he received a phone call from his attorney that he had to take. I could tell right away the news wasn't good. I'm not sure I had ever seen Ian turn so red, and I won't even talk about the swearing. I was glad we were at the park and not at a restaurant. He got up from our blanket and began pacing around while ranting to his attorney on the other end. I sat there and watched. I knew better than to try and intervene.

After several minutes, he sat down and joined me again. I was afraid to even ask what that was all about, but I wanted to make it better for him. I reached up and placed my hand upon his still reddened cheek. "Ian..."

He reached up and touched my hand with his own and then slid it down my arm. "I didn't mean to ruin our lunch."

"Don't apologize. Just tell me what's wrong."

"I don't want to involve you."

I dropped my hand. "Why?"

His features softened, as did his tone. "Numbers eight and nine on your list."

I half grinned. "I already know you come with a lot of baggage, buddy."

"Well that phone call just added to it."

I took his hand in mine. "If you want us to be a couple, you can't hold things back from me."

He brought my hand up and kissed my palm. "Kelli, you know that's what I want. Why do you think I moved to Nashville?"

"I thought you came to run Chandler," I teased.

He pulled me to him and groaned against my ear. "Fine, apparently my ex-wife and Alexa have teamed up in an attempt to take more of my money. Alexa is now claiming we had an affair while she was at IAG and I was married."

I pulled back and looked into his troubled eyes.

"Kelli, please tell me you don't believe that," he begged.

I ran my fingers through his hair. "Well…I know how you like blondes and big boobs."

He pecked my lips. "You drive me crazy."

"I know." I grinned. "And I also know you didn't have an affair with *Ms. Manselle*. But even if you did, not that I would be okay with it, what's the fuss about? Didn't your ex-wife cheat on you?"

"Marissa," he snarled, "and I had a prenup in place. It kept our property separate, namely IAG and her family's wealth. The investment her father's firm gave me was paid back with interest as agreed upon several years ago, removing any claim he might have on the company. Of course, his venture capital firm that Marissa worked for still got a lot of leverage out of the success of IAG. This was all well and good until IAG outperformed any of our expectations and our marriage went south. My wealth increased as theirs decreased because of bad investments, and things just got out of control from there. She's lobbed accusation after accusation at me. She's desperate to get her hands on the money I received from selling IAG. She's trying to paint me as manipulative and a liar."

He was beyond tense. Every muscle in his face was tight. I moved, knelt behind him to rub his shoulders, and whispered, "I'm sorry."

He kept lamenting. "I already offered her a hefty sum so she'll go away, but I think this has become more of a vendetta for her. I never should have married her."

I kept rubbing his back and shoulders while he kept ranting. Next on his list was Alexa. I had a few choice words for her as well, although I kept them to myself. Ian was doing a good enough job. It was also nice to hear him say what a mistake he made in bringing her here. I couldn't have agreed more, but again I kept my mouth shut. There was no sense in making him feel worse.

He finally had it out of him. He reached up and grabbed my hands that were on his shoulders and pulled me over onto his lap. He searched my face silently for a moment. Worry lines were etched into his forehead. "Kelli, your name has been brought into it too."

"What do I have to do with it?"

"They're going to claim that I have a pattern of having affairs with women that work for me."

I tugged on Ian's tie and brought our faces as close as they could get without us actually kissing, which was coming, but first I had something to say. "Well, they just messed with the wrong Southern girl."

Ian closed the small distance between us. He kissed me until I saw stars in the middle of the sun-filled day. As soon as I was out of breath, he kissed his way over to my ear. "Have I mentioned lately how much I love you?"

Oh, he had, and I knew he was waiting patiently for me to reciprocate. Someday I would, but not today. "I'm here for you," was all I could offer.

"I know that, but this is my battle."

I sat up and leaned away from him. "We're a team now. If Alexa and Marissa want a fight, then we're going to give them one. And I don't plan on losing." Alexa Manselle wouldn't even know what hit her after I was done.

"Hell, you're sexy."

I leaned my forehead against his. "What's the game plan?"

Ian was already planning to go to Colorado the following week for what he hoped was the final step in the litigation process, but now he wasn't so sure. I decided I was going with him. He wasn't sure if that was a good idea in light of the accusations that were being tossed our way, but I was certainly not going to let someone drag my reputation through the mud and not have a say about it. Besides, Ian had some great contacts in Colorado that we had been talking to. This would give us the opportunity to dazzle them in person, so Ian eventually gave in. Not like I was really giving him a choice in the matter.

I was looking forward to going back to Colorado. I missed it, and there was nothing like late springtime in the Rockies. I was hoping, too, that after the litigation ridiculousness there would be some time for romance. After all, Colorado is where it all started for us.

Ian was stressed out more than usual, which was saying something. He couldn't stand not being able to predict or control the variables. I think he mentioned it was kind of like being in love with me, but horrible. I took that as a compliment.

We had Delfia set up some appointments for us in Colorado with two large banks. This way, being gone together looked like it was a business trip, even though I was pretty sure Delfia didn't believe it, just like she didn't believe that we weren't a couple. I never said we weren't, I just never validated her relentless claims. I knew we weren't fooling her, but for Ian's sake, I didn't advertise it.

Of course, my family knew, and so did Boss and Holly. Ian felt he should be on the up and up with Gary about it. I wouldn't have kept it from them anyway, they were like family to me. In fact, they weren't surprised at all. I guess I was the only one who was.

Ian made all the travel arrangements. It was the first time I had ever flown first class, and it was the best flight I'd had to date. I had forgotten what it felt like to be in a relationship that made every aspect of my life better, even mundane things like a flight. I missed being able to talk to someone who I felt I could be just me with. The ease and contentment I felt with him I'd never been able to duplicate with anyone else, and now, almost fourteen years later, he still made me feel that way.

The only downside was Ian was beyond tense. He was worried about this ludicrous lawsuit. It wasn't the money that was bothering him. No, what worried him was me. He felt this need to protect me, and I think he was more than ready to put this chapter of his life behind him. He wanted to get rid of his baggage per se. I tried to put his mind at ease that I wasn't going anywhere. Besides, I had a few tricks up my sleeve. Marissa and Alexa were going to be sorry they messed with me and mine.

Ian let me have the window seat, and I couldn't help but feel excited, even under the circumstances, when I saw the big, white, peaked rooftop of Denver International Airport. It was the strangest looking airport I had ever seen, but oddly it made me feel, in a sense, that I had come home. I turned and grinned at Ian. He looked past me out the window and smiled, too. It was his only smile the entire flight.

"Have you missed Colorado?" I asked.

"I've missed being here with you."

I'd missed it too. The more I was with him, the more I realized how much I truly missed him, missed us. He was like the harmony to my melody, and together we created a more complete and richer sound. I felt the more we were together, the more in tune we would become. At least I hoped. I was still having a hard time separating our personal and professional lives. While we were away, my plan was to be mostly Kelli and Ian.

Ian proved once again why he was the perfect boyfriend. We had just picked up our luggage in baggage claim when I heard two familiar voices call my name. I looked up to find Ian's parents, Tony and Sheila.

I dropped my suitcase and hurried to them. "Tony, Sheila, what in the world are you doing here?"

They simultaneously hugged me. It was amazing to be in their arms.

Sheila kissed my head. "Ian told us you were coming to town with him, and it has been too long since we've seen you."

My eyes began to water. "Yes, it's been far too long."

They looked almost the same as they had fourteen years ago, maybe a little more weathered and worn, but they were perfect in my mind. Tony was an older, grayer, jollier version of Ian, and Sheila reminded me of Jamie Lee Curtis, with her short, gray, spiky hair. She and Noelle shared the same mischievous gleam in their eyes as well as in their nature. Boy, had I missed them.

Ian sidled up to me carrying all our luggage. His parents stood back and beamed at us.

"It's about time," Tony said.

Ian put his arm around me. "I would say it's long overdue."

I leaned into him, but what I really wanted to do was grab his face and kiss him senseless. It didn't seem like the appropriate venue, but he better watch out later. Ian did peck me on the lips. It would have to tide me over.

"Well, let's get out of here so we can catch up," his mom said.

Ian took my hand and Tony grabbed some of our luggage before we headed to our rental car. Sheila gave me one more hug. "It is so good to see you, honey."

She had no idea how good it was to be seen.

Chapter Twenty-Four

IAN'S PARENTS FOLLOWED US TO our hotel where we were going to have lunch. I smiled to myself, thinking about how Ian thought maybe it would look better if we stayed in separate hotels. I didn't care what his ex-wife and Alexa thought. It was none of their business what we did. We were consenting adults. Though we weren't consenting to everything. I was still starring in the *Virgin Tales*. Ian didn't seem to mind playing the role of costar. He said he wanted to give me what I wanted and deserved. Though he did book us five floors apart, like that was really going to stop us if we wanted to do something. And let's be honest, we both did; but I had waited this long, and I wanted all the ingredients to be there and so did Ian. I was beginning to think I was falling in love with him all over again.

When we pulled into the hotel's parking lot I leaned over and kissed Ian. "Thank you for inviting your parents down."

"They didn't wait for an invitation when I told them you were coming."

I rested my hand on his cheek. He was acting so subdued. His chocolate eyes swirled with worry. I was going to make sure, before we returned to Nashville, that those babies would be all alight. "It's all going to work out. I promise."

Ian's lips landed on mine. His tongue slid across my lips. "Mmm," he groaned before deepening the kiss. It was over too quick. "I guess we better not keep my parents waiting."

I hated that he was so melancholy. I knew part of him was happy to see his parents and to have us all together, but when there was a problem to be solved, Ian had a hard time focusing on anything else.

When we sat down to lunch it reminded me of the nights at the Greyson's table playing games and eating leftovers from Thanksgiving. It was amazing how fourteen years could be erased in the course of lunch. There was no awkwardness or lulls in the conversation. It still puzzled me after all this time how such carefree individuals ever raised such an uptight person like their son.

Tony and Sheila were both loud and laughed easily. They had great stories to tell about goats getting on roofs and chickens escaping and finding their way into their kitchen.

Poor Ian barely cracked a smile. He was beyond uptight. He was meeting with his attorney after lunch.

When it was time for Ian to leave, I walked him out to his car. His parents were going to stay with me for a while before they had to head back to Glenwood Springs, a few hours away.

"I'll go with you if you want. You know I was raised by a lawyer, and I have some good ideas."

He squeezed my hand. "I have it under control. Please don't worry."

"I don't appreciate being handled with kid gloves, and I'm going to worry either way." I stopped in front of his car. "Don't you get how much you mean to me? How could I not be worried?"

He took me into his arms and pressed me against the car. "Kelli, I love you." His eyes finally had a little light in them as he looked into my own. "Can you please just trust me and let me deal with this?"

"If the roles were reversed, would you stay out of it?"

His lips turned up slightly and he released an over-exaggerated breath. He knew I was right.

"I'm not some pretty little airhead or nineteen-year-old kid anymore, and—"

His laughter stopped me from finishing my thought. I narrowed my eyes at him in frustration.

He brought his hands up and cupped my face. "Kelli, you're the most capable woman I've ever known, so you can get that thought out of your pretty little head."

I rolled my eyes.

"You're so sexy when you're irritated." He ran his hands down my curves before pressing his lips to mine.

I had no choice but to reciprocate. Okay, I had a choice, but why would I choose not to? I leaned into him and enjoyed a few minutes of bliss.

He reluctantly pulled away. "Please, let me fix my mistakes. Enjoy today with my parents, and I'll be back to you as soon as I can," he said it with love, but also with finality. He was done arguing. He kissed me once more and left without another word.

I watched him drive off and smiled to myself. He was crazy if he thought I was going to stand by and be an observer. Unbeknownst to him, I had already taken action. I was hoping he would agree on the front-end to let me be involved, but I guess I was going in from the back-end. In the meantime, I did as he asked. I walked back in and joined his parents for a wonderful day of sightseeing and catching up.

I don't know how many times his parents expressed how thrilled they were to see us back together and to see me again. They had thought of me often through the years and wondered many times about the "what ifs." Me too, but there was no going back. I wasn't quite sure what the future held yet. All I knew was that I wanted Ian to be in it, and I knew that's what he wanted. He was patiently waiting on me to decide when we should move forward. It really was odd to hear him say that he loved me on a daily basis, and it was weird for me not to reciprocate the sentiment. It's not that I didn't love him. I think I always had, but I wasn't ready to admit that to him. I still needed time, and he was more than willing to give it to me. He didn't seem bothered in the least that I wasn't saying those three little words.

His parents had to leave after dinner, but before they did they extended an invitation to Ian and me to come and spend the weekend with them. I accepted, without consulting with my absentee boyfriend. I hoped he didn't mind. I knew we had planned on going back home on Friday, but there was no way I was turning down the opportunity of spending the weekend with Ian in one of my most favorite places. I had a feeling that after this week, we were both going to want the getaway. His parents were beyond delighted.

I spent the rest of my evening in my hotel room going over my notes for my presentation. Ian would text me intermittently and say he was missing me, or he would apologize for being delayed. At nine, though, I got a text asking me to meet him in the parking lot. I took no time slipping on my shoes and hurrying to meet him. He was waiting for me by the car with the passenger door open.

He grinned as I approached, but he looked tired and worn. "Hello, beautiful." Even his words sounded tired.

I smiled warmly and touched his cheek. "Hi, handsome."

He caught my hand and kissed my palm before helping me into the car. He jogged over to the driver's side, got in, and took off.

"Where are we going?" I asked when we exited the hotel parking lot.

He glanced over at me. "I believe there are still some swings with our names on them."

I could feel my own face erupt with delight. This was why he was perfect for me. Even though he had more money than most and could afford to take me anywhere in the city, he still chose the one place I adored more than any other. It cost not a thing, but it was priceless to me.

Not much was said on the drive over. Ian held my hand the whole way to "our" park, while I looked out the window at all the changes that had occurred in the last ten years. Denver had definitely grown. I didn't remember the traffic being this bad this late at night when I lived here. It reminded me why I loved Nashville so much. Nashville was the perfect-sized city in my mind. Don't get me wrong, I loved Denver, but I don't know if I could stand to live here again.

As the park came into view, I felt eighteen again. My motto was, "You are never too old for the park." I was glad Ian still agreed with me, or at least went with it. "I hope my butt still fits in the swing," I worried out loud. I was barely back to belly dancing after the accident.

"You have nothing to worry about, I check out your backside plenty, and it looks great." He swung our hands between us in the park's parking lot.

We laughed about the first time I saw him at Chandler, when I was telling Delfia to check out my butt. I couldn't believe that was only three months ago. It seemed like a lifetime away, so much had happened since then. But we didn't come to the park to talk about Chandler or lawsuits. We agreed we would only talk about us, or even better, we would occupy our lips and there would be no need for words.

As soon as we hit the cool grass, we both removed our shoes and rolled up our pants. There was nothing like cool grass beneath your feet and holding hands with your special someone. As we walked toward the swings, I looked around. The trees had grown taller, and it looked like the playground equipment had been painted, but it was still our park. Thankfully, we were the only ones there. Not like we would have noticed anyone anyway; we only had eyes for each other as we walked hand-in-hand with a slight swing in our arms and a spring in our step.

When we were several paces from the swings, I dropped his hand to race him. He must have anticipated my move as he was quick to grab me and pull me back. Kissing was way better than racing or swinging any day. When he kissed me, I could feel a release of tension. I don't think he could have pulled me any closer. He kissed every inch of my face and neck. He was driving me crazy, in the best sort of way.

"Ian, are you okay?"

He kissed my neck once more before leaning his forehead against mine. He simply breathed deeply for several seconds.

"I'm here for you," I whispered.

"I don't deserve you."

"Yes, but regardless, I'm still here."

He chuckled. "I do love you."

"I know. Let's swing."

We spent the next hour swinging, laughing, and talking. It was there I divulged our new plans for the weekend. He seemed genuinely pleased with the idea.

We only needed to make it there.

Chapter Twenty-Five

GLENWOOD SPRINGS WAS THE WORD of the week. Whenever Ian was tense, I would whisper the beloved place and remind him what was waiting for us in a few short days. Tuesday morning we spent going over our presentation for Norwest Bank. We spent the afternoon meeting with their big wigs in downtown Denver in their oddly shaped skyscraper that I swore looked like a cash register on the top. The meeting went mostly well, but they were super stringent about security issues. They wanted us to change our contract and terms and conditions for them. Ian took it all in stride and didn't promise them a thing.

"I never thought I would meet anyone more anal than you," I remarked to him on our way out through their lobby.

He laughed, and for a moment, he forgot I was Ms. Bryant. He reached down and took my hand.

"Mr. Greyson, I'm not sure how to take that," I teased.

He dropped my hand, but at least he smiled. I really did miss being just Kelli.

That night I was left alone as Ian met with his attorney again. They were going to court the next afternoon. He didn't know it, but I was too. I was also working on this ridiculous case. Ms. Manselle was about to be very sorry.

I dressed in my finest business suit the next morning before I met Ian for breakfast. He hadn't gotten in until almost midnight the night before.

He had come up and lightly rapped on my door when he got back. "I needed to see your face," he'd said before he kissed me.

I happily obliged. He had looked so worn, and this morning he still did. It made me more determined to go with him. He had been so adamant about me staying out of it that he didn't even discuss what was going on with me, but like he said, he had never known anyone more stubborn than me.

As soon as our breakfast was cleared away, I reached into my satchel and pulled out a large manila envelope. I slid it across the table to him.

His brow quirked. "What's this?"

"Your insurance policy."

He still looked confused.

I pushed it more toward him. "Open it."

He picked it up, carefully opened it, and pulled out the contents. I watched him as he read through the small stack of papers. I could see his chocolate eyes brighten as he read the lawsuit Chandler was filing against Ms. Manselle for breach of contract, corporate espionage, and violating her NDA. He looked up from the papers with the biggest grin I had ever seen on his face.

I took that as my opportunity to hand him a DVD. "This video shows Ms. Manselle taking pictures with her phone of your laptop screen showing the framework of our software. It also shows her talking to who I assume is your ex-wife, discussing their 'plan.' I've asked Ms. Ayers, Chandler's attorney, to subpoena Ms. Manselle's and Marissa's cell phone records. I also have Delfia's handwritten statement that she overheard the conversation and her plans to 'take you down,' for lack of a better term."

He shook his head at me in amazement. He was positively speechless.

"So, can I go with you to the courthouse now?"

He leaned over and planted a kiss on my cheek. "I love you."

"I'll take that as a yes."

Ian called his attorney and insisted on meeting immediately, if not sooner. His attorney agreed, and we were on our way. I watched him as we drove over. I could visibly see that his stress level had diminished. He looked so relieved. I even teased him that I would be willing to get up and swear, under oath, that I was still a virgin to put to bed any talk about his nefarious relationships with women in the office.

He laughed and briefly looked my way when we stopped at a red light. "You say the most absurd things sometimes." He took the opportunity to peruse me from head to toe with his hungry eyes. "Unfortunately, no one would believe you."

I raised my brows.

"Except for me, of course," he added. "Besides, I had no intention of letting anyone come near you. I would have given it all up to protect you if needed."

I reached up and touched his cleanly shaven face. "Ian, you don't have to protect me, but thank you."

"Maybe I don't have to, but I want to, for the rest of my life."

My eyes began to water. I flipped down the visor mirror and tried to keep my makeup in place. It wasn't that I was embarrassed to cry in front of him, especially not a happy cry, but I wanted to make sure I gave my best impression today.

"You're beautiful," Ian said as I dabbed at my eyes.

"Stop being so sweet, you're going to make me cry some more."

He laughed at me. I was happy to hear him really laugh.

The attorney's office wasn't far from our hotel, so it didn't take us long to get there, even with Denver's insane traffic. On our walk in, he held my hand.

"So, I get to be Kelli today?"

He gave me a wry smile and applied gentle pressure to my hand. I squeezed back. I hoped someday he would get over all of this separation nonsense. I mean, I get why he did it, but this was me. I wasn't Marissa or Alexa. I fell in love with Ian long before he was ever wealthy or successful, at least in the worldly way. He could trust me, and it wasn't like I wanted to make-out in the office or anything. I just wanted to be us. Okay, if he felt the urge and it was behind closed doors, I wouldn't mind at all if he kissed me in the office.

Ian's attorney, Mr. Nathaniel Clark, ushered us in right away. By the looks of his opulent office, he did very well for himself. I expected no less, considering who had solicited his services. He was probably around Ian's age, maybe a tad older. He had a commanding presence to him. I could see instantly why Ian had chosen him.

Ian introduced me and then took no time getting down to business. He handed over the packet to Mr. Clark and explained the contents.

Mr. Clark grinned at me. "Are you sure you're in the right profession, Ms. Bryant? I could use someone like you."

"She's taken," Ian replied for me.

Mr. Clark smiled at the two of us before he continued to look through the documents. "This is amazing leverage," he commented. "And why we didn't think of it, Ian, I don't know."

Ian beamed at me.

Mr. Clark made a couple of phone calls to the opposing lawyers, and then the fun began. After an hour, we all headed over to the courthouse that was conveniently across the street from Mr. Clark's firm. Ian surprised me and held my hand as we made our way over. I couldn't wait to see the looks on the faces of his ex and that snake Alexa.

As this wasn't a jury trial, we met in a conference-style room. Apparently, the opposing side wanted to meet without the judge first. Shocker. They knew they were in trouble.

We got there first and took seats on the hard-wooden chairs at one end of the table. Ian looked more relaxed than I had seen him in days. That was until the Bobbsey Twins, more like the boob twins made their appearance. His demeanor changed in a split second. I wasn't sure if I had ever seen such a look of disdain on anyone's face.

The twins didn't look happy either, especially when they saw me. I couldn't help but wickedly grin at them. Oh, yes... they were going to be very sorry. They turned away from me, and I smiled lovingly at the man by my side. He grabbed my hand under the table and held it firmly. I so badly wanted to get out my phone and take a picture of the painted ladies for my sister. They both overdid the hair and makeup today, and for some odd reason, it looked like they color coordinated. They were each wearing navy blue and red and were showing a lot of cleavage. I didn't think that was going to help them today.

Besides their lawyer, there was an older gentleman with them. I think he was Marissa's father. I take back my previous comment, he was the winner for the look of disdain. I couldn't tell who he was unhappier with, Ian or his daughter. It was a toss-up as he looked between the two. Ian didn't flinch though.

I leaned over to Ian. "You are so sexy when you're trying to play it cool," I whispered low enough for his ears only.

His lips twitched but then he was back to business and staring down the opposing side. I found it interesting how Alexa refused to make eye contact with Ian. In a way, I couldn't blame her. I knew what it felt like to be rejected by him, and it was devastating.

The opposing side kept chatting and arguing amongst themselves as we stayed cool and collected on our end. They were scrambling. I took way too much pleasure in it. They had obviously been very confident about a different outcome. Finally, after about twenty minutes, their lawyer asked for a meeting between the two parties, meaning Alexa and I were asked to leave. I was honestly looking forward to a little time alone with Ms. Manselle. She, on the other hand, looked a little worried, as she should be.

Ian stood up with me, and I couldn't help it, I kissed him once on those sensuous lips of his. "Make sure you ditch the baggage, okay?" I gave him a playful nudge.

He smirked before I turned around to find all eyes on us, even Ms. Manselle's. I plastered a huge smile on my face, held my head up high, and walked out like a boss. Ms. Manselle joined me in the hall that was lined with large paintings of judges of the past. We both took a seat on the bench outside the room. She on one end and me on the other. She kept nervously glancing between me and her phone. For a moment, I took pleasure in watching her squirm. I wasn't sure how long my window of opportunity would be, so I slid closer to her on the long bench. She tried to ignore me by turning away from me, but I wasn't having it. "Ms. Manselle."

She refused to turn and look my way.

"Cat got your tongue? Well, no matter. I don't need you to say anything, but you will listen to me."

She turned and glared at me.

My eyes bore into her. "I'm sure they're in there cutting a deal right now to keep Chandler's lawsuit against you from going forward, but know that if you even think about causing harm to Ian again, you won't know what hit you. And if I see a hint of my software design anywhere, I'll make sure you see prison time."

Her mouth fell and she swallowed hard. She looked like she wanted to scream at me, but she knew better.

I smirked. "That's right, I think orange would suit you well."

Without a word, she stood up and marched away in her hooker heels and short, tight skirt. Was it evil for me to wish she would slip and fall on the gleaming tile floor?

She never returned, so I took the time and texted my sister while I waited. I didn't even have to hear Amanda's voice to know that she was completely amused with my report. I couldn't wait to see her next week when we could have a face-to-face conversation.

Within a half-hour, Ian emerged looking quite pleased. I couldn't say the same for his ex and her daddy. I wanted to yell out, "Cheaters never prosper!" and "Take that!" Once Ian put his arm around me though, I suddenly couldn't have cared less about anyone else at that courthouse.

We didn't say a word until we were outside. There he let me know that the ridiculous lawsuit had been dropped. "You're a genius," he kept repeating over and over. Apparently, Ian had also warned his ex-family that if any part of Chandler's software showed up, they would be very sorry. I told him of my conversation with the "contractor." By this time, we were to his car, and before he opened my door, he made me see stars. And like always, I knew how he felt by his kiss. He loved me.

Chapter Twenty-Six

IT WAS SO HARD TO keep my mind focused on our presentations over the next couple of days knowing that we would be spending the weekend together in our place, as I thought of it. By the time we were done on Friday afternoon, I was more than ready. The only thing that stood between the glorious mountains and us was rush hour traffic. Good thing my view inside the car was excellent. Ian looked great with his tie and suit coat off and white shirt slightly unbuttoned. I found, even though I missed the Clark Kent version, I more than liked the sexy boardroom version in front of me.

When we finally made it up the I-70 corridor into the foothills, I sighed. I missed these mountains. I was thankful to have the early evening sunlight during our drive. It was so beautiful. Nothing compared to the Rocky Mountains, from the pine tree lined mountains to the tiny waterfalls that cascaded down the rock walls near the highway. It even smelled like heaven. There was a crispness and freshness that filled the air. I think I took at least a hundred pictures with my phone as we drove. I texted several to my sister and told her we needed to take a family vacation here. She agreed.

It was around 7:30 when we arrived in Glenwood Springs. Our first stop was the hot springs. Neither Ian nor I could wait to revisit that beloved place together. I brought extra Chapstick and lotion for the occasion.

"I haven't been back since the last time I took you here," he said as we walked in.

That did my heart good.

We entered the water just as the sun was starting to set and the cool air highlighted the steam rising from the naturally hot water. It was breathtaking. No picture could do it justice. It was something that had to be experienced, not seen through a lens. As soon as I hit the water, Ian wrapped me up. I sank into his arms and stayed there for the next two hours until the hot springs closed.

There wasn't a lot of talking, but what was said I found quite interesting.

After about the hundredth kiss, Ian stroked my wet hair and slid his hands silkily down my arms to where we interlocked hands. His hungry eyes added to the heat from the water. "You know," he said, "this is where I fell in love with you."

"Really?" I could hardly believe it.

He nodded, and for a moment I saw regret in those beautiful eyes of his. "But I knew I couldn't have you. I knew I would have to let you go. I tried to think of everything I could to make it last as long as possible. I knew I shouldn't have and it was selfish of me, but I wanted you, so I started telling you I was crazy about you, instead of how I really felt. I hoped you would go with it, because I knew if ever you felt about me the way I felt about you, I would have to walk away. And for a while you went along with it. I tried to keep you at arm's length, but in the end, you weren't having it." He placed our still entwined hands behind my back and pulled me closer.

"I wish you would have been honest with me."

"Kelli," he nuzzled my ear, "you were so young. I didn't want you to wake up fifteen years later and regret that you never lived life or that the only real relationship you had was with me." He dropped my hands, brought his wet hands up and held my face. "And let's not forget how innocent you were and still, amazingly, are. I didn't want to do anything to ruin that, but believe me, you pushed my self-control to the brink sometimes. You still do."

I placed my hands on his toned bare chest. Did it ever feel nice. I too had to use self-control around him. "Ian, thank you, but I always knew you were the one for me. The only thing I regret is that I missed out on being with you these past thirteen years."

He ran his thumbs gently across my cheeks. "Me too."

I slid my hands up his bare skin and placed them around his neck. "I guess we better quit wasting time then."

His lips crashed down on mine and proved to me why the extra Chapstick was a good call.

His parent's home was about thirty minutes west of the hot springs. I felt bad we kept them up waiting for us, but after the week we had, the water and closeness was exactly what the doctor ordered. In fact, the whole weekend was.

The next morning, after sleeping in Ian's old room that looked identical to the way it had almost fourteen years ago, I got up early to watch the sunrise. I tip-toed past Ian, who was sleeping on the couch. I guess the old sofa bed had seen better days, since it was long gone. I didn't want to disturb him. I knew he hadn't been sleeping well.

I wrapped up in a blanket I had taken from the bed and sat on one of their patio chairs on the weathered deck. The air was clean and crisp with a slight chill. I could barely make out the ridge that sat behind their home, but it didn't take long for the sun to begin its slow rise over it. At first, it was only a few strands of light. It was almost as if the night was fighting for control, but it was no match for the powerful beams that broke through. It was breathtaking, but not quite as breathtaking as the man who slid open the glass patio door. He looked disheveled with his untidy hair and wrinkled pajama bottoms and t-shirt, but it was perfect to me.

He didn't say a word. He sat on the chair next to me and pulled me over onto his lap. I curled up against him and listened to his heartbeat.

He held me tight as we watched the sun take her rightful place in the sky and illuminate the fields that surrounded his parents' home. The warmth of the sun's rays burned off the dew of the night, and steam began to rise across the landscape. It was a moment of pure perfection.

The rest of the day we spent walking through those fields and picnicking near the riverbank. Dinner was spent on the deck with his parents. As I looked at each person of the Greyson clan, I wished I could have made the weekend last longer. I didn't want to go home to reality and to being Ms. Bryant during working hours. But reality called, and on Sunday morning we made our way back down to the busyness of the city, back to that oddly shaped airport, and back home.

When we arrived back home, things started to feel different to me. For several weeks I couldn't put my finger on it. Don't get me wrong, I was happier than I had ever been, but something was missing. Then it hit me one day as I was going over the sales numbers for last month. I realized I didn't want anything standing between Ian and me. And now that my baby was making a name for itself, I wanted some of the domestic bliss I had been craving—that something else boss talked about, right down to picking out the perfect suburban house. I knew who I wanted to live in that house with me, but I knew we couldn't have any boundaries between us, professionally or otherwise.

So, I decided to seize the day. After our weekly account managers meeting, Ian was riding high. Sales were up and our pipeline was full. It was then I walked through the adjoining door. I hadn't bothered knocking in weeks. I headed straight for Ian.

He looked surprised to see me, but I didn't let that stop me. I strode right over to him and really surprised him by spinning his chair around, sitting on his lap, wrapping my arms around his neck, and kissing him like a woman who was in love. He hesitated at first, but he nicely fell in line, if only for a brief moment.

"Ms. Bryant—"

I put my finger over his mouth. "I don't want to be Ms. Bryant anymore."

He hung his head. "We've been through this."

"I know," I smiled, "but you're not listening to me."

He cocked his head to the side. "Are you saying what I think you're saying?"

"If you think I'm saying I love you, then yes." It was the first time in thirteen years I had said those words to him, or any man for that matter, but his response was so much better this time. I had never seen him grin so wide. He even decided to cross the professional boundary line. He kissed me deeply and thoroughly. By the time he was done, I felt like I had just done a marathon session of belly dancing.

"Ian," I whispered, "I want to be Kelli to you all the time."

"Kel," he pled, "just because I call you Ms. Bryant in the office doesn't change the way I feel about you."

"It says you don't trust me."

He was taken aback. "I trust you more than anyone."

"You're going to have to prove that," I said in my come-hither voice.

His hands inched slowly down my back, drawing me closer to him. "How do you propose I do that?"

"Well... I suppose you could change my last name. You said you'd never call your wife Mrs. Greyson in the office."

"Mmm. Mrs. Greyson, I do like the sound of that." His lips skimmed mine.

Oh, so did I, especially when he said it. My lips played above his, teasing them. "So, do we have a deal?"

"A lifetime one."

Epilogue

One Year Later

SMILED WHEN I WALKED OUT of the master bath to find my husband propped up in bed typing away. I assumed he was working on a new proposal for a prospective client out of Rhode Island. We had done a demo for them last week and they were ready to sign on the dotted line. Our marketing software was making waves across the nation.

I tiptoed toward him, hands behind my back. "I thought we agreed not to bring our work home anymore." We had both been guilty of it, though I had to say there was something sexy about him working with no shirt on.

He gave me a sheepish grin before closing his laptop and setting it on his nightstand. He pulled back the covers on my side of the bed, inviting me to join him. I casually sauntered toward him.

He tipped his head to the side. "What's behind your back?"

"Oh, since our merger, I've acquired another acquisition."

His brow crinkled. "Are you talking about the Salinger deal?"

We were working on acquiring a design firm, but that's not what I was referring to.

I stood by the bed and slowly brought my hands around. "I was talking about *our* merger." I held up the pregnancy test I had just taken.

Ian blinked, and blinked some more before he came to and lunged for the test to make sure he was reading it right. "You're pregnant?"

"Apparently, you do good work." We had only been trying for a month.

He tossed the test to the side and reached for me, pulling me onto the bed with him. I curled up next to him and rested my head on his bare chest. "Are you happy?"

His hand glided down my bare arm. "I couldn't be happier. How are you feeling?"

"Great so far. But..." I brushed my fingers across his chest. "I was kind of thinking that once the baby comes, I might want to be a full-time domestic diva. What do you think?" It wasn't that I didn't love my work but being with Ian filled something in me I didn't even know I was missing. I think there was more to that something else Boss talked about.

Ian thought for a moment. "I would miss you in the office, but I want you to do whatever makes you happy."

I kissed his chest. "I love you." And I did. I don't think there was a more supportive husband around than mine. Even if we still butted heads from time to time.

"I love you, Mrs. Greyson."

"That's my favorite name, outside of the office, of course."

He chuckled.

"You know, you never did say what you were planning on calling me in the office after we got married had I not been so demanding about you calling me Kelli."

"That's because I was never planning on working with my wife."

"What?" I propped myself up on his chest.

He ran his hands through my hair. "I was going to quit once we got married."

"Why didn't you?"

"Because," he impishly grinned, "I love pushing all the boundaries with you."

Oh, so did I.

About the Author

Jᴇɴɴɪꜰᴇʀ Pᴇᴇʟ ɪꜱ ᴛʜᴇ ᴀᴡᴀʀᴅ-ᴡɪɴɴɪɴɢ, bestselling author of the *Dating by Design* and the *More Than a Wife* series, as well as several other contemporary romances. Though she lives and breathes writing, her first love is her family. She is the mother of three amazing kiddos and has added the title of mother-in-law, with the addition of two terrific sons-in-law. She's been married to her best friend and partner in crime for a lot longer than seems possible. Some of her favorite things are late-night talks, beach vacations, the mountains, pink bubble gum ice cream, tours of model homes, and Southern living. She can frequently be found with her laptop on, fingers typing away, indulging in chocolate milk, and writing out the stories that are constantly swirling through her head.

To learn more about Jennifer and her books, visit her website at
www.jenniferpeel.com.

If you enjoyed this book, please rate and review it on
Amazon & Goodreads

You can also connect with Jennifer on
Facebook & Twitter (@jpeel_author)

Other books by Jennifer Peel:

Other Side of the Wall

The Girl in Seat 24B

Professional Boundaries

House Divided

Trouble in Loveland

More Trouble in Loveland

How to Get Over Your Ex in Ninety Days

Paige's Turn

Hit and Run Love

Sweet Regrets

Honeymoon for One

The Women of Merryton Series:

Jessie Belle — Book One

Taylor Lynne — Book Two

Rachel Laine — Book Three

Cheyenne — Book Four

The Dating by Design Series:

His Personal Relationship Manager — Book One

Statistically Improbable — Book Two

Narcissistic Tendencies —Book Three

A Music City Romance
Best of My Love
Beck and Call
Midnight Promises

More Than a Wife Series
The Sidelined Wife — Book One
The Secretive Wife — Book Two
The Dear Wife — Book Three (Coming Soon)

A Clairborne Family Novel Series
Second Chance in Paradise
New Beginnings in Paradise — Coming Soon
First Love in Paradise — Coming Soon
Return to Paradise — Coming Soon

Not So Wicked Series
My Not So Wicked Stepbrother
My Not So Wicked Ex-Fiancé
My Not So Wicked Boss

Made in the USA
Monee, IL
06 October 2021